PRAISE FOR THREE CHORDS OF CHAOS

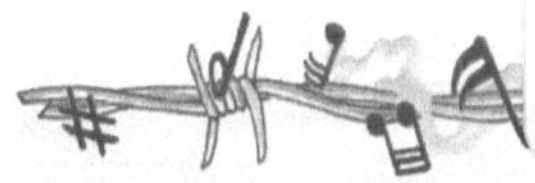

"Three Chords of Chaos is a darkly rich story, starring an exiled faery and his lady love. Mr. Chambers has created a cast of intriguing and charismatic characters in a music and magic fueled world."
– Bibliophilic Book Blog

"Three Chords of Chaos is a well-written, compelling story interwoven with an authentic description of the famed punk rock culture that developed in the early 80s. A very entertaining and enlightening novella. Highly recommended."
– Gene O'Neill,
author of
The Cal Wild Chronicles
and *Frozen Shadows*

"In this dark urban fantasy James Chambers plays a thrilling riff on the razor's edge where music and magic meet. Sex, drugs, Faustian bargains, and rebellious Fae make Three Chords of Chaos my kind of faery tale."
– Douglas Wynne,
author of
The Devil of Echo Lake
and *Red Equinox*

Other Bad-Ass Faerie Tales

The Halfling's Court
by Danielle Ackley-McPhail

The Redcaps' Queen
by Danielle Ackley-McPhail
(re-release forthcoming)

THREE CHORDS OF CHAOS

A Bad-Ass Faerie Tale

REMASTERED EDITION

James Chambers
with illustrations by Ed Coutts

PAPER PHOENIX PRESS

Pennsville, NJ

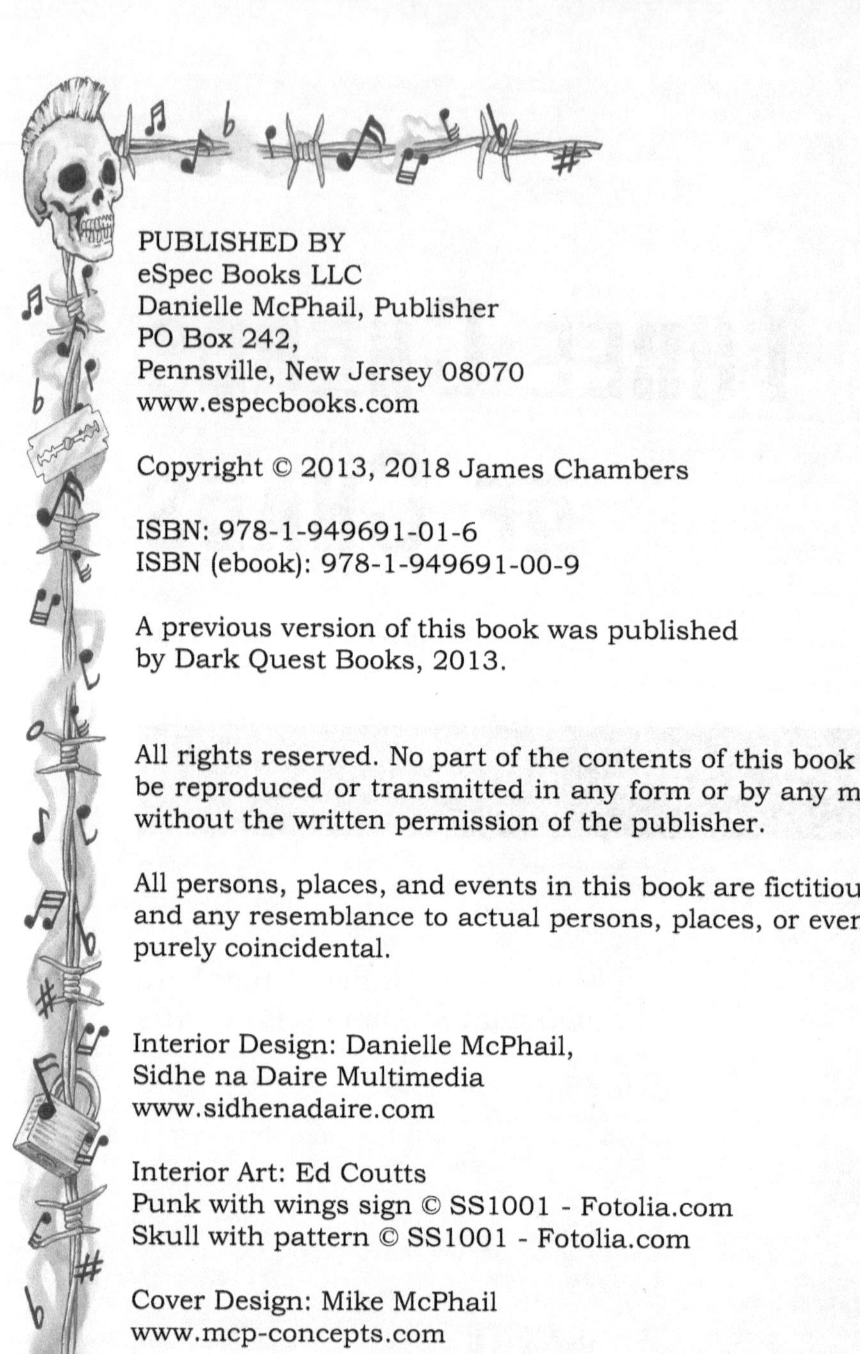

PUBLISHED BY
eSpec Books LLC
Danielle McPhail, Publisher
PO Box 242,
Pennsville, New Jersey 08070
www.especbooks.com

ISBN: 978-1-949691-01-6
ISBN (ebook): 978-1-949691-00-9

A previous version of this book was published
by Dark Quest Books, 2013.

All persons, places, and events in this book are fictitious
and any resemblance to actual persons, places, or events is
purely coincidental.

Interior Design: Danielle McPhail,
Sidhe na Daire Multimedia
www.sidhenadaire.com

Interior Art: Ed Coutts
Punk with wings sign © SS1001 - Fotolia.com
Skull with pattern © SS1001 - Fotolia.com

Cover Design: Mike McPhail
www.mcp-concepts.com

Cover Art: Musician with an electronic guitar enveloped in
flames on a black background © Sergey Nivens
www.shutterstock.com
Back Cover Art: Realistic Flames © Julia-art

DEDICATION

*This book is dedicated to Danielle,
Gorge's faerie godmother.*

*Special thanks to Greg Schauer for his wonderful
editorial input and much gratitude to all those who
read and supported the first edition of this book.*

My thanks too, as always, to Laurie, Lily, and Will.

Past Publications

A version of "Faerie Ring Blues" was previously published in *Bad-Ass Faeries 3: In All Their Glory*. Danielle Ackley-McPhail, Lee Hillmann, L. Jagi Lamplighter, and Jeff Lyman, eds. Cincinnati, OH: Mundania Press, 2010; reprinted in *Three Chords of Chaos*, Dark Quest Books, Howell, NJ, 2013.

A version of "The Way of the Bone" was previously published in *Bad-Ass Faeries 2: Just Plain Bad*. Danielle Ackley-McPhail, Lee Hillmann, L. Jagi Lamplighter, and Jeff Lyman, eds. Marietta, GA: Marietta Publishing, 2008 / Reissued, Cincinnati, OH: Mundania Press, 2009; reprinted in *Three Chords of Chaos*, Dark Quest Books, Howell, NJ, 2013; reprinted in *The Best of Bad-Ass Faeries*. Danielle Ackley-McPhail, editor, Stratford, NJ: eSpec Books, 2017.

Portions of this book were previously published in *Three Chords of Chaos*, Dark Quest Books, Howell, NJ, 2013.

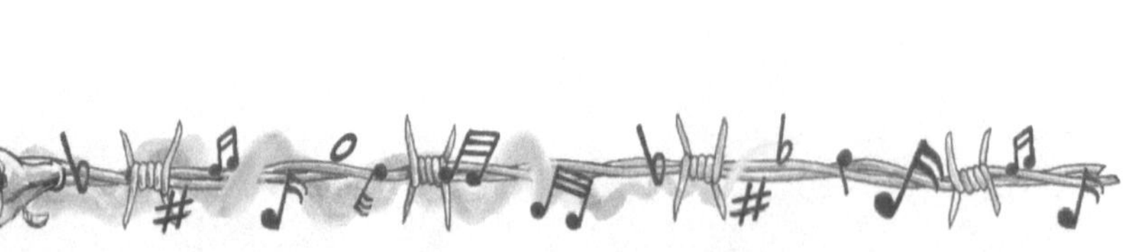

CONTENTS

*New content exclusive to this edition

THREE CHORDS OF CHAOS
—FIRST VERSE

GORGE RELEASED NOTE AFTER BLISTERING NOTE FROM HIS guitar, and the audience soaked up his music like a rain of razor blades. They danced, whirled, and smashed together; they bled magic that flowed across smoky air, shimmering red and yellow with flashing stage lights, to feed the hungry core inside him. He hadn't felt magic this pure and vibrant since his days in the Kingdoms; *how ironic*, he thought, *to find it among these nihilistic, rebellious, angry young mortals.* His left hand throttled the guitar neck, fingertips gliding among the frets, tapping and pulling the strings to slash out biting riffs until he reached a crescendo—

—and then let it all come crashing down.

Gorge dropped his hands to his sides as his last notes reverberated.

Caught off guard, Social Contract Dispute lost the beat, faltered. Someone in the audience shouted, "Fuck you!" into the lull. Another threw a beer bottle at the stage.

Gorge grinned.

Even their praise was crude and furious.

He screamed into the microphone, then let D.S. Dent pick up the song.

He worked the strings again, exploring a scale he'd learned as a child, perfecting Social Contract Dispute's music. The notes didn't belong in this world; they rose from his guitar in crude remembrance of music he'd played a long time ago in a place now lost to him, a ghost of what they were meant to be—yet they drove the crowd wild. Gorge led them to undiscovered sounds more potent and thrilling than anything else they had ever heard. Their energy surged. Into the stink of hot sweat and spilled beer drifted a whiff of burning copper, the scent of an invisible charge only Gorge understood as magic. It flowed into the crowd on the music then returned amplified by their love, worship, envy, and awe. He reveled in the parasitic feedback loop, the power so chaotic and electrifying it overflowed him and spilled into Dispute, elevating their music to the sound of demigods. The amplifiers vibrated and roared; the song soared; the club quaked; and the crowd snapped their heads back and forth, waved their arms, and twisted their bodies in hot, kinetic spirals.

Dent's voice sliced through the din:

Thou shalt not kill
We have a pill
to make sure you're a gooooood boy
And when it's time
for you to die
you'll die because we saaaaaay so—
and you better not cry about it!

The rest of Dispute and Gorge joined in for the chorus:

No crying
No crying
No, no, no crying
Why are you such a crybaby?

Social Contract Dispute would never again play this well or feel so deeply connected to an audience. Playing this gig, Gorge was giving them both gift and curse, one that would launch their legend only to destroy them when they realized they could never live up to it without him. He didn't care. Tonight he played to lay down everyone in the club with the force of a neutron bomb. He hungered for their magic, and they gave it with pleasure.

He watched faces in the writhing crowd.

Skin pierced with shining steel.

Eyes adorned with savage swatches of make-up.

Hair teased into spikes, Mohawks, and bursts of color, or swirling like stringy shadows.

Pale complexions, thin lips, and gaunt cheekbones.

Clean-shaven heads.

Bright eyes surrounded by dark circles.

They wore loose T-shirts and torn jeans. Black jackets and short skirts. Leather and ripped denim stitched together with safety pins. Button-down shirts stained with perspiration. Anarchy symbols, Union Jacks, and band logo patches sewn pell-mell onto vests, sleeves, and jackets. Death's heads and angular letters scratched in white marks onto dark cloth. Chains hanging from necks, wrists, waists.

Tattoos on soft flesh crept out from beneath the edges of flapping clothes.

All of it bounced and swayed, a crest of human energy riding a wave of sound. Hardcore, Metal, New Wave, Punk, Post-Punk, all of pop music's new rude children pulsed in their blood.

And Gorge saw that it was good.

He stopped thinking about the music and let his hands roam where they wanted. Notes and melodies welled up unchecked from the part of his soul that always hummed. As Social Contract Dispute ripped through one song after another, Gorge drove the crowd into a deeper frenzy. Struggling to keep up, the band dropped into a bare-bone, attack-dog rhythm. Mickey's bass machine-gunned notes; Reynolds' drums thundered. Dent punished the same three power chords again and again as he abandoned his lyrics for raw shrieks and groans.

The music mushroomed over the crowd like a slow-motion explosion.

The floor shook, and the walls quavered.

The club throbbed; to Gorge's eyes alone the walls seemed to weaken and bow as the music pushed them outward onto a surrounding darkness. A new song began, and he played a series of lightning-fast arpeggios, picking out an intricate melody that pushed even harder against the walls. The darkness seeped into the club, bringing with it a hint of bitter cold. He shunted magic through himself, sent it probing into the black.

They're out there.

They hear.

I can almost sense—

A discordant crash shattered Gorge's spell.

The darkness and the cold retreated; the walls snapped back into place.

Behind Gorge, Reynolds had beaten his snare off its stand. He fought to stay upright in his seat while he whaled on his remaining drums to keep up with Gorge's lead. Dent no longer sang but only flailed around the stage, twirling his mic at the end of its cord, his guitar slung around his back. People in the crowd tripped over each other, fell to the floor, or propped each other up, exhausted, off-balance.

Gorge smiled and chose mercy.

He fired off a last burst of notes then slowed the pace like a music box winding down, bringing everyone back to earth.

Social Contract Dispute followed his lead and finished the song.

The air thrummed with its echo.

The stage lights darkened. Blackness filled Motormouth's.

When the houselights glared, everything returned to normal; solid wood and fogs of cigarette smoke replaced wavering walls and cold darkness.

Gorge dropped his guitar—a black Stratocaster with a red anarchy symbol painted across its face—into its stand and flipped the audience the bird.

They cheered in response.

Dent jumped to the microphone, raised his fists above his head, and yelled, "*You* are the disenfranchised! *We* are Social Contract Dispute—with *Max* effing *Chaos on guitar!*"

The audience howled for Gorge. He didn't linger to enjoy it.

Their adulation meant nothing without their magic pouring into him, and the less interest he showed in their acclaim, the more they heaped it upon him. He set his sights on a raven-haired woman at the bar, the only placid face in a sea of orgiastic expressions.

Delilah.

Her cool-ember eyes drank in Gorge, darting between him and her sketchbook as she scratched a charcoal pencil over the pages. Catching him looking, she lifted one of the two beers beside her, drank, and then saluted Gorge with the bottle.

Gorge pushed through the crowd to her.

He cupped the back of Delilah's head with one hand, twining his fingers in her soft hair, as he kissed her, soaking in her warmth. After their lips parted, he grabbed the other beer bottle, tilted his head back, and drained it. Slamming the empty on the bar, he tapped Delilah's sketchbook.

"Show me," he said.

Delilah ignored him, her smile a spotlight. "I *felt* that."

"You'd have to be dead not to," Gorge said. "You're sitting less than a hundred feet from the amps."

"Uh-uh, not the music. The magic." She flipped open her sketchbook. "Look."

Gorge riffled the pages. Delilah's sketches leapt off the paper. The faces of the audience took on a second life in charcoal lines and textured smudges. Gorge's face rose from the stage, surrounded by tangles of his silver-black hair, a giant with spidery hands wrapped around his guitar, ten blurry fingers drawn for each one to show the motion of his music. Delilah had captured the shapes of his body as it twisted to the rhythm—and rising from his back was the faintest outline of wings.

"You saw my wings?" Gorge said.

Delilah nodded. "Not only that."

She flipped forward a few pages.

Gorge studied her sketches of the club. The crowd rendered in muddy blurs, the stage a burst of light broken by the shadows of Gorge and Social Contract Dispute—and behind them a black cloud speckled with white flecks like feral eyes glowing in the night, its inky tendrils streaming through the air, the walls disintegrating into it.

The darkness.

The Way of the Bone.

The stage and the audience seemed to float in it.

"You saw *this*?"

"The magic was so *bright*. It lit up my whole body. It was like... god, it was almost as good as sex."

"Did they see my true face?" Gorge's fae features sometimes bled through the perpetual glamour he cast over himself to make his appearance more human.

Delilah shook her head. "It was faint, even for me, and I know what to look for."

"And you have so much of my magic in you already. There was more power than I could hold onto tonight. I let some spill into Dispute. Poor bastards. Next time they pick up their instruments they'll wonder where it all went."

"What'd you do to these people?"

Gorge glanced around. Everyone looked fine, everything back to the familiar grind and hustle between sets. People who'd appeared ready to faint or cry or scream while he played seemed unfazed now. He shrugged.

"They believe," he said. "Shitty as this world is, they *believe* in this music like their lives depend on it. They punched the power off the charts. I've never felt magic this strong before in the mortal world, only in the Kingdoms. To have actually seen the darkness—I wasn't sure it was possible from this world even to touch the Way of the Bone—"

Three women interrupted Gorge. Eighteen years old at best and wrapped in patchworks of tight clothes layered over Tartan skirts and stockings spotted with holes tucked into high, laced boots, they fidgeted with excitement. They wore their hair shaved over one ear and long on the other side, each girl's dyed a different flare of color: pink, green, and red.

"Could we...?" one of them said.

"Couldwegetanautograph?" the second one said.

Gorge squinted at them. "Got a pen?"

The third one giggled and handed him a marker, her hand shaking.

"Where do I sign?" Gorge asked

The girls tugged down their shirt collars for Gorge to sign above their cleavage.

He looked to Delilah, who laughed and shook her head.

Gorge scrawled "Max Chaos" on each girl's skin then returned the marker. The girls blushed and thanked him. One darted in and kissed him on the cheek before they rushed into the crowd to show off their autographs.

"Don't let *that* go to your head," Delilah said. "And don't get any ideas about groupies."

"I don't play with children. I'd only break them." Gorge offered Delilah his hand. "And why would I need to when I already have the perfect woman? You're the only one I want. And it's time for us to get out of here so I can prove it."

Delilah smiled and reached for Gorge's hand, but then she paused and shot straight up in her seat. "Damn, look who just walked in."

Making his way through the club, surrounded by a mosquito cloud of hangers-on, walked a man in a white suit, a red handkerchief blooming from his chest pocket, black leather vest shining beneath his jacket. Hair surrounded his head in a meticulously wild fashion that looked as if it took hours to style to appear careless. He carried an ebony cane with a silver top.

"Peter Peters," Gorge said. "Bastard."

"Hush. That man's going to put me in his gallery if it kills one of us. Wait here." Delilah kissed Gorge and stroked the back of his neck. "You don't mind, do you?"

"I'd wait a thousand years if you asked."

As Delilah moved off into the crowd, Gorge ordered another beer and sighed.

He felt eyes watching him, tickling the back of his mind.

Somebody wanted something from him. Someone always did in these places, and when a man with a short, scraggly beard and aviator-frame eyeglasses parked himself on the next stool, Gorge braced himself to put him in his place. A few years older than the rest of the crowd, the man wore clean blue jeans and a threadbare sports jacket over a Misfits T-shirt. He ordered a beer. The sound of his voice rankled Gorge.

Without looking at the man, he said, "Fuck off, record man."

The man gaped. "What...?"

"I said, 'Fuck off, record man.'" Gorge glared at him.

"Who pissed in your beer, asshole?" the man said—but he didn't leave.

"You can shove whatever you think you're going to pitch me right up your ass," Gorge told him. "Not interested."

"Relax," the man said. "I'm not pitching anything. I don't work for a record company."

"Then you want *something* from me. You stink with want. Like a hungry dog."

"Like a... what?" The man shook his head and extended his hand. "Jake Blaze, hungry dog."

Gorge ignored the hand. "That's your name?"

"Max Chaos is giving me shit about my name? What's in a name anyway? Everyone here? We're all who we want to be even if that isn't who we are. That's why this shit matters."

"What shit is that?"

"The music—especially the way you play it." Jake drank some of his beer. "That's all I want is to talk to you about your music. You're a hard gig to catch. I watched you play with Bonzo's Pajamas at CBGB, like, what, three months ago? Been trying to catch you again ever since. Out almost every night, club after club, hoping you'd sit in for a set somewhere. I'm not the only one. You have any idea what kind of crowds you could draw with a little publicity?"

"More than a dive like Motormouth's could hold. Is that your thing? You a promoter? Want to help me take my career to the stars, make a million dollars, buy five cars? You've got dollar signs and limousine lights in your eyes, Jake, and you drink shitty beer. Again, I say *fuck off.*"

Jake eyed the label on his beer bottle. He'd picked the cheapest brand. "No, that's not me, I'm only a fan, and—"

Gorge tipped over his empty beer bottle so that it fell with a hollow *thunk* pointing at Jake. "Liar."

He stood, but before he slipped away from the barstool, Jake grabbed him by the arm.

"Okay, I'm a writer. All right? I write for *Music Maze.* But I'm not trying to milk the golden calf. All I want's your story."

"What makes you think I have one to tell?"

"Seriously? You're Max Chaos. Totally unknown until this year. You're a phantom except when you're on stage, and no one but you ever knows where or when that will be. And when it happens it's like a bomb going off. I've interviewed musicians from My Revolver, Out of Step, TV Party—all the bands you've jammed with. Even they didn't know you were sitting in till you showed up. If you're trying to make yourself into a legend, it's working. People are calling you the musical bastard love-child of Eddie Van Halen, Andy Summers, and Sid Vicious."

"Fucking nonsense. I drank Sid under the table in London last year and Eddie's a coked-out peacock. Andy's all right, though. Plays for the music not bullshit hoopla."

"See? And you say you've got no story to tell? Man, I break *your* story, I get the scoop on who Max Chaos is, what he's all about? Forget *Music Maze*, I'm writing for *Rolling Stone*."

"You come to me to juice your pathetic career and wonder why I say 'fuck off,' which, by the way, you still haven't done. Or don't you understand what 'fuck off' means?"

Jake gave Gorge a dismissive wave. "You'd benefit too. You don't even have to give me your real name. I can help you spread the word, grow the legend. People have been coming in from LA, Nashville, even Seattle to catch you play. Bands are driving here from Minneapolis and D.C., sleeping on couches to catch a few gigs on the chance you might sit in with them. Hell, man, I saw Robert Quine out looking for you last week. Like it or not, you're on fire. A little press could fan the flames. I don't want to blow out your game, but feed me enough to light the fuse and take whatever you want out of it."

"What the hell would a pisswater-drinking writer know about what I want?"

Jake sighed and shook his head. "Whatever, man. I spent too long looking for you to be put off by you bitching about my choice of beer. Are you going to give me an interview or what? Or are you waiting for me to throw some money on the bar? You want to get paid? You act all about the music, but maybe you're all about the money. Maybe you're nothing special after all, and we're wasting our time. So, tell me, which is it?"

Gorge flagged another beer from the bartender and let Jake wait.

He watched Delilah sitting with Peter Peters and his retinue of sycophants, wannabes, drug connections, and whores. They laughed and waved cigarettes in front of their faces. Gorge hated how the talentless prick dangled his gallery to manipulate hopeful artists. The lucky bastard had made his rep off connections to Basquiat and Warhol, and his gallery had launched a couple of up-and-comers, making it a hot spot, but mostly he showed crap. Gorge wished he could drag Peters to the Kingdoms to show him real art and true beauty. The pompous fool might break down crying from despair when he returned to this world. Delilah exceeded them all, a true artist with a creative heart and soul worth more than any thousand of the so-called artists Peters promoted. Gorge wanted to yank Peter Peters' head back by his hair and scream in his face to give Delilah a show—but he couldn't. A show would only mean something if she landed it on her own.

Gorge squinted at Jake. "Seems I've got a few minutes to kill. You want my story?"

Jake nodded. "That's all I want."

"Order yourself a decent beer and a good whiskey for me, and I'll tell you."

"You bullshitting me?"

"Only one way to find out."

Jake waved for the bartender, ordered the drinks, and paid. He slid the whiskey to Gorge. "So where are you from?"

"I'm not from around here," Gorge said.

"I figured that. You've got that look. What are you, Middle Eastern, Asian? Dye your hair, right? That silver-black thing can't be natural."

With a withering stare, Gorge said, "I'm not from your world."

Jake groaned and threw his head back. "You *are* shitting me."

Gorge shook his head. He placed his left hand open on the bar. A flicker of green light flared in his palm.

"What the hell's that?" Jake asked.

Gorge touched the light to Jake's chest, above his heart. Jake flinched then froze and grew calm. Gorge sang: "Two things you will do for me/the first, you will believe/all the words I have to say/all the wonders I will tell." He withdrew his hand and sipped his whiskey. "And I'll tell you the other thing when we're done."

Jake looked stunned. "What was that? It felt *so* weird...."

"I told you. Not from around here," Gorge said.

"Where from then?"

"The Enchanted Kingdoms, the Realms of the Sidhe."

Jake smirked. "What's that, like, Disney World?"

Gorge sneered. "That this world allows ignorant morons like you to call themselves 'writers' has never ceased to piss me off. No, you witless skid mark, the Enchanted Kingdoms, the land of the Fae. I'm a faerie."

"A... *faerie.* But you're a guy. Oooooh, you mean, like, you're from the West Village."

"No," Gorge said. "I mean the kind that steals your children and screws up your house if you don't leave us a little milk and honey. Despite what mortals think they know from movies and storybooks, we're not all tiny, cute, and female."

Gorge's spell compelled Jake to believe, but Gorge saw in his eyes that deep down he didn't understand.

"Humans think of us that way because the truth is scary," Gorge said. "How afraid can you be of something small enough you can crush it underfoot? Fortunately for you all, we don't find mortals all that interesting, and we don't give a damn what you think of us."

"If you're a faerie, why don't you have wings?"

"That, Jakey, is a long and painful part of my story." Gorge drained the last of his whiskey and signaled the bartender for another, indicating to add it to Jake's tab. "I was the greatest musician the Kingdoms ever saw, but the royal twats who ruled everything thought there was some music that should never be played. So, fuck them, I played it anyway. As punishment, they took my life and wings away from me and banished me here."

"To... Motormouth's?"

"No. To your world. The *mortal* world. Turn on your brain, and stay with me. The Flock of Eternity—the assembled kings and queens of the Kingdoms—couldn't kill me outright. There are *some* rules about these things, after all. So they compromised with exile. They figured I'd go mad and die here, problem solved. Except I brought more magic with me than they knew. That was more than thirty years ago. When I'm strong enough, I'm going back to the Kingdoms, and I'm going to shove all the Flock's rules and their prissy fears right back in their faces, and if tonight's any indication, that might be a lot sooner than I expected."

"What happened tonight?"

"Magic happened."

Delilah returned from Peter Peters' table. She leaned against Gorge and slid her hand along his back. "What a talentless prick."

"Still a 'no'?" Gorge asked her.

"I've got him up to a maybe. He wants to see new work. So that's good news, and I should be excited, but he's still a talentless prick with trash friends."

"Who's this?" Jake asked.

"Jake Blaze, meet Delilah," Gorge said. "Delilah, this brain-dead rock zombie is Jake Blaze. Calls himself a writer. He sure as hell doesn't drink like one."

"She your girlfriend?" Jake asked.

"Girlfriend? That's quaint," Gorge said. "Delilah saved my life. Now she *is* my life."

"Oh," Jake said. "That's, um... deep."

"Deeper than the deep, blue sea, Jakey, and at the moment, I sense my life would like to be elsewhere. So ends our little convo." Gorge stood and wrapped an arm around Delilah's waist. "Thanks for the drinks."

"Wait," Jake said. "You told me there were two things."

"True. I said I'd give you my story. I never said I'd let you keep it." Gorge touched Jake's chest again, the green light flickering in his palm, and sang: "Your loss is my gain/your pain my reward/when I lift my hand /all I told you will be *gone*."

Jake's face blanked then refocused on Gorge. "Wait, you're leaving? I thought you were giving me an interview. I ordered drinks."

"Ah, Jake, how do you remember to breathe and stay out of traffic? Nighty-night, writer-man."

Gorge walked to the stage and put his guitar in its case.

Dent, Reynolds, and Mickey thanked him for the gig and invited him to jam again. Gorge knew he never would, though.

Dispute put their heart into their music, but they simply didn't have the talent to keep up with him. Gorge gave them a few words of encouragement and then left them to pack up their gear.

Stares and whispers followed him and Delilah across the club.

Gorge didn't like attention off-stage. He fixed an extra glamour around both of them so that no one noticed them actually leave—and then they ducked out a side exit.

Outside Motormouth's, New York City hummed with nightlife.

"Sort of shitty what you did to that writer," Delilah said.

"Vacuous minds must be made to suffer," Gorge said. "How else will they grow? Besides, it passed the time."

"Seems risky to me, talking to people like that then taking it back."

"No risk. All he'll have left is the nagging sense he's forgotten something very important," Gorge said. "If that sharpens his thoughts and opens his mind then I've done him a favor. People who can't change how they think are dead on their feet."

Halfway down 5th Street to Bowery, Gorge froze at the mouth of an alley. Days old trash spilled out of it, a symptom of a city still recovering from the financial malaise of the 70s.

"What is it?" Delilah asked.

"Something from the Kingdoms," Gorge said. "See it? Open your senses. Use what I taught you."

Delilah relaxed, closed her eyes for a second, then opened them and scanned the sidewalk back the way they'd come. She looked around the street, up at the buildings, then into the alley—and stopped. "By the dumpster."

"Good," Gorge said. "What is it?"

Delilah squinted. "It's... a sprite."

"A wretch of a one, too. A garbage-picker," Gorge said. "We call them scrape sprites because you're liable to wind up scraping them off your shoes. He shouldn't be here. He's spying on me."

Gorge entered the alley, Delilah by his side.

The six-inch tall sprite paid them no attention. Stains and debris from rooting through the trash peppered its skin, hair, and clothes. It struggled to excavate the carcass of a roast turkey from a torn garbage bag and a pile of paper plates sodden with grease and soggy vegetables. It grunted and whistled. It swore, then kicked a bottle cap into the air.

Gorge caught it.

When the cap didn't strike the ground, the sprite looked up from its food.

It wiped the back of its hand across its brow, knocking away some crumbs, and then stared at Gorge, one eyebrow raised. "Oh, you can see me," the sprite said, his voice gruffer than his size suggested.

"Clear as day," Gorge said.

"Well, you're drunk and I'm a hallucination! Wooooo! What the hell do you want? This is the Big Rotten Apple. Don't you know better than to make eye contact with strangers in alleys?"

Gorge laughed.

"What's funny!? Go on! Get out of here! Mind your own business, or I'll—" the sprite faltered as realization spread across its tiny, soiled face. "Huh. You're from the Kingdoms."

"I am," Gorge said.

"You look sort of familiar." The sprite squatted on the rump of the turkey and rubbed its chin. "Did we know each other, attend the same court perhaps?"

"No garbage-eating scrape sprite would ever have been allowed into the courts I attended," Gorge said. "Did the Flock send you to check up on me? To make sure I'm be-having myself?"

Wide-eyed, the sprite said, "The Flock of Eternity? Send me? To check on you? Hah! Who the hell are *you*? And why would the Flock waste their time with a sprite like me?"

"You're exactly the kind of bottom-feeding vermin I might overlook even in a mortal city," Gorge said.

"Okay, true, but why do you need checking up on? You steal someone's gold?" The sprite threw its hands up in the air. "Unless you're in exile, or—waitaminnit! I know who you are now. You *are* in exile."

"You're a terrible liar." Gorge snapped his hand out quicker than the sprite could react and snatched him off the turkey. "*Snitch.* Were you going to report back about me? To who? Soniella?"

"I never heard of her!" The sprite tried to wiggle free. "And I'm no snitch, blagnabbit! I only come here for the garbage. Get a hankering for mortal trash now and then. Give you my word!"

"I don't believe you," Gorge said.

"It's true. Why would anyone in the Flock listen to me anyway?" the sprite said. "I eat garbage, for crying out loud. You *have* to believe me."

"No, I don't," Gorge said. "Nor do I want to."

Gorge hurled the sprite to the ground. Before it recovered, he stamped his foot down on it and crushed it to the pavement, grinding it in with the refuse and slime. The sprite shrieked.

Delilah flinched, glanced away.

When the screaming stopped, Gorge grabbed a cardboard scrap from the dumpster and used it to wipe what was left of the sprite from his shoe and flick it onto the garbage pile.

Delilah made a face. "Ew, *gross.*"

"Sorry you had to see that."

"Did you have to kill him? What if he was telling the truth?"

"Doesn't matter," Gorge said. "I couldn't let him tell anyone in the Kingdoms that he saw me. Whether he'd been sent here or not, he never could've kept that to himself. The more they know about me back home, the sooner the pieces will form a picture, and I don't want them to figure out what I'm doing."

"He didn't see you until we walked over here and interrupted him."

"Maybe. Maybe not. Sprites are tricky," Gorge said. "Never trust a sprite. Besides, no one will miss a scrape sprite. In some parts of the Kingdoms, fishermen use them for bait."

"Oh." Delilah shuddered. "Can we go home now?"

Gorge put his arm around her and walked her to the corner, where he hailed a cab.

In the shadows of the car, Delilah leaned into him, pulled his arms around her, and held his hands in hers. Gorge let the night's energy drift through his senses, seeking signs of other Sidhe in the city. They were always around, often closer than he liked, and until he gathered the power he needed to open the Way of the Bone, he and Delilah needed to be like ghosts to them.

Three nights later Gorge hit the stage with Shake Appeal at Donnie D's, a hole in the wall too small to provide a stage. The staff cleared away a few tables and chairs for the band to play next to the bar. Shake Appeal's fans jammed the place, and even more people poured in when word spread via the payphone outside the ladies' room that Gorge had joined them. By the time the band finished half their first set, the crowd overflowed onto the street.

Gorge played low key at first and let Shake Appeal lead, building anticipation for him to cut loose. They ripped through song after song, most of them under two minutes long, and Gorge's eyes roamed the crowd while he played. He recognized familiar expressions in the young faces, stark hair, and torn clothes. Intoxication, elation, anger, hope, and lust for something better, for one moment when the world was honest. For as long as the band played, all of them lived free from whatever bullshit baggage they'd left behind that night, and magic blossomed in them. It streamed out of Gorge, washed through the audience, and then ran back to him in an amplifying feedback loop. He fed their souls and they fed him power. The air quivered with its intensity. For these people, music equaled religion, and they'd appointed Gorge their high priest for the night.

Fuck that, I've become their god.

The notion inspired him to let go of caution.

A sonic eruption burst from his guitar and broke apart Shake Appeal's song.

The sequence of power chords and screeching riffs Gorge unleashed stopped Brimmer Riggs, Shake Appeal's guitarist, dead in his tracks. After several measures, he dove back in as Gorge drove the tempo faster, forcing the band to improvise to his lead. Panic flashed across the band member's faces—Marty Martin on bass, Jack Daniels on drums—but when the crowd roared approval, all their worry vanished. They channeled every bit of energy they possessed into their performance, all of it together combined to only a fraction of what Gorge offered. He was the only star in the room, and, as if to prove it, he felt more magic than he could absorb gush into him. It overflowed into Shake Appeal, who launched into a frenzy of blitzkrieg rhythms and strained melodies as they punched through one song after another after another with barely an empty beat between them. The building trembled as the crowd danced. Gorge glanced at Delilah, seated at the bar.

The nascent magic cast a blissed-out light in her eyes.

Time slowed down. The music expanded and became the world. Gorge floated inside it, staring down at Shake Appeal, at himself, the audience, and the stained walls of Donnie D's like a circling hawk. The walls shimmered. The darkness appeared in the cracks and corners. It pressed against the music. Gorge sensed cold things out there, listening, things he hadn't felt since his darkest days in the Kingdom, his last days before the Flock cast him out. Their presence thrilled him. He played faster, harder, rougher, reaching for them. He pushed his mind through the cracks in the walls and pressed into the edge of the darkness.

So cold.

So empty.

He strained to see through absolute blackness.

The void crackled with sound. Between thundering notes of the music that carried him there, he heard the tumult of the things that lived in the Way of the Bone, the cacophony of a universe full of planet-size insectile things hissing, clicking, and rustling over each other.

He pushed further, astounded the music launched him so far—

—and then a fast-breaking wave of cold surged against him, shoving him back into the world.

A discord of sour notes and crashes wrecked the music and the flow of magic. The sudden disruptive shock blinded Gorge as it wrenched him back to reality. He staggered, almost dropped his guitar then regained his balance and played on through his disorientation. Steadying himself, he wound down the music and eased out of the song.

His vision returned, fading in on the sight of violence.

Three feet in front of him, a brawl boiled in every direction.

More than a dozen men and women shoved and kicked each other, knocking some into the band, making it impossible to play. Three men yanked Brimmer's orange flying-V guitar from his hands and fought over it before the crowd sucked it away.

Others grabbed for Marty's bass, but he dodged them and ran. Trapped behind his skins, Jack speared his drumsticks at anyone who approached him.

A widening circle formed in the audience as the fighting spread and people crammed into the front doorway. A group of young, shaven-headed punks, hands marked with black Xs, rushed into the thick of it, trying to clear the doors to let people out, but the crowd overwhelmed them, and thrust them back.

A man in a leather vest grabbed at Gorge's guitar; Gorge punched him in the throat and left him gagging on the floor. Two more rushing him veered off in fear when Gorge extinguished for a second the touch of glamour around his face, letting them glimpse a faerie with enough anger and power to tear them apart with his bare hands. Gorge slung his guitar on his back and leapt onto the bar. He jumbled bottles and glasses, kicked the faces of a skinhead and another man with a Mohawk who grabbed at his feet. Delilah crouched behind the far end of the bar where the bartenders beat back against people trying to loot the booze. Gorge reached her and pulled her up beside him. The front entrance was thronged with people shoving to get through, and smaller fights had broken out everywhere. The back door offered the only escape.

Gorge led Delilah along the bar then jumped down by the band. Brimmer and Jack fell in beside them. Marty vanished into the rear of the club, cut off and swept against the doors of the restrooms by the crowd. Gorge sent a touch of magic his way, hoping it would protect him. He urged Brimmer and Jack to go for the back door, and then the four kicked and shoved their way to the storeroom. Gorge tried to shield Delilah, but the melee pressed against them from all sides, forcing her to fight people trying to grab her by the hair.

They reached the storeroom and slipped inside, slamming the door closed behind them. It jumped and rattled against the pounding mob. Brimmer, Jack, and Gorge moved a filing cabinet and cases of liquor piled in front of the back door, and then Gorge kicked it.

It didn't open.

The storeroom door cracked and splintered. Fingers poked through then disappeared as another blow struck, cracking more wood.

Gorge worked the back door, but it held tight, locked. Pissed off and fed up with the bullshit and stupidity all around him, he sent a flare of magic into the door then kicked it again. This time it jolted open onto an alley. Everyone ran outside. Gorge shoved the door closed and used another touch of magic to freeze it shut.

"Fucking savages," Gorge said.

"What the hell was that?" Jack said.

Brimmer rubbed his head. "Damn, man, they took my ax. That's cold."

"I mean it: *What the hell was that?*" Jack's voice rose. "We were in the middle of a set. That is *not* fucking cool."

"We should go back for Marty," Brimmer said. "He was trapped."

"Marty's a big boy. He can take care of himself," Gorge said. "You go back in there, they'll beat the hell out of you for sure." He turned to Delilah and rubbed her shoulders. "Are you all right?"

Delilah avoided looking Gorge in the eye. "You did that?" she whispered.

Gorge nodded. "I didn't mean to, but, yeah, I think so."

"How?"

"I pushed into the darkness. I heard what was out there. I wanted to see it," Gorge whispered. "I must've channeled it back through the music, and it drove them crazy."

"What are you talking about?" Brimmer asked. "You think your music started that? You arrogant prick. Like you're so fucking amazing, people riot when you play?"

"Fuck off, Brimmer," Gorge said.

Jack stepped between them. "Shut up, both of you. It wasn't the music. Some shithead dropped a bag of blow in the crowd then started shoving people around to keep them from stepping on it. The more he pushed, the more they pushed back. Then that guy with the green Mohawk and the Bad Brains T-shirt threw a fist, someone else kicked, and... *boom*... explosive mayhem."

"Whatever," Gorge said.

"What was that glowing thing with the door?" Jack said. "How'd you to get it open?"

"You've never seen magic?" Gorge said.

Brimmer shook his head. "Delusional prick really does think he's magic."

"Enough," Gorge said. "Time for us to go."

"You're walking away?" Brimmer said. "Not even knowing if Marty's okay? And leaving all our gear in there? They're probably stomping it to pieces. It'll cost us a fortune to replace it, and you couldn't care less."

"I'm not Marty's mother. And that's Shake Appeal's gear, not mine." Gorge tapped his guitar. "I've got mine right here. Cases are cheap."

"You have any idea how psyched Marty was to play with Max Chaos? Now you just blow him off after he takes a beating? Where's your sense of, like, a conscience?"

"Brimmer, cool it, man, ease off," Jack said. "Max, hold up, don't go."

"I'm already gone," Gorge said.

He walked Delilah to the end of the alley. It opened onto the next block, but it was shut by a locked iron gate with barbed spikes atop its bars. Gorge rubbed his fingers over the lock.

"Sonofabitch," he said.

"Can't you open it like the door?" Delilah asked.

Gorge shook his head. "It's cold iron, no good. Damn gate must be a hundred years old. We're trapped unless you want to climb over."

Delilah eyed the barbs atop the gate rails. "No, thanks."

Gorge whispered, "I'd fly us, but I've showed off more than I should've already."

"It's okay," Delilah said. Distant police sirens wailed, approaching. "The cops can sort it out. Then we'll walk out the front door."

"Stuck, huh?" Jack said, when Gorge and Delilah returned. "Don't be too pissed at Brimmer. He shoots off his mouth, but if he didn't know you were right, he'd have gone back in for Marty. They've been tight since they were kids."

Gorge eyed Brimmer slumped down in the corner by the door, back to the wall, head down on his knees. "I don't give a shit what Brimmer thinks of me."

"Yeah, I get that, man," Jack said. "But do you have to be such a hard case all the time?"

Gorge glared at Jack.

"All right, something I gotta talk to you about," Jack said. "Figured it could wait until after the gig."

"Yo, Jack, don't even do it, man." Brimmer lifted his head and glared at Gorge. "This asshole doesn't deserve it. Let him go be a fucking recluse or whatever stupid game it is he's playing."

"S'not for us to decide, man," Jack said.

"This is getting tiresome," Gorge said. "Spit it out already."

"Fine," Brimmer said. "Whatever."

Jack said, "You got an invitation from Bruno Rice we're supposed to pass along."

"Yeah? And?"

"You know who Bruno Rice is?"

"I'm not an ignorant child," Gorge said. "What does he want with me?"

"Wants to meet you," Jack said. "The invitation is to a party. We'll bring you there. It's at Bruno's house out on the Island."

"I'm not going."

"You know what meeting with Bruno Rice could mean for you? For Shake Appeal?"

"I know," Gorge said. "I don't care. I don't want to meet him."

"See, man, no fucking loyalty," Brimmer said. "This is our shot. If Rice signs us, we *are* the next big thing. We're fucking made for life. All you gotta do to help us stay in his good graces is go to a party and meet the guy. That's, like, *nothing* to ask. Going to a big fancy house, drinking free booze, eating free food, taking free drugs, and all you have to do is say hello to the guy—that's not even doing us a favor. We're doing *you* a favor."

Gorge softened his voice. "Yeah, Brimmer, I know, and it's no small favor. I get that. I'm not the asshole you think I am, all right? But I want nothing to do with Bruno Rice or his people. I play what I want, when I want, where I want. I like it that way. If you want to be an indentured servant to a bloated, coprophilic bean counter, that's your business. Go ahead and sell out. Don't put it on me."

"Like you put this shit on Marty, leaving him in there? Are you gonna pay his hospital bills?" Brimmer said.

"Marty'll be fine. I didn't see you leading the charge to rescue him."

"Asshole." Brimmer spit at Gorge, his saliva falling short and splatting the concrete.

"Nice, man," Jack said. "Real persuasive."

Brimmer flipped Jack the bird and slid back to his spot in the corner.

"Delilah, can you talk some sense into him? It's Bruno Rice. The big time doesn't get any bigger," Jack said. "We do this, we all make good."

"Sorry, Jack," Delilah said. "Gorge does what he wants, and he's got his reasons. You have to trust they're the right ones. He wouldn't say no to screw you over."

"Not good enough," Jack said. "We hooked you up, man. When you first came around and nobody knew you from a shit stain on the men's room floor, we introduced you to people, we spread the word, and we got you gigs. We all vouched for you so you could have this mystery man bullshit to build your rep. You *owe* us, Max."

Gorge bristled. His body tensed as if he might hit Jack, but then a calm came over him, and the tension faded. "I owe you. I know it. And I pay my debts. *Always.* Shake Appeal's the only band I've ever sat in with more than once. All those people showing up for your shows want to hear me. You think you haven't become better musicians by playing with me? I won't sing for my fucking supper in front of the likes of Bruno Rice. He wants to hear me play, let him come down here with the people who believe, let him smell the sweat and feel the heat, let him hear what he wants to castrate and pack in plastic to sell to the brainless masses. Let him show it some respect. If you're serious about your music, you'll demand the same."

Jack stared at Gorge, speechless.

"Don't hurt yourself too badly when you fall off that high fucking horse," Brimmer said.

"Don't worry about me," Gorge said.

"Max," Jack said. "We've been scraping by on nothing for a lot of years, making records maybe a thousand people buy. No one's playing anything like our music, and we know it's good, man. We know it in our hearts that we kill it every time we pick up our instruments—but when we toured last winter, we slept in a run-down van and twice we played to single digit audiences. This isn't about selling out. It's about surviving. We need to hit another level here or this thing will end, and I'm not ready for it to end."

"I'm sorry," Gorge said.

"Okay, listen, I don't know what this means, so be cool if it's some bad shit from your past or *whatever*—I've got no idea, understand?—but Bruno said if you wouldn't come to tell you you'd be missing the most amazing party ever thrown outside the Kingdoms."

Heat flooded Gorge's face. He glared at Jack, remembering in an instant to reinforce his glamour to hide the full extent of his faerie features before they came raging through in his anger. Even with the glamour in place what Jack saw unnerved him enough to flinch two steps back from Gorge.

"What exactly would Bruno Rice know about the Kingdoms?" Gorge's voice rang high-wire tight.

"Told you, man, I don't know. Is that a place, like a club?" Jack shook his head. "You know what? I don't need to know. I don't even *want* to know. That's your business. The party is two nights from tonight. We'll take you there. Brimmer'll be on his best behavior."

"Fuck that," Brimmer said. "Crash the car if this callous motherfucker is in it."

The back door of Donnie D's jolted and scraped open. Everyone tensed, expecting the angry crowd to stampede through. Instead, a single face appeared—Marty's. He stepped into the alley, his clothes disheveled, a scratch above his right eye, but otherwise unharmed.

"You stupid mugs lock yourself out?" he said. "S'all clear now. Cops are throwing everyone in the paddy wagons."

Brimmer jumped to his feet and shoved Marty. "Thought you were dead, brother."

"Not me, man. I'm golden. I'm a ninja," Marty said. "Weirdest damn thing but those morons couldn't lay a hand on me. I was all Bruce Lee and Rocky and Snake Pliskin dodging and blocking their shit." Marty eyed Gorge for a moment. Without understanding how or why, Gorge realized, Marty intuited that his coming out unscathed had something to do with him. "It was like magic. *I* was magic."

"You got hit in the head," Brimmer said.

"Telling it like it is," Marty said. "You coming back inside or what? We got gear to salvage. I found your guitar, uh, what's left of it at least."

"Not sure I want to see," Brimmer said, throwing Gorge a nasty look as he followed Marty into the club.

Jack walked after them. "Two nights," he said to Gorge. "Meet us outside Donnie D's at eight. Rice hooked us up with wheels for the night."

"Jack," Gorge said, stopping him halfway through the door. "Watch yourself with Bruno Rice and people like him. You're only their friend as long as they've got their foot on your throat."

"We can cover our own asses," Jack said.

In the middle of the night Gorge woke to the noise of cars driving by outside the open bedroom window. Complete quiet never touched the fifth floor apartment, but he'd grown accustomed to the din of the city. The coolness of the sheets, not the noise, had woken him when he reached for Delilah and discovered her side of the bed empty. He slid out from under the covers and found her in her studio in front of a canvas, brush in hand, bringing life to lines and daubs of color in a painting that resembled a half-focused glimpse into hell. Intent on her work, she didn't notice Gorge's presence. She wore a long, red T-shirt, spotted with paint. Gorge lingered in the doorway to study her, admiring how her body moved when she was relaxed and immersed in her own world. All her defenses were down, all the walls they both erected when they went out into the world gone. Her energy and her light filled the studio. She hummed one of Gorge's songs so casually he wondered if she even noticed it.

Gorge stepped into the studio. "Couldn't sleep?"

"I thought I felt an extra set of eyes." Delilah daubed a few finishing touches onto the canvas then smiled at Gorge. "Miss me?"

"Like I'd miss my own heart," Gorge said.

He rubbed her shoulders and eyed the painting. Despite the bold composition and bright colors, a dark and uneasy tone possessed the image, the suggestion of a terrible chaos blurred by Delilah's painting style. A world in flames seen through a rain-smeared window. Madness rising, inescapable.

"Something for Peter Peters?"

"We'll see when I'm finished."

Gorge touched a corner of the canvas, tracing its edge. Delilah settled against him.

"What was that tonight?" she asked. "What was it *really*?"

Gorge smothered his face in Delilah's hair, slid his lips against her neck, and inhaled her scent. It soothed him. She had taken him in and given him life when the Kingdoms had discarded him. She contained his home, his country, his world. He embraced her tighter and laughed.

"What?" Delilah said.

"I was thinking," Gorge said, "about how the Flock of Eternity thought they were punishing me by exiling me here, but they were really giving me the greatest gift I've ever received because they sent me to you."

Delilah twisted around in Gorge's arms and kissed him. He returned the kiss. They stood pressed together, holding each other, their breath mingling, until Delilah slipped free and set to cleaning her brushes. While she worked, Gorge approached a canvas on an easel in the corner, covered with a paint-smeared sheet.

"What's this?" He reached to lift the sheet.

Delilah threw a watery paint brush at him. "Hands off. That one's special. You don't get to see it until it's done. And you're avoiding my question. I've seen a lot of terrible, incredible things since we've been together, but that riot tonight—that *scared* me. What happens if you set people off like that when you're playing to more than a couple hundred? That power can't be controlled."

"All power can be controlled if you've got the balls to control it." Gorge retrieved the paintbrush from the floor and brought it back to Delilah. "I wasn't ready tonight. That's all. I was testing the limits, and I didn't realize what I'd sparked. It went wild into the air. But it also opened the darkness for me. With enough magic, I can break the walls down—open the Way of the Bone— and keep it bound to my will. It'll take years to gather the power I need, but now I know it can be done. I can open the dark way, the way home, the way of death that makes gods of men, and then I can shove all its horrors down the throats of the fae."

Delilah gasped and dropped her brush. "You're bleeding!"

Gorge looked at his feet, surrounded by a slowly widening puddle of blood.

Delilah grabbed a clean rag from her table and rushed across the studio. Streams of blood trickled down Gorge's back and the backs of his legs, flowing from the scarred knobs above his scapulae—the vestiges of his wings. Delilah dabbed them, wicking away the blood, then she ran back to the table for another fresh rag to wipe Gorge's skin. She staunched the bleeding until the rags dripped blood then got others and wrapped his wounds in them. The blood kept flowing.

"Does it hurt?" she said.

"Like my flesh is on fire," Gorge said. "But I don't care. They sent me here to suffer. I won't play along. Forget the rags. Let's get in the shower, let it bleed down the drain."

The bloody rags fell away as Gorge left the studio. He tracked sticky, red footprints along the floor. Delilah followed him into the bathroom. Gorge stepped into the shower and turned on the water, pumping it steaming hot. Delilah stripped off her T-shirt and got in beside him. The water stung Gorge's back and carried his blood away in a pink stream that circled the drain before it vanished. He stood with his back to the spray of water and leaned into Delilah's welcoming arms. She held him, kissed his neck, and caressed the scar tissue around his wounds. Gorge jolted at her touch. Anger flared through him, a sudden heat radiating from his body. He pulled Delilah's hands away from his back, startling her, and pressed them to his chest.

"I won't be their wounded, cast-off child," he said. "I'm alive. I'm going to live like it."

Gorge kissed Delilah and pulled her against him. Delilah slid her body against his, the water letting their skin glide together.

Gorge lifted Delilah; she wrapped her legs around his waist as he pulled her onto him and entered her. She clung to him, her body straining as tension built in every muscle. Gorge pressed his face to her flesh and touched her with his lips. He let the water coursing through her black hair run down across his eyes and into his mouth. Steam and heat filled the shower. Water mingled with their sweat. On and on it lasted, their bodies moving together, apart, and back, Delilah rising and falling, over and again while their muscles grew taut and time seemed to slow down. Then suddenly Delilah's body drew ripcord tight before she shivered with release, dug her fingers into Gorge's sides, and half-screamed, half-moaned in his ear. Gorge let go at the same time, giving up a touch of magic to suspend them in that perfect bliss for what seemed like minutes, maybe hours, before he bent to his knees and let Delilah part from him.

She stood over him for a moment, trembling, pressing his head to her belly.

Overwhelmed by the intensity of the shower, which had become like a sauna, she panted. She staggered out, wrapped herself in a towel, then handed one to Gorge as he turned off the water.

She checked his back. "The bleeding stopped."

"Good," Gorge said. "It hurts less when they aren't bleeding."

He took her to bed, and they made love again.

They finished as the sun rose, and they lay half awake, Delilah's head resting on Gorge's chest, in the hazy light.

"I don't want you to be afraid of me or anything I can do," Gorge said.

"I'm not," Delilah told him. "It's the magic."

"The magic is part of me. It's part of you too."

"And what you do with the magic? Or what it does to you? To me? Should I fear that?"

Gorge caressed the side of Delilah's thigh. "Do you believe in me?"

"Yes."

"Then you should only worry about what the Flock might do to us when they figure out what I'm going to do to them. If we're careful that won't be for a long time," Gorge said. "But being careful sometimes means taking obvious bait."

"Bait?" Delilah lifted her head and pushed hair from Gorge's face. He always let his glamour down when they were together, and his faerie features never failed to captivate her. "You mean we're going to Bruno Rice's party."

"I have to know what he knows about the Kingdoms and how he knows it," Gorge said. "I've no doubt they sent spies after me, and you never know what bullshit comes about when people like Bruno Rice go screwing around with the fae."

"At least it'll be free food and drinks," Delilah said.

"Let's just hope it isn't boring," Gorge said.

SECOND VERSE

Jack, Brimmer, and Marty arrived on time outside Donnie D's, all three spilling from the back of a gleaming limousine as it braked at the curb, dressed as if they were going to a gig in full makeup with their hair in wild spikes and waves.

"Sweet wheels or what?" Jack said.

"Bullshit wheels," Gorge said. "Seduction in steel and leather. You'll have your hand down Bruno Rice's pants before you know he's got you by the balls."

Jack's smile faded. "Enough bad-ass, downer shit, Max. It's a long drive. I don't want to listen to it all the way to the party."

"This could be a show of respect. Ever think of that, Max?" Marty said. "You're on fire, and we're, like, your unofficial band. Maybe Bruno's just giving you your due."

"You've got a good heart to think that, Marty, but people like Bruno Rice aren't capable of respect—only of owning things and destroying them," Gorge said. "If you don't want to listen to me tell it otherwise then stop trying to convince me he's a prince among men. I'm going with you. That makes you all look good for Bruno. Count your victories and let go of the rest."

"Fine with me if we don't talk at all," Brimmer said.

"Still sore about your gear?" Gorge asked. "Not my fault you can't keep a guitar in your hands when the crowd gets rowdy."

Brimmer shook his head and slipped back into the limo. The others joined him, Gorge and Delilah sitting together across from the members of Shake Appeal. Jack shut the door, and Marty cracked open the mini bar and poured everyone drinks.

"Don't think Rice sent this car for you three," Gorge said as he sipped the whiskey Marty handed him. "He's using you to get to me. If you don't like it, all I can say is sometimes the truth hurts."

"Whatever, man." Jack rapped on the glass divider behind the driver, and the car rolled away from the curb.

"Hate me or not," Gorge said, "but you're the only band I've gotten close to. I could've chosen any group on the scene. Hell, I could've gone solo, but I picked Shake Appeal because I like what I hear when you play. I've sent your reputation into the stratosphere. We helped each other. But if you think you're not using me now—and that Bruno Rice isn't using you—you're naive. Or is Brimmer going to take the high road next time I come to jam with you and draw the crowds? Should I take my guitar and find someone else to play with? What do you say, Brimmer?"

"I say shut the hell up and let it be already," Brimmer said.

"So be it." Gorge settled into his seat, reclining against Delilah.

Brimmer slipped a joint from his jacket, cracked the window, and lit up.

City lights rolled past, muted by tinted glass. The limo crossed the East River on the 59th Street Bridge and took it to the Long Island Expressway. It seemed to float through the night. For most of the ride, no one spoke, letting Marty's music play on the limo's tape deck and occupy the awkward silence. Marty cycled through a handful of cassettes—Black Flag, Killing Joke, The Clash, The Germs, Motörhead, The Ramones—naming his favorite song from each one while he sipped vodka on ice. Brimmer and Jack passed another joint. The alcohol and weed mellowed the harsh mood, and even Brimmer seemed to relax. They were far from the city when the car left the LIE for winding back roads. Gorge lost track of their location, but he knew they were somewhere on Long Island's north shore, where the homes stood far apart and the woods grew thick among them. He had been out this way before. He knew of the lightless streets full of shadows draped in sparse moonlight, of the houses well hidden from the road, of the nearby cliffs and beaches on the Long Island Sound.

Magic lingered here.

More than one kind.

He sensed the thread of common background magic emanating from the natural world, the aura of trees and plants, of stones and living earth, intermingled with the steady presence of the Sidhe that persisted even in semi-wild places like this. Despite the houses, roads, and humans, faerie rings and secret doors stood hidden in the stands of birches and maples, in hollows ringed with pines, in the overgrown brush, and the hills no one ever climbed. For those who knew how to approach them, the barrier between the Kingdoms and the mortal world fell away there. Only the Sidhe could sense them, but plenty of Sidhe occupied the woods tonight—fae and others from the Kingdoms. It put Gorge on edge. He hoped they wouldn't notice him; it was harder to conceal his magic out here than in the city.

Another magic thread interested him more. It ran weak. Crude. Polluted.

It carried a soft sting, like touching your tongue to the end of a dying nine-volt battery.

Gorge's awareness of it grew as the car turned through an iron gate and traveled up a long, twisting driveway. Then the limo rounded a curve, and Bruno Rice's house appeared like fireworks exploding from the night, a mirage of spotlights and strings of colored lights, paper lanterns, and torches mounted on stakes, all of it cocooned in the raucous noise of the party and an amped-up ska band playing somewhere behind the mansion.

The limo stopped at the front entrance. A man in a tuxedo and oversized gold sunglasses with slats across the lenses opened the door. A red-haired woman in a green silk gown with a neckline that dropped to her navel gestured to everyone from the top of the front steps as they climbed out of the car. They followed her into the house. Her white feather boa fluttered as she led them into a foyer as big as all of Donnie D's. She handed them each a flute of champagne from a tray on a marble pedestal. The place echoed with party noises.

"I'm Sharon, your hostess," the redhead said. "Mr. Rice is pleased you all could come. He has many guests to entertain tonight, but he'll make a point of spending time with each of you. Until then, make yourselves at home. There's only one rule for tonight's party: *No rules!* Indulge yourself and let everyone else do the same."

"Got it, thanks." Making no effort to hide how he eyed Sharon's figure as she moved to welcome the next arriving group, Jack whistled. "Gorgeous."

"Try not to have too much of a good time, Max," Brimmer said. "I'm sure that won't be hard for you." He then walked off and disappeared into the party. Marty went after him.

"Our ride home splits at two a.m.," Jack said. "Cool with you?"

"Whatever," Gorge said.

Jack nodded, drained his champagne, and then left for the backyard, discarding his glass on an empty table.

Gorge asked Delilah, "Feel it?"

Delilah nodded. "I've got goose-bumps. There's magic here."

"Rancid magic." Gorge scowled. "I felt it more clearly the closer we came to this place. Now it's all around us. I want to know what it is. Ready for some seek-and-destroy?"

"Lead the way."

They walked into the next room, crowded with people, drinks in hand. A dozen or so partiers knelt around a coffee table, snorting lines of cocaine from the mirrored tabletop. A mound of the white powder waited piled in the center, shining razor blades fanned out around it. Gorge and Delilah moved on to the next room, where they found a spread of catered delicacies on a dining table, people milling around it, shoving bits into their mouths, spraying crumbs when they spoke. The third room they entered, a den with a built-in bar, featured two men and two women, dressed only in tight, metallic satin shorts, pouring cocktail after cocktail for the horde pressed against the bar rail. The party sprawled through the house, each room a different offering, and as he and Delilah moved from one to another, Gorge felt the steady presence of the sour magic.

It turned his stomach.

Like sniffing a piss-drenched wino in a subway station.

Its miasma hung over the house, but only he and Delilah seemed to notice.

They encountered a room where people sat around hookahs, getting high. Another, lit by dozens of lava lamps, accommodated an orgy with pillows and mattresses scattered on the floor. A smoke-filled room hosted gambling tables. One offered chains and leather straps bolted to the walls and a rack of whips and masks with zippers, which several people were squeezing into. Yet another was dark except for the soft glow of black-light artwork, quiet except for random moans and sighs, and steaming with the acrid scent of incense. Whatever kinks or perversions his guests might desire, Bruno Rice provided. Debauchery overtook the entire mansion, but nowhere did Gorge find what he sought.

After an hour, his frustration fermented to anger. He wondered if Rice meant to taunt him. First, he'd told Jack to mention the Kingdoms, and now this taste of hidden magic made his skin writhe. No doubt Bruno wanted more from him than his music. Gorge needed to learn what he really sought; he had to make sure Rice was only human.

He bulled his way down a corridor, jolting partiers. No one recognized him. People knew Max Chaos by reputation, but few knew what he looked like. Then a familiar face appeared in the crowd: Jake Blaze. Dressed in the same Misfits T-shirt and sports jacket, he clutched a bottle of the same cheap beer from Motormouth's while he chatted up a mini-dress-wearing brunette giving him a tepid smile.

"Your cheap tastes never change, do they, Jake?" Gorge said as he shoved past, jostling him.

Jake grabbed Gorge's arm. "Hey, what the hell? You shove me and insult us and walk by like it doesn't matter? You owe the lady an apology."

Gorge eyed the frowning brunette and then tapped Jake's beer bottle. "The beer, Jakey, you drink cheap beer. The lady's out of your league and far too good for anyone who drinks this swill. Same shit brand you were drinking at Motormouth's."

Jake's eyes narrowed. "I know you?"

Gorge eyed Jake, evaluating the glassiness of his eyes. "You knew me well enough the other night." The spell Gorge had sung at Motormouth's should've robbed Jake of his memory of most of their conversation but not of anything before or after he'd cast it.

"Yeah, well, wannabes like you are easy to forget," Jake said.

"Oooh," Gorge said. "The hungry dog finds its bark. Too bad your memory is as weak as your mind." Gorge jerked his arm free and plunged back into the crowd.

"Asshole," Jake shouted, giving the brunette a welcome chance to slip away.

Gorge pushed deeper into the party, yanking open doors, glancing into rooms, then slamming them shut again when they didn't yield what he wanted. Delilah hurried to keep pace with him. Ignoring the puzzled glances of the party guests, he tapped walls, touched windows, searching for hidden spaces; he lifted framed paintings and photos; he knocked over stacks of books and CDs.

In a corner room on the third floor, Gorge stopped dead.

A wall of windows on the far side of the room overlooked the backyard, where the ska band played beside a swimming pool silvery with light. Soundproofing dampened their music, and tinted windows muted the sparkle of the torches outside. No one here indulged in the vices offered in the other rooms, and except for a group of ten by the corner window, most lounged on the sofas and armchairs in twos or threes, sipping drinks during the empty spaces of their conversations. No one clamored for the food spread out on various tables, and no one lusted obviously after drugs or sex. Gorge knew some of their faces from magazines, movies, and television. Beautiful people. VIPs. Too famous to mingle long with the general mass of partiers. *People with something to lose*, he thought. Then he realized the group in the back corner sat gathered around the lead singer from a triple-platinum supergroup—a band whose music Gorge despised.

Missing, though, was any sense of the magic he tracked.

Its presence had grown more powerful on his approach to the door, but inside the room he felt cut off from it. Defensive spells placed on the room blocked it out. He was about to step back out when a voice called out, "Gavin? Is that you? No way, man, that can't be you!"

A tall, gray-haired man in jeans and a linen sports coat stood and squinted at Gorge. His pony tail trailed down his back. He crossed the room like his bones and joints were made of pipes and gears, his muscles of wires and belts, all of it in need of a tune-up. He bumped his knee against an ottoman, nearly spilling his drink onto the shoulders of a woman in a backless gown but then recovered and approached Gorge, pointing a knobby finger at him.

"Shite. Do you know something?" The man spoke with a soft British accent. "You're a dead ringer for Gavin Gray, which I guess is the only kind of ringer you can be since Gavin's a decade in the ground. But, blimey, you could be his twin brother if his twin was born thirty years after him. I was about to ask if you remembered me. But you couldn't if we never met, now, could you?" The man wavered and exhaled. "Rich Taber, by the way."

"It's cool." Gorge laughed. "I get the Gavin Gray thing often enough I might have wondered who my real father was if Gray had ever played my hometown. Only coincidence, though."

"Hell of a coincidence," Taber said. "I played with Gray three times in the studio before I was in Gold."

"You were in Gold? No way," Gorge said. "You're *that* Rich Taber?"

"That's me, the one and only." Taber grinned. "Singer and drummer for Gold from '66 to '69, which was as long as we could keep our egos in check. We made some damn good music while it lasted, though. Gavin Gray's how I wound up in that band. You know that?"

Gorge shook his head. "No. Tell me."

In truth Gorge knew the story as well as Rich Taber, if not better, because he'd been Gavin Gray for twenty years—up until he got tired of being him and "killed" Gavin in a plane crash. His glamour changed his appearance now yet somehow Taber saw through it enough to catch the resemblance.

"I jammed with Gray three times." Taber steadied himself with a hand on Gorge's shoulder. "Two of those sessions I was tripping. The third I was too drunk to get up from my drum set. If I were another man, you might say it's a bleeding miracle I remember Gray at all—but faces are something I *never* forget. I meet you once your face is with me forever, etched in the old gray matter." Taber tapped the top of his head then noticed Delilah holding Gorge's arm. He did a half double take. "There's a very beautiful face right now. M'lady, forgive me for being such a rude—and mildly intoxicated—old fart. Didn't mean to ignore or bore you. Do you know who Gavin Gray was?"

"I've heard of him," Delilah said, smirking.

"Then you understand my shock when I thought he'd walked in here. I thought someone might have slipped a little something extra into my drink to make me see things. Sadly not, though." Taber paused to grin. "Anyway, to make a long story short, I figured I'd screwed my reputation after my sessions with Gray. Not that my performance was any less than perfect. No matter how screwed up my head was I could always keep a beat and play like the Devil himself. You can rely on Rich Taber to pull it out a hundred and ten percent when it comes to music. But Gray was a nut job. Brilliant, no question. Greatest musician I *ever* played with. He made anyone who played with him *better*, you know? You always played the *best* you could when you played with him, and he deserved every bit of fame and fortune he had—*but...* the guy was so angry *all* the time. He played like he wanted to punish the audience and lay down tracks that would set people off. Hardly ever had anything nice to say to anyone during the sessions until the last time—that time he made a kind comment to me. Totally out of character. So I thought, well, he doesn't much care for me, or that I've been intoxicated in his presence, or whatever the hell it is about me that rubs him the wrong way, and I figured I was done because in those days, Gray could sink your studio career with a word, and I didn't have a band at the time."

"How'd it work out?" Gorge asked.

"About two months after all that, Eric Ginger rings me up out of the blue and tells me, 'Rich, I've got Alan Desmond here, we want to form a band, and you're our drummer—you in?' Of course, I said 'yes,' and the rest is history. They made me the singer when it turned out I had a better vocal range than Ginger. Found out while we were recording our first album they'd picked me because Gavin Gray told them he'd never played with a better drummer. Called me a 'mad genius.' I always intended to thank Gavin for that, but I never saw him again. And I'll tell you a sad truth: I cried the day he died."

"A lot of people did," Delilah said.

Taber nodded. "You could do worse than having a passing resemblance to Gavin Gray."

"One thing I know about him." Gorge winked at Taber. "The man never spoke a word he didn't mean. If he liked your drumming then you must be the true prince of percussion."

"Shite, you sounded exactly like him then." Taber's face turned white. "Why'd you say that? 'Prince of percussion,' I mean? That's what he said to me the last day we jammed. How could you know...?" He glanced down at his glass. "Shite, how much *have* I had to drink?"

As if Taber's question had summoned him, Bruno Rice entered the room and pushed into the conversation with a booming voice. "Not nearly enough, I'd say, eh, Rich? Go nab yourself a refill. It's a party after all. You don't want to go about dry, or people will think you're on the prowl for a fresh liver again. Can't have more rumors spreading, can we?" Rice slapped Taber on the back and pointed him toward the bar against the wall. "Chin, chin."

"Thanks, Bruno. Suppose one more can't hurt. It's not like I'm driving." Taber laughed then nodded to Gorge and Delilah before he toddled off to the bar, saying, "Lovely meeting you two. Don't let Bruno take advantage now."

"Who's to say they won't take advantage of me?" Rice, too, had a British accent but louder and brassier than Taber's. He took Delilah's hand, kissed it, and then offered his hand for Gorge to shake. Gorge merely studied Rice from head to foot, assessing his meaty figure.

Rice was taller than Gorge had expected, almost as tall as him, and he wore a tailored black suit with an electric orange silk shirt and a black necktie. He was past middle age with thinning, blond hair cut close and styled to give him a casually ruffled appearance, as if he'd stepped in from the wind only a moment ago. His fair skin and red cheeks added a deceptive touch of youthful vigor. His smile never settled on his face but squirmed there, untrustworthy. But Gorge saw even more reason to distrust Bruno Rice because the second the man had entered the room, he'd found the source of the magic.

Rice himself.

He stank of stale, rotting magic, so much so that a wave of nausea rolled through Gorge. If the magic hadn't been fading and attenuated, he might've vomited. The power wasn't native to Rice, who Gorge saw was human. That meant Rice came by it through the old rites and disciplines or by trickery and theft. Either means made him a wizard.

As if the man didn't already disgust him enough.

Rice dropped his hand to his side, ignoring Gorge's snub. "Here's Max Chaos in the flesh and blood. Not an easy man to reach, are you? I'm thrilled we got you out here tonight thanks to our mutual friends. They're a talented lot, Shake Appeal, aren't they?"

"They do all right," Gorge said.

"I hope you're enjoying yourself." Rice nodded to Delilah. "You, too, miss. Ah, I'm afraid I haven't had the pleasure."

"I'm Delilah," Delilah said. "Great party. You've got a lot of... *interesting* friends."

Rice laughed. "No, I don't. I've got a lot of interesting sycophants, wannabes, employees, and other trained monkeys, but when it comes to friends, I'm sorely deficient. I do hope *we* can be friends, though."

"Don't get your hopes too high," Gorge said.

Frowning, Rice said, "Something wrong?"

Gorge felt a gentle pressure touch his mind and spirit: Rice probing his magic, testing it, perhaps thinking himself subtle enough that Gorge wouldn't notice, but the man's clumsy efforts betrayed his lack of skill. Gorge entertained pushing back with crushing force, blasting the magic out of Rice and turning his brain to jelly, but then that would show his hand, maybe even give Rice what he wanted—whatever that was.

"What could be wrong?" Gorge said. "We're at a party full of people more dedicated to wasting their bodies and souls than to the music that pays for them to do it."

"Don't be a prude," Rice said. "Everyone's entitled to a wild time now and then. Gets the creative juices flowing, doesn't it?"

"Then it's a crutch," Gorge said. "If you have to blow your mind or get your rocks off to play good music, that's pathetic."

Rice's foul magic got under Gorge's skin and rattled him. He took a deep breath and let Delilah hold his hand and trace circles in his palm to soothe him. He couldn't afford to let Rice put him off balance.

"Nothing personal, of course," Gorge said.

Rice scowled. "No, you're absolutely right. We're supposed to be about the music. But we've lost our way and made it about…" Rice waved a hand, indicating the mansion and the party, "…temptation, sin, pleasure. That's why I wanted to meet you, Max. Because it's all so *utterly real* in you. Your music *lives and breathes* like it's the only thing in the world that matters to you. That's what everyone who's heard you play says. Even if you think I'm some bloated, old corporate desk-jockey, you've got to realize it all started for me with the music. I came up from a cold-water flat in Hackney. I fought, clawed, and leveraged my way to build Disharmony Records from scratch with sweat and blood. It *all* began with the music. I know what real music can do. I understand bloody well the difference between that and some of the shit my company peddles to pay the bills."

"Do you? Good for you, record man," Gorge said. "You trying to convince me or yourself? Not that it matters. I don't care about your pitch. I write and play on my terms."

"I wouldn't change that for—wait, shit, Max, where are you going?" Rice said.

"Back to the fucking city," Gorge told him. He stepped through the door, leading Delilah by the hand. "All the trees and nature out here make me edgy—and there's a sickening stench."

Rice came after them, but with the partying crowd for interference, Gorge and Delilah soon lost him. They wound their way through the jam-packed celebration until they reached the foyer. The redhead in the green gown and the man in the tuxedo were gone. People crammed the foyer, drinking champagne from the tray on the marble pedestal. The front doors hung open; a crowd milled around on the steps shadowed by a canopy of cigarette smoke. It wasn't yet midnight, and their limo waited nowhere in sight. Gorge searched around for a phone to call a cab.

A blonde woman in a clinging, diaphanous, white gown with a diamond-studded collar broke from the crowd.

"Lost?" she said.

"Looking for a phone," Delilah told her.

"There's one in the next room," the woman said. "Are you leaving already? I wish you'd stay a little longer. My name's Cleo Rush, Bruno's wife. He's ticked you off, hasn't he? If anyone knows how pompous and abrasive he can be, it's me, but I promise you it's all for show. All he wants is to talk music with you."

"With me? Is that so?" Gorge asked. "Who am I to interest the great Bruno Rice?"

"You're Max Chaos, aren't you? And you're Delilah?" Cleo said. "Brimmer pointed you out for me earlier."

Impatient to leave, Gorge's anger flared, but when he met Cleo's stare, her beauty melted his glare. Pure, clear skin stretched tight over high cheekbones and a perfect symmetry of lips and eyes refined her expression to living poetry. Gold and platinum hair shimmered around her face in perpetual, gentle motion while light danced on its sheen. The white gown fit her body as if it had been sewn onto her, and Gorge found mementos of the most beautiful fae in how her limbs fit together, how she moved, and how she tipped her weight on one foot and threw her sensuous curves into stark, seductive lines. He could've written ballads about the arc of her slender neck or the fragile shapes her delicate fingers made and the twinkling rings that decorated them. Aside from Delilah, she was the most physically perfect mortal woman he'd ever met.

Gorge found himself disarmed, and, in a very rare occurrence, speechless.

Noticing this, Delilah laughed.

"Yes, I'm Delilah." She offered Cleo her hand.

"So nice to meet you," Cleo said, taking it. "Then you must be Max."

Gorge gave Cleo a bow. "Max Chaos. A pleasure to meet you."

"Will you stay?" Cleo said. "I've heard so much about your music, Max. The guys in Shake Appeal say you're both incredibly talented. I thought Delilah and I could talk art. I've got some fantastic pieces in my collection I could show you."

Delilah touched Gorge's shoulder, signaling that she wanted to stay.

Gorge glanced around for Rice, expecting him to emerge in a panting bluster from a door or alcove at any minute.

"All right," Gorge said. "We'll hang around a bit."

Cleo smiled. "Wonderful! Come on, I'll take you where we can talk."

Although Rice was out of sight, his magic vibrated in the air, and Gorge wondered if he'd sent his wife to salvage the situation he'd blundered. If so it was a cheap shot to play on Delilah's passion for art—but then maybe it was only what it seemed. He sensed no magic in Cleo. She seemed sincere, her interest in Delilah's art genuine. Maybe, as he did the members of Shake Appeal, Rice played her like a pawn. Gorge heard only fragments of Cleo and Delilah's conversation over the din of the party. The seemingly tireless ska band outside butchered an obscure song he loved. After a few bars, he recognized it as Mucous Membrane's "Venus of the Hardsell"; the realization only deepened his foul mood.

Cleo led them through the house, which proved even larger than Gorge had realized.

They passed through the party in full swing, opportunities for sin and gluttony arrayed like carnival games, only the barkers missing.

Rice had been right about one thing: The party reminded Gorge of the Kingdoms.

Like Rice, the kings and queens in the Flock of Eternity liked to burn through fortunes to put on endless festivals of indulgence. They invited their subjects to partake only so they could laugh at them afterward. The fae possessed so much— beauty, magic, riches, talent, near immortality—yet they too often wasted it on petty pleasures and grudges instead of creating worthwhile and wonderful things to push the boundaries of art and life. Rice was worse. Exile in the mortal world had opened Gorge's eyes to what made life worth living, and none of the things with which Bruno Rice surrounded himself counted.

Cleo took them into a long, wide room and closed the door, shutting out the music and the noise. The quiet surprised Gorge. As he had upstairs, he lost touch with Bruno's magic as the same dampening sensation kicked in—but he sensed different magic here.

Only a flicker, but unmistakable.

Power contained by the room.

Cleo held her arms out and spun around slowly. "This is our favorite place to unwind. In here, Bruno can shed his image. He's a different person, more down to earth. I want you to see that side of him. I'm sure you'll warm up to him if you do."

Gorge doubted it. The cavernous room oozed undiluted opulence and excess.

Wide, soft chairs upholstered in leather and silk. A crystal chandelier suspended above a dining table of oak with inlays of cherry wood. At one end of the room, a huge fish tank built into the wall; at the other, a giant-screen, projection television and four theater-style lounge chairs. Between them and beside the dining table stood a full-size pool table. A well-stocked bar occupied one corner. An array of framed artwork—all contemporary or at least twentieth century—hung on the walls. Pieces by Keith Haring and Ralph Steadman. One from Andy Warhol. A Peter Max and a chaotic splatter by Jackson Pollock. A row of black-and-white comic book pages by Robert Crumb, Jack Kirby, and Harvey Kurtzman. Gorge knew all the artists' work from what Delilah had taught him in the hours they'd spent in museums, poring over art books, or visiting the studios of artists she befriended. Art covered every inch of wall, a priceless collection, and if Delilah's reaction gave any indication, every piece in it wondrous in some way.

"Incredible," Delilah said. "How'd you gather all this?"

"It's taken me years. Not everything is here now, though. I loaned a few pieces to museums in Berlin and Madrid. I don't mean to brag, but it gets me so excited," Cleo said. "I got a lot of it through Peter Peters. He gets a line on almost anything. Says I have a natural eye for signature pieces."

"You know Peter?" Delilah said.

Cleo nodded. "Do you?"

"I'm trying to talk him into giving me a show."

"That would be *amazing*," Cleo said. "I'd love to see your work."

She led Delilah along the wall, pointing out her favorite pieces while the two women chatted.

Gorge leaned against the doorway. The soft carpet tempted him to slip off his shoes and dig his toes into it.

Lights from the backyard stage flashed dimly through floor-to-ceiling windows and French doors with tinted glass. Not a note of music drifted into the room, soundproofed like the room directly above it. Yet Gorge sensed magic bleeding into the space—magic besides Rice's, which was blocked out by the same defenses that shielded the upstairs room.

He pushed his senses to sample more of the energy.

It possessed a component Gorge couldn't unwind. Feedback. A static charge. Some type of interference. An artifact, perhaps. Some faerie relic or rotting grimoire or blessed bit of bone Bruno had hidden away while he tried to draw the power out of it.

On the opposite end of the room, Cleo and Delilah huddled deep in conversation beneath what Gorge thought—incredulously—was a Picasso. He tuned them out and searched through the layers of energy that infused the house, picking out the thin thread of magic tethered to the room. The artifact wasn't far but obscured by further concealment spells. Poorly configured ones, at that, or Gorge wouldn't have felt it at all. He assumed Rice had cast them. The cycles of energy led his senses around and then down, tugging from beneath the floor, from the basement... the only part of the house he and Delilah hadn't seen. He hadn't even noticed a door or stairwell to get there. A sneaky bastard, Rice had made it off-limits, maybe so he could dip in here every so often to pick up a charge, Gorge thought.

He concentrated on the space below the house, lacing his senses into the surrounding earth, then drawing them back, bringing them up through the foundation, passing his senses through cracks in the spells. He encountered blank spots in the basement, voids where perhaps Rice had done a better job of hiding things, but without knowing more, Gorge couldn't force them to reveal themselves. Then his senses touched music.

A song.

Someone down there singing with bare-bones musical accompaniment.

Powerful and heartfelt.

A bluesman with his lonely guitar.

A torch-song seductress stretched across a gentle piano.

A mother singing to a sickly child. A father scratching out a dirge at the side of a grave.

Sadness.

Loss.

Grief.

The voice itself eluded Gorge.

He caught only bits of the melody, certain he knew it one moment, then lost the next. Soft and dark. It lifted magic on its plaintive notes and cast it into the room.

Gorge followed the magic until the song became clearer, but he still couldn't nail it down or who was singing. He got down on hands and knees and pressed his ear to the floor.

He could almost make it out.

"Max?" Delilah said. "Are you all right?"

Her voice snapped Gorge out of his exploration, and he lost the song.

The interruption ignited a burst of rage in him, but the concern on Delilah's face rendered it dead on arrival.

"I'm fine," Gorge said.

"You're sure you're all right?" Cleo looked skeptical. "We called you three times before you heard us."

"Only trying to get a different perspective on things," Gorge said.

The door bumped open then and Bruno Rice entered. "What perspective would that be, Max, the worm's-eye view?"

Gorge stood up and put his arm around Delilah.

"Let me guess. It's one of those 'creative-type' things. So glad I caught up with you again. Have you been enjoying Cleo's art?" Rice walked to the bar and poured himself a drink.

"Can I get anyone a tipple?" he asked.

"White wine for me," Cleo said.

Delilah followed her to the bar. "I'll take the same."

Rice served them, then glanced at Gorge. "Anything for you, Max?"

Gorge seated himself, tilted his chair back, and kicked his feet up on the table. "Whiskey, Bruno. Make it a double."

Rice faltered a moment at the sight of Gorge's feet on the table, but he poured the drink and brought it to him without losing his twisted smile. Gorge took the glass, drained it, and then handed it back to Rice.

"How about another?" he said.

"Sure, why not?" Bruno said. "It's a party, after all."

Rice carried the glass back to the bar, refilled it, and returned it to Gorge, who again drained it then offered it back to Rice.

This time, Rice didn't take it. "You're pulling my strings now."

"Am I?" Gorge stamped his feet down, got up, and poured himself more whiskey. "I thought I was enjoying your hospitality. *It is a party after all.* Didn't you say you wanted us to be friends?"

"Yes, of course," Rice said. "I apologize for being so presumptuous earlier. That's what this is about, isn't it? I overstepped, assumed familiarity where none existed, pressed too hard, and you, Max, are a man who won't be pressed. You do what you want to do, and no one's going to glad-hand you. I respect that. So let's lay our cards on the table, shall we? You play music I want to record—simple as that. In a studio or live, with or without Shake Appeal or any other band you choose, an album of *your* music, or a session with another artist. Anything at all, anyway you want it, whenever and wherever you want it. You call the shots."

"I already do," Gorge said. "Sadly for you, though, my wherever, whatever, and however don't include singing to you for my supper."

"Don't think of it like that," Rice said. "You'll be well paid, of course. Overpaid, even. Hell, any music we release will make millions. One album and you'll be set for life. Money's no object. Does that hold no appeal for you whatsoever?"

"Tell me, my dear, new friend Bruno," Gorge said. "How many millions do you have? Look at this fucking place—it's an emperor's palace in an era when all the emperors are dead. When is it enough? A man must know what matters most to him.

Everything else is distraction. Leeches draining your soul. Have you got any soul left to lose?"

Rice trembled, and his face flushed red. His hand white-knuckled his glass until it seemed it might shatter in his grip. Gorge's words had sliced into Rice like stilettos. He saw it all laid bare: Rice had put on this insane, overblown party for Gorge's sake to match the kind of celebrations that went on in the Kingdoms.

He had meant it to impress Gorge.

Except Gorge didn't give a shit, and Bruno had no idea why.

Gorge thought for a moment that Rice would smash the glass or throw it across the room and kick over some furniture. A temper tantrum from a big man unused to being told no.

It disappointed Gorge when the heat faded from Bruno's expression as he regained his composure.

"As I was saying, don't think of it like that," Bruno said, voice brittle with control. "The money doesn't matter? I'm not sure I believe you, but I'll take you at your word for now. How about reaching an audience? Don't you want to bring your music to millions rather than hundreds? These clubs you're playing, Max, anyone with talent uses them to pop their cherry and then moves on, and anyone without talent dies there on the vine. I'll admit your influence has upped the ante, but you'll never come close to what you can do with my help."

"Come close to millions of brain-dead, tone-deaf idiots who won't understand what they're hearing," Gorge said. "The mindless mass market, the sing-along society. Let's all dance and bop and not think too hard what it's all about. Mood music for drinking and fucking. You think that's what I'm about?"

"I—" Bruno stammered and fell short.

His face paled. He gritted his teeth, locked in a moment of intense anger and confusion.

Gorge tipped himself another whiskey then said, "Screw it, Bruno. I'm only giving you shit. I mean, c'mon, man, you've never even heard me play."

The tension drained from Rice's body. The color returned to his face, flush with shame. He set his glass on the bar and seated himself on a stool. "Bollocks, you're right. I've made a fool of myself. What can I say?"

"Say nothing. Forget it," Gorge said.

"How can I make it up to you?" Rice asked.

"I don't want you to," Gorge told him.

"I must. I'll think of a way," Bruno said. "If you still want to go home, Cleo will call you a car right now."

"Thanks, that's very human of you, Bruno." Gorge leaned in close to Rice and whispered in his ear: "Don't think you know anything about the Kingdoms or the powers you're toying with. This party wasn't even a pale echo of things I've seen in the Kingdoms. If you fuck with me, I'll make sure you regret it."

Rice tensed again. He glared at Gorge, but he didn't speak.

Delilah said goodnight to Cleo, and Gorge kissed her on the cheek.

"Thanks for the art show," he said.

"You're welcome," Cleo said. "Delilah, I'll call you about Peter Peters."

"Thanks," Delilah said.

As they walked out the door, Gorge paused and glanced back at Rice. "Bruno, if you're really interested then come out some night and hear me play."

Gorge took his guitar to Dresden Underground.

Glamour hid his and Delilah's arrival. The first anyone noticed them they slid into seats at the bar, half-hidden in shadows, while an all-girl group, Your Uncool Niece, rocked the end of their first set. It had been more than a week since Bruno Rice's party and longer since Gorge had last performed. Meeting Bruno had made him wary of exposing himself, but tonight he itched to fill himself up with magic.

He decided he'd come to the right place.

The crowd at the Underground wanted an excuse to cut loose.

Yet despite how hard and fast they played Your Uncool Niece failed to throw down the fierce sounds and defiant energy the audience craved. The crowd's need sparked the magic in Gorge and stirred the music in his soul. He waited until Niece finished their first set then asked Nancy Asp, their singer, if he could sit in on their next one. The request lit Nancy up with excitement, and when the band returned to the stage half an hour later,

Gorge slid from the shadows and let his guitar announce him.

The crowd roared.

By the time Gorge played through the first chorus, the audience heaped wild applause on them and danced hard enough to shake the floor. Gorge dug deep into the song, keeping his lead tight, elevating Niece on his playing, helping their full potential shine in their music.

The magic kicked in, surged through Gorge, and laced itself through the crowd.

He smiled at Delilah, who sat at the bar, serene, beautiful, drawing in her sketchbook.

Word spread about Max's appearance, and the crowd bloomed as Niece worked through their set. Within an hour the place was packed tighter than a rush-hour subway car. Even Brimmer and Marty showed up, and Gorge wondered if Brimmer had ditched the chip on his shoulder only to realize he hadn't when Rice and Cleo joined him. To turn up that fast, Bruno must have been slumming it, with Brimmer playing lookout between kissing his ring and kissing his ass. The group kept to a back corner cut off from the crowd behind a cigarette machine. Deep into the music, Marty and Cleo danced and tapped their feet. Brimmer lit up a smoke and made a point of looking bored. Rice stood still, eyes glued to the stage, hands clasped at his waist like a prince surveying his future domain. Gorge couldn't read his emotions, but he seemed transfixed by what he heard.

Gorge played an eruption of breakneck riffs, weaving them through Niece's music like secret assassins hiding in plain sight. The magic feedback loop spiked. The crowd kicked their dancing into overdrive. The building rumbled and ceiling fixtures swayed, adding to the disorienting dazzle of the stage lights. Gorge glimpsed shock in the faces of the bartender and the bouncers as the sudden jolt of motion startled them. They scanned the crowd for trouble. No doubt they'd heard about the riot at Donnie D's.

Delilah flashed Gorge a warning look. He blew her back a kiss.

Impossible as it seemed, Brimmer looked even more tense than usual as he too checked out the crowd, ready for another melee. But Gorge held control. Neither the music nor the magic had driven the Donnie D's audience over the edge—it had been the darkness.

Tonight, Gorge wouldn't touch the Way of the Bone.

Not with Rice, dilettante wizard and money-grubbing *nouveau riche*, in the club.

Shitty grasp of magic or not, Rice would likely sense the cold energy rippling out of the Way of the Bone and wonder about it. And while his magic was no secret to Rice, the darkness—the knowledge to reach it, or even that it existed, and what it could do—needed to be kept close to Gorge's heart. But that didn't mean Gorge couldn't taunt Rice.

He pushed harder, played faster, sent more magic into the members of Niece to help them keep up and tighten their playing. So much magic flowed into Gorge he sent a touch out to Cleo and Marty to make them feel as if they floated on the music.

Gorge played hard, reckless chords laced with bright melodies that dragged in bits of music from the Kingdoms and forced them into shape within the limits of sound in the mortal world. Niece hung with him through every note. *I've been wasting my time with Shake Appeal,* he thought, *and won't it give that hypocritical prick, Brimmer, what he deserves if I kick them off for Niece. Piss off Bruno, too, to lose the one hook he'd managed to land in me.*

Gorge grinned. Contempt crept into the music, bled into the magic.

Rice and Brimmer's faces soured.

They turned pale and broke out in cold sweats.

They wiped their brows, opened their shirt collars, and fanned their faces. They looked woozy and faint, and he laughed at their frailty, his laughter lost in the roar pouring from the amplifiers. Gorge fingered notes from a potent minor scale he'd learned in his youth; it made Rice and Brimmer even more uncomfortable.

Rice rubbed his head. Brimmer clutched his gut.

With the right notes Gorge could kill them.

The thought delighted him.

Nancy wheeled around, confused by the harsh change of tone in the music. Gorge winked at her and took it in another direction. He pushed Rice and Brimmer from his mind, dissipated his hate, and then dropped back into the sheer joy of the song. Niece exploded in the spotlight; their music flared in the hearts of the audience. They played with abandon, full of passion, as if nothing in the entire universe mattered more than the music they drove through the speakers—and for as long as they performed, nothing did.

Gorge played things close for the last few songs, gracing them with short, blistering solos and improvised riffs, until Niece wound it down and ended the set.

Nancy kissed him on the cheek and hugged him before he left the stage.

Delilah hugged him at the bar. "Thought we'd have another riot on our hands."

"I didn't take it there," Gorge told her. "But I didn't think it'd hurt to make a point for our new *friends* who came out to hear me play."

Delilah tilted her head. "Who?"

Gorge, sensing Rice approach, took a swig of beer, and gestured over his shoulder. Delilah glimpsed Rice, groaned then brightened when she noticed Cleo. Brimmer and Marty came with them.

"Delilah, Max," Rice said as he pressed up to the bar beside them. "Incredible! You were right, absolutely right. I *needed* to hear you play. Stupid of me not to have done it sooner. But then you don't make it easy, do you? We've been driving around this neighborhood every night for a week, counting street people and waiting for *the call* from Brimmer on my car phone. So damn glad we did. Amazing! And that band, wow, brilliant, talented ladies."

"You really think so?" Gorge said.

"Best I've heard in a year."

"You're full of shit," Gorge said.

"No, I mean it," Rice said. "You pushed them to the edge, and they stayed right there with you. Variations on a three-chord theme, layers so deep I felt like I was swimming in the song, tempo changes, contrapuntal melodies, and all of it on improv? I haven't heard brilliance like that since Joy Division—*god rest Ian Curtis*. It's not the kind of music one expects from a four-piece punk band that's relying on their tits and asses more than their music to draw a crowd."

"Ugh, asshole." Delilah shook her head.

Cleo slapped Rice's arm. "Don't be crude."

"Sorry, but it's not crude if it's true," he said.

Gorge sat back and studied Rice. "At least you really listened."

"That's why I came," Rice said. "Breathtaking. Tremendous."

"So sign them."

"Ah, hey..." Rice's smile wavered and began its dance. "It's not that simple. I've never met them. Are they reliable? Do they have a following? I don't even know their name."

"Your Uncool Niece," Gorge told him.

"All right, fine," Rice said, "but it was only one performance."

"One breathtaking, tremendous performance," Gorge said. "They're as good as you think they are. Better, maybe. Sign them. Throw lots of money at them. Release their records. Make them stars. I'll introduce you."

Gorge raised his hand, palm facing the crowd. A tongue of green fire flickered in his palm, a flash of magic that burned too fast for anyone else to notice but long enough to carry a summons across the smoky room and make Nancy look his way. She nodded and pushed through the crowd.

"How do I know they're as good without you?" Rice asked.

"Because I say they are," Gorge said. "That's all you need."

"Come on, there's more to it than that. They may be talented, but have they got enough songs? If I book them studio time, will they show up?"

"Don't worry about those things," Gorge told Rice. "All you need to consider is that if you don't sign them then Delilah and I won't talk to you. Tonight or any other night. Put your damn money where your mouth is, or we'll leave here, and you'll never find us and never hear me play again."

Rice swallowed; his eyes hardened as he squelched his outrage.

"You said you know good music, said you wanted to get back to it. If Niece is the best you've heard in a year then it's a no-brainer," Gorge said.

Licking his lips, Rice frowned, and a dark tension crept into his voice. "Take it easy, Max, we come bearing a gift."

"What gift?" Gorge said.

Cleo pushed Bruno aside. "What he means—I'm so excited, Delilah!—is that I made some phone calls, put in a word or two, and convinced Peter Peters to meet with you one-on-one—you, him, your art, no bullshit. He promised. Peter trusts my taste. If he likes what he sees, he'll give you a show before the end of the year. I know you would've won him over if you kept wearing him down—and this is no guarantee, it's only a shot—but you won't have to waste more time convincing him. I can't imagine he isn't going to love what you show him. Isn't it great?"

"I... that's—wow, *thank you,*" Delilah said.

Gorge assessed her eyes for a clue to her true reaction. He hoped she might be pissed by what Cleo had done, by its implication that she needed strings pulled to get what she wanted, but she only looked overwhelmed and excited. Her acceptance disappointed Gorge, but he held his tongue. Cleo had only done her a favor—sparing her jumping through Peters' hoops and more time suffering among his retinue. Delilah's art would win him over or not on its own. It impressed him that Cleo had helped Delilah in a way he couldn't.

"Thank you, Cleo," Gorge said. "Great timing, too. Delilah finished some new pieces."

"I know," Cleo said. "They're fantastic. That's why I called Peter."

"You've seen them?" Gorge glanced at Delilah.

Cleo nodded. "I dropped by the other day. You were out."

"Delilah forgot to tell me," Gorge said.

"It was only Cleo," Delilah said. "You went to the music store, so we grabbed some lunch, and I brought her up to the studio."

"Sorry I couldn't tag along," Bruno said. "Big meeting that day with one of my distributors. Got to keep them happy."

Nancy, standing almost forgotten beside Gorge, touched his arm.

"You floored us tonight," she said. "*So* intense. *Any* time you want to play like that again, we're there."

"Thank you," Gorge said. "I'd love that. You guys blew me away. You played brave music tonight. People will never forget what they heard."

Nancy blushed. "Thanks."

"Listen, I've got good news." Gorge pointed at Rice. "This ridiculously rich, powerful record executive is going to give you a recording contract if you want one—and he's going to play fair on all the terms and give you full artistic control."

"Not funny, Max. You know how long we've been hoping to hear that?" Nancy eyed Rice. "Way too long. So don't screw around with me like that."

"Bruno?" Gorge said.

"No one's screwing around, dear." Rice handed Nancy a card. "Your Uncool Niece has what it takes. I know it when I hear it. Call my office tomorrow. We'll iron out details. Do you have enough material for an album?"

"Yes...." Nancy nodded as she read the card and recognized Rice's name and the Disharmony Records logo. She screamed, hugged Gorge, and then she bounced from him to hug Rice, who staggered, surprised.

Over Nancy's shoulder, Rice eyed Gorge. "Maybe Max will record something with you, guest artist and all that."

Nancy whirled back to Gorge. "That would be fantastic! I mean, if you want to."

"You never know," Gorge said.

"I have to tell the band." Nancy ran across the bar to share the good news.

"You'd record with them?" Brimmer said.

"Do good things and good things happen to you," Gorge said. "Hey, wait a sec, Brimmer, didn't you date Nancy last year, until she dumped you?"

"Dick." Brimmer walked away, lighting a cigarette.

"All right," Rice said. "By my count, we've done you two favors tonight. Plus I've heard you play, and you've sufficiently chastised me. I'd say that earns me a little of your time to make my case for why you should let me record you. Agreed? I've been told by the members of Shake Appeal that you always honor your debts."

Gorge wanted to go on hating Rice, to lash out and reduce him to nothing, but the smile on Delilah's face stopped him. She and Cleo, tight at the bar, going over how best to show her work to Peter Peters, the happiness in her eyes. Gorge suffocated his anger, stuffed it deep inside.

"Agreed," he said.

"Excellent!" Rice beamed. "I've got a car outside and the perfect place we can go."

He took Cleo's arm then led them all across the club, waiting while Gorge retrieved his guitar and said goodnight to the ladies in Niece. They wanted him to go out and party with them. Strong temptation, but Gorge wanted only music from them. Everything else he could ever want from a woman he had in Delilah.

For once, he didn't throw a glamour over himself and Delilah to hide their departure.

Despite his contempt for Rice, he wasn't above ratcheting up his legend by letting people see them leave together.

Rice's limo waited at the corner.

Its plush interior made the car that had taken them to his party look like a yellow cab. A perfectly soundproofed cabin of fine leather and polished maple with flawless climate control and thick carpeting isolated them from the city. Not a whisper of street noise reached them. The bar was twice the size of the one in the other car and fully stocked, and the built-in television and a stereo system represented every audiophile's wet dream. Music played over the speakers—a band Gorge knew from the sixties, one of Disharmony Records' first breakthrough stars. Good music. Gorge had liked it new, and he liked it now. He couldn't deny Rice had an ear for music, and Gorge suspected he'd put that band on to remind him of that.

The limo pulled into traffic and cut into the night.

Rice poured them all drinks, recalling their preferences from the party.

He tipped his glass to Gorge. "I'll keep my word with Your Uncool Niece. Count on it. They have the sound, you're right about that, and they have the look to be stars as well. A few rough edges, but nothing we can't fix. Tell you the truth, I'm kind of excited. I can't remember the last time I signed an act on the spot like that. They'll be my personal project. I told you I wanted it to be about the music again. I hope this convinces you."

"It doesn't hurt," Gorge said.

Rice raised an eyebrow. "Your hard edge never softens, does it? I suppose that's what it takes to play the way you do, what the *magic* calls for."

Gorge refused the bait. "Good music is always magic."

He sipped his drink and listened to Delilah talk art with Cleo, shutting out everything but the joy in her voice. It had been a long time since he'd heard her like that. Her years with him took their toll—kept young by his magic, never aging, the world changing around her. The last person from the life Delilah had lived before she found Gorge had died three years ago. Her sister. Delilah hadn't seen her for more than a decade before she died, afraid for her to see how she hadn't aged a day since the 1940s.

Gorge wanted to be everything for her—*he had to be*—but what if he wasn't enough?

His senses sampled the passing city. Streaks of shadow and light. Gray shapes on dark sidewalks. He tasted magic and recalled a time when the magic of the Kingdoms was unknown in cities, when scrape sprites haunted farmhouse compost piles and town dumps instead of alleys and steel dumpsters. The green places weren't what they'd once been, but the Sidhe—like any other living creatures—adapted or died. He noticed more and more of them in the city. The fae themselves had always had a presence, but the pixies, sprites, and others who preferred more elemental surroundings were all too commonplace now. Gorge had spied a kelpie and a few naiads in the water off Battery Park when he and Delilah had gone walking there, and the city's great Central Park provided a sprawling haven for nymphs, gnomes, and faerie rings. Even as they drove through Lower Manhattan he picked up flickers of stray magic in the air—one kind of Sidhe or another nearby. He had spent so much of his exile living in cities to keep his distance from places where the mortal world overlapped with the Kingdoms, but now they encroached on him. He worried he might not have the time he needed to gather the magic to give the Flock what they deserved.

"Max," Rice said. "You looked lost in thought. Anything you want to share?"

Gorge frowned and handed Rice his glass. "Wishing I had more whiskey."

Rice nodded, filled the glass, and then replenished Cleo's and Delilah's drinks.

They travelled through the financial district and Tribeca, down along the Hudson River, a neighborhood of light traffic, darkened warehouses, and desolate sidewalks.

"Where I'm taking you is open only to the elite of the elite, so exclusive you won't get in unless *I* approve you—that's because I own it." Rice grinned and winked. "You think music is the only thing in the world that matters, Max. At least, you play like it— like you could live *sans* air, food, or water as long as you have music. Tell me something, though. Why mess around with these punks and hardcore bands, these guitar bangers and shriekers? You've got the talent for anything. Symphonies. Operas. Musicals. You could shoot to the top of the pops, but you're lurking in the gutters."

"The gutters are where the music is real," Gorge said. "No one cares about classical music anymore. When was the last time a fistfight broke out over a show tune or a pop song? I'm not interested in soothing the savage breast. I want to play for people whose lives depend on a song."

"Fair enough, but music's only part of the equation," Rice said. "There's power and freedom to consider as well. That's what I offer you. Sure, I want to record you, absolutely, and I want us both to make a rude fortune selling those recordings. What really matters, though, is the position in which you find yourself once we've done that. You've got to have a long-term perspective. Fame and fortune are stepping stones. There's always a higher goal. I want to know what that goal is for you. I want to help you attain it."

Gorge stared at Bruno and drank half the whiskey in his glass.

An uncomfortable silence filled the limo, shaped by Bruno's anticipation.

Reacting to the rising tension, Cleo and Delilah fell silent.

Gorge let the awkward moment drag on while he reassessed Rice, wondering whether the man possessed somewhat more depth and ambition than he'd imagined. Maybe he knew more about Gorge's magic than he'd let on and hoped to pry something out of him. Yet no matter how he viewed Rice, he always came off in his mind as a cheap, mortal imitation of the royalty in the Kingdoms.

"I'm fairly certain," Gorge said, his voice soft, but his words hard, "that you actually see that working the other way around. You need me, Bruno, but I don't need you. That's your position."

Rice grimaced and sat back in his seat.

Cleo frowned. Delilah hid a smirk by pretending to yawn.

The limo entered a warehouse garage, slowed, then wound down a ramp into an underground parking lot. Two guards waved them by from a booth when they recognized the car. The driver drove through a dark patch where the overhead lights flickered on and off, steered into a dim corner, and parked by a battered, metal door flanked by two hulking men in black leather suits. A pathway delineated by velvet ropes strung from brass poles led from the curb to the door. One of the leather men opened the limo. Rice got out. He handed Gorge a red business card as Gorge followed him.

"You'll soon see position is everything."

Rice grinned.

On the card, printed in black, were the words "Compromising Positions—An Elite Nite Spot" and below that "By Invitation Only." Gorge flipped it over to see the symbols for male and female printed in a suggestive overlap.

"What the hell is this place?" Gorge said. "I've had enough of your parties."

Cleo, who exited the car with Delilah, touched Gorge's arm and smiled. "If we tell that would spoil the surprise. You have to see for yourself."

One of the bouncers opened the door, which squeaked and scratched the pavement. Rice swept Gorge, Delilah, and Cleo into an entrance clouded by drapes and lit by electric candles in wall sconces. They pushed through the thick curtains and walked down a corridor with blood-red velvet walls lined with more light sconces. Square mirrors in gilt frames caught and enhanced the light. Halfway down the hall, they passed the first of five doors, two on either side, the fifth at the end. Gorge heard voices beyond the doors. Laughter. Excited squeals. Ecstatic moans. Angry words too muffled to understand. A deep *thud* reverberated through the floor, and Gorge flashed Rice an inquisitive look. Rice only shook his head, smiling, and directed them through the last door.

They entered a lounge suffused with a haze of smoke. Along one wall stood a bar, tended by a man in a skin-tight, latex body suit and a woman wrapped in wisps of transparent silk tied loosely around her limbs and torso. Sofas and plush armchairs squatted around the room with tables placed among them. Off the bar loomed a grand piano, where a man wearing a black tux and a leather mask with eyeholes zippered shut played a light, up-tempo piece. People sat scattered about on the seats. All of them noticed Rice, who seemed to set their nerves on edge. Those who were dressed wore expensive clothes and bright jewelry. Rice nodded to them all on his way to the bar.

"Good evening, Mr. Rice," the lady behind the bar said.

"Hello, Becky," Rice said. "I'm afraid I've upset the mood a bit. Do me a favor, and you and Sean do a round on the house, would you?"

"Sure thing, Mr. Rice."

Becky moved down the bar to prepare the drinks. Her silks fluttered, covering little of her slim, yet curvaceous body. She and Sean prepared a batch of drinks then brought them around on two trays, passing them out with Bruno's compliments. The guests accepted them, most with a tip of the glass to Rice, and the mood settled again.

Gorge knew he'd seen many of the people in the lounge before, but he wasn't sure where. He recognized only one—a tall, blond-haired, blue-eyed man—the star of a movie Delilah had taken him to see. The others' faces he'd glimpsed on television or magazine covers. Delilah looped her arm through his and pulled him close. Her body hummed with excitement.

"All these people are famous," she whispered to Gorge. "Superstar, private-jet, *private-island* famous."

Gorge sighed. "Been there, done that."

Becky brought them the tray, and Gorge and Delilah each took a glass.

"They look vaguely familiar," Gorge said.

"You'd know them if you watched TV or went to the movies more often."

"It's hard enough living in the mortal world as it is," he told Delilah, "without trying to wrap my mind around your childish fantasies of how you wish it was."

Delilah frowned. "Party-pooper." She giggled then kissed Gorge.

He pulled her tight against him.

Rice approached them, drink in hand. "Max, Delilah, welcome to my club. Come on, then. I've got a private room where we can talk."

Every eye in the lounge followed them as Rice took them through a black door behind the bar. It led to a short corridor that ended in a flight of stairs up to a loft area furnished with more sofas and lounge chairs arranged in a semi-circle around a pair of velvet curtains on the opposite wall.

"Get comfortable," Rice told them. "I'll prepare the night's entertainment."

"Did you bring us here to show off your movie-star friends?" Gorge asked.

"Not exactly," Rice said. "But aren't we all the stars of our own movies?"

Cleo and Delilah settled onto the central sofa. Gorge sat down beside Delilah.

Rice opened a wall panel, manipulated a series of switches behind it, then closed it and picked up a pair of remote controls from a table. He sat beside Cleo, activated the first remote, and the wall curtains drew back like stage drapes to reveal a bank of television screens stacked five high and six across. Icy light filled the room. Moving images in blue and white took shape in the dark. Miniature ghosts trapped in glass. Delilah squeezed Gorge's hand. Gorge tried to make sense of what he saw on the TVs.

Each showed something awful or private. Camera feeds, views into rooms Gorge assumed stood behind the closed doors of Compromising Positions, but the people onscreen were doing things people simply did not do for public consumption. The screen grid reminded Gorge of Bruno's party—a room for each perversion—but much worse because what he saw here went far beyond sex, drugs, and rock and roll. These people wanted to hurt themselves—or others—physically or otherwise. They intended not to satisfy their desires but to destroy their hungers. Bruno pressed a button and the volume came up, weaving a sound cloud of inarticulate voices crying out in pain and pleasure. Gorge tried to match the voices to the faces, but he couldn't tell who enjoyed themselves from who suffered or even who simply put on a show. The images blurred into a sequence of flesh and shadows, black lines lashing air, glints of sharp silver, and legs, arms, and torsos entwined and sliding together. Gorge recognized the face of a man engaged with three women in nothing but spiked leather collars, bracelets, and belts. Scratching and scraping each other. Drawing lines of blood.

"Is that... the guy from the six o'clock news?" Delilah asked. "No, it can't be."

"Oh, but it is." Rice set his drink on a table and walked up to the screen grid. "If we see him later you can ask him for an autograph." Rice pointed to a man and a woman working another woman from front and back, each of them wearing red scarves knotted around their necks and pulling on them gently. "Here's a couple of state senators, married—not to each other, mind you—but they still like to party together even though they're from different parties." He gestured to three more screens. "Here's the governor, here's everyone's favorite local sportscaster, and here's one of the city's best known movie stars. Even shorter in real life than he looks on screen." Rice picked another row. "Academy Award winner, Grammy winner, Pulitzer winner, tennis star, real estate magnate. She used to own this building." He tapped a lower screen. "Assistant commissioner of police. Comes in often. Lots of frustrations to work out." He pointed to another row. "She's got a daytime talk show, she's on the city council, and she's had work shown in MOMA. It's fantastic, isn't it?"

"You're sick. These people are sick. Why are they letting us watch them?" Gorge said.

"They don't know they're putting on a show." Rice retrieved his drink and sat down, eyes glued to the array of screens. "I'm showing you this because I want you to see what power looks like. Power is knowing all the dirty little secrets of powerful people—and having the videotape to prove it. Everything you see on these screens is recorded via a feed to a secret location. No one knows that when they first they come here. Some never find out. I offer them a secure, elite playground where they can tuck away their public persona and indulge themselves and I charge dearly, by the way. In many cases, they get precisely what they pay for. You'd be surprised how easy it was to sell the idea once I got the movie stars on board. Everyone wants to be a movie star—or fuck one. I stockpile the videos until I need something. Having trouble getting some permit or other? Want drug charges against your top star to go away? Want that penthouse on Park Ave. at a criminally low price? Show the one who can make it happen a good time, and once you've got a recording of them doing... whatever they do while they're here... your problems vanish, your desires are fulfilled." Rice slunk down in his seat, resting his glass on his belly, eyes tight on the television grid. "As long as I don't need something from you, the tape remains a secret. But if I do, then you'd better have the stomach to watch yourself getting your rocks off and the spine to do what it takes to make sure no one else watches it—or you're going to have a massively bad day. You have no idea what kind of power I have in this city, the things I can make happen."

"Are you threatening me?" Gorge asked.

Rice jolted up, sloshing some of his drink on his shirt. "No, I— for fuck's sake, you cynical bastard, I'm trying to be your friend. Why would I threaten you?"

"Then why are you showing us your dirty, little secret?"

"I'm showing you what I've built with my own two hands." Rice raised his hands to his chest and curled the empty one into a fist. "I'm inviting you in. You've got power. I want you to know that I do as well. I want us to be on equitable footing."

Gorge walked to the screens and ran his fingers over one of them, sensing the prickly pull of static electricity.

Scattered magic swam through the air.

Gorge felt a wave of it as he connected with the people in the rooms as living beings rather than pictures in glass and light. Sex energy birthed potent magic, but the people wasted it, let it spin out of them and diffuse into the air. They took nothing except the little high that came from building up tension and giving it release. Not that sex magic ever lasted long. It was unstable, passion-fueled energy that faded soon after the desire of its creators died.

While it lasted, though, it could work wonders.

Gorge laughed at the stupid, oblivious people—and then it came to him that this could be why Rice's magic stank of rot and weakness. If he gathered it here, he didn't fully understand the power his victims produced. He'd been trying to stockpile something with an expiration date measured in minutes or hours at best. Now he was even showing it off to Gorge.

Equal footing? Poor Bruno, you imbecile wizard of bad garage rock, I don't think so, not in this world or any other.

Gorge turned his back to the screen grid and glared at Rice. "Point made. Mute the damn things and close the curtains. Some of these poor bastards are not pleasant to see naked."

Rice chuckled. The curtains blotted out the television light. Rice punched another button and the sound gave way to music from hidden speakers. He grabbed a phone, spoke a few words, and a seconds later, Becky opened the door and brought them a tray of food. She set it on the table by the sofa. Her silk strips whispered as she moved. Rice plucked a chocolate-dipped straw-berry and popped it in his mouth.

After he swallowed it, he said, "We can do great things for each other, Max. It's obvious. Here, let me get you another drink."

Gorge let Rice take his glass, fill it, return it.

"Let's quit dancing around the question," Rice said. "You're far better acquainted with some types of power than I am. I want access to that power. Give me that, and in return, I'll give you whatever you most desire. Let's dispense with secrets, shall we? Cleo and Delilah know what we're really talking about is *magic*. You told me I don't know the Kingdoms. True, I've never been there, never seen them for myself. I've met more than a few who have, though. Your kind. Creatures of the earth, woods, and waters. I've attracted them, talked with them, sometimes even traded with them. Some of them know you. None would divulge your name, of course, names being power and all—but I know you aren't really Max Chaos. You've been around a long time. I've had very interesting chats with our mutual friend, Rich Taber, about that. Shame he never did give Gavin Gray a proper thank you. And I've known Jake Blaze since he was a pup wet behind the ears. All those things you wanted him to forget were still locked in his mind, ripe for me to pull them out. Wasn't hard to do once I felt the magic on him and realized you'd screwed with his head. I've been searching for you for a long time. I feared I'd lost you when Gavin Gray died. The thing is nobody else in the world plays the way you do. You'll never be able to hide that no matter what you call yourself or who you pretend to be."

Delilah squeezed Gorge's hand. An uneasy silence fell over the room.

Gorge broke it: "So that's it—your cards on the table?"

"Yes." Rice said. "Better to get things in the open. You can't go back to the Kingdoms, and if I had to guess, I'd say you're not especially keen to have them know about the amazing levels of magic you've been accumulating here. That's not normal for the mortal world, is it? I can help you. Power is something I understand."

"Bruno," Gorge said. "You don't know the first thing about the kind of power I have or what I most desire, and so all I have to say to you is the thing I say to all of your kind: fuck off."

Rice only laughed and shrugged. The reaction puzzled Gorge.

"You can't blame a lad for trying." Rice flopped onto the sofa beside Cleo, sighed, and pushed hair from his eyes. "A partnership would serve us both well, but I'm used to getting what I want one way or another. Doesn't really matter if it's given willingly."

Rice's hand slid onto Cleo's thigh. Magic flowed from him into her. Cleo glanced at Rice then turned back to Delilah with a strange euphoria and naked lust in her eyes. She caressed Delilah's shoulder. She leaned close, parted her lips, and kissed her on the mouth.

Delilah stiffened; her eyes widened. Gorge raised an eyebrow.

Cleo held the kiss, dragged it out, Rice massaging her thigh the whole time, and then she broke it off and nuzzled Delilah's neck.

Staring at Cleo with shock and confusion, Delilah said, "Shit, Cleo. What the hell—?"

Cleo touched a finger to Delilah's lip and shushed her. She shifted her body and straddled Delilah, grinding herself onto Delilah's hips as she took her face in both her hands and kissed her again. Rice's hand traveled up Cleo's leg, to the small of her back, where he lifted the tail of her shirt and rested his palm on her skin.

This time, though, Delilah's confusion didn't slow her reaction.

"Get the hell off!" she said.

She pulled away then grabbed Cleo by the waist, shoved her onto Rice, and surged to her feet, spilling Cleo even further off balance and onto Rice's lap.

Delilah took Gorge's hand and wrapped herself in the ring of his arm, pressing as tight to him as she could. Rice grunted and pushed Cleo onto the sofa.

He stood up, trembling, red-faced, eyes burning.

The moment he broke contact with Cleo the euphoria and lust in her expression gave way to fatigue and fear. She curled into a ball on the sofa and began to cry.

"I've got to hand it to you, Bruno," Gorge said. "I figured you couldn't possibly be an even bigger, sleazier prick than I already pegged you for, and there you go proving me wrong. Did you think that was my tawdry, little fantasy—or was it yours? Or did you think you'd have me quaking in my boots because you can manipulate a mortal woman? Is that how you got Cleo to marry you, how you keep her? A cheap spell to keep her hung up on you? Even for a piece of trash like you that's low."

Rice slammed his glass down on a table. "What the hell do you know? The great Max Chaos—you're nothing! No one! And you never will be. Your own people don't want you. *I* don't need you. *You* need me. I *know* what you are, and you and everyone else where you come from is a pampered, self-absorbed, gluttonous imbecile. You come to our world like it's where you can go be bad and leave behind all your nasty business. But the things that protect you in the Kingdoms don't matter for shit here. In this world, we're in charge. Do you know how many people would kill for the chance I'm offering you?"

"I make my own chances, and you have no idea who you're dealing with," Gorge said. "But since we're being honest, you reek of bad magic, Bruno. I've smelled it on you since the moment I met you. You're a weak excuse for a wizard. Do you come here to draw power from the sloppy seconds of your pathetic victims? Do you bring Cleo here to punch up whatever spell you've cast on her and keep her how you like her? What you've done to her is worse than stringing her out on dope. She'll be lucky if she's got half her mind left when you get tired of her and let her go."

Rice burst onto his feet, glass clutched in his fingers, hand swinging to smash it against Gorge's head. Gorge pushed himself between Rice and Delilah and sent a bit of magic in Rice's direction. The glass erupted into shards, cutting Rice's hand, and throwing him off balance. Gorge's faerie senses kept him well ahead of Rice, and he sidestepped the blow. Rice's momentum carried him forward until he slammed his knees against a table, lost his footing, and fell sideways over one of the chairs. He rolled himself onto his feet and came at Gorge again. Sending Delilah toward the exit, Gorge kicked a table into Rice's path, tripping him up but not stopping him. Rice swung at him again but missed. He took another swing, then a third, neither connecting. Gorge snatched him by the wrist and twisted his arm, spiking pain up the limb, and driving him to his knees.

Gorge stood over him, basking in Rice's hatred.

Cleo stopped crying and sat up, watching.

"You fat loser." Gorge dropped his glamour and let Rice see his true face, an inhuman and beautiful face full of rage and power; Rice paled. "I've fought in wars. I've killed things stronger and more monstrous than any human could ever hope to be. I've played music that would turn your mind to jelly, wither your bones, and melt your flesh. You picked a fight with the wrong, fucking ax man." Squeezing Rice's arm, Gorge touched his face with his other hand, spreading his fingers in an arc across Rice's forehead, his thumb settling on his left cheek. His fingertips glowed with a deepening green light. He bent low to look Bruno in the eye and sang: "These are the fingers that make the thing you covet/the hand that plays the tune that steals your soul/but the music's all mine, and so you won't forget it/I'll leave my marks upon your face before I go."

Rice screamed. Wisps of smoke drifted from his skin beneath Gorge's fingers.

Gorge held him locked in place for seconds that seemed to drag into hours.

Cleo whimpered and tried to dissolve into the sofa.

When Gorge let go, five red, blistered welts remained where he'd touched Rice's skin. Rice clutched at his face and fell onto his side.

"What did you do to me?" he said.

"Only what you deserve," Gorge said.

Delilah walked to the sofa and knelt by Cleo. "Come with us," she said. "You don't have to stay with him. We'll help you. You owe him nothing."

Cleo recoiled, her eyes wet with terror. She pulled her knees up to her chest and kicked herself away from Delilah.

"Please," Delilah said. "I don't want to leave you here like this so he can hurt you again. Don't let him control you."

She reached for Cleo, but Cleo slapped her hand away.

Delilah grimaced. "Fine then, stay."

She kicked Rice twice, the toe of her boot biting him hard enough to make him yelp. He swatted at her and crawled behind the nearest chair.

"Last thing before we go," Gorge said as Delilah moved to his side. "If you screw with any of my friends—the girls in Niece, or the guys in Shake Appeal, or anyone I've jammed with—I'll know even if you so much as spit in their direction, and I'll come back and teach you more than you ever wanted to know about my power and how it works."

Gorge grabbed the whiskey bottle from the bar as they left and tucked it into his jacket.

Downstairs he told Becky and Sean that Rice and Cleo were spending some *intimate* time together and not to disturb them for at least an hour.

As he and Delilah walked down the club's main hallway, Gorge banged on all the doors, and shouted, "Pay attention morons, he's video-recording everything you do. There are cameras in all your rooms. I've seen you all naked, and I was not amused!"

One of the doors cracked open, and the governor's face peeked out.

Gorge pointed at him. "Especially by you. Put some clothes on, old man."

The governor frowned and slammed the door shut.

Outside the club, Gorge glared at the bouncers. "Where's our fucking limo?"

The two men traded glances, uncertain. Gorge tweaked his glamour to convince them.

"Our car, right now."

One of the men waved. The limo rolled out of the darkness to the curb.

Gorge and Delilah got in. Gorge yanked the cap off the whiskey, drank from the bottle.

"Driver," he told the chauffeur. "Go. I don't care where. Drive until you run out of gas. Then park the car, get out, and walk far away and never come back."

The chauffeur twisted around and glared at Gorge. "Who are you to give me orders? Where's Mr. Rice?"

"Indisposed," Gorge said. Then, pushing a touch of magic into his voice, he added, "Now go. Drive like I said."

The chauffer looked confused for a moment. Then he settled into his seat and drove.

Gorge raised the solid divider screen, cutting them off from the front of the car.

"Bruno's going to be a problem," Delilah said.

"No, he won't," Gorge said. "I put him in his place. He's weaker than me, and now he damn well knows it. Also, he's a wizard, and the day I let the likes of him get the better of me is the day I turn to dust and blow away."

Delilah slid next to him, kissed him. "What if he tells someone in the Kingdoms what he knows?"

"No one in the Kingdoms will pay attention to a wizard." Gorge slid his hand under Delilah's shirt and stroked her back. "They're considered about as trustworthy as a junkie. Now, forget it for the rest of tonight and remind me why we're perfect for each other."

The car rolled through the dark city. Gorge and Delilah unaware of the lights and the noises, of the buildings and the other cars, shucked their clothes and fell into one another. Delilah's touch and her sweet scent chased from Gorge's mind all the twisted things Rice had shown him.

The limo ran for hours before it spent its gas, and when it did, right around dawn, the chauffeur parked and then walked away, leaving Gorge and Delilah alone.

"Time to go," Gorge said.

Delilah lifted her head from his chest and kissed him.

They dressed and then left the car. It sat on a cobbled street, outside a warehouse near the East River, in the shadow of the Manhattan Bridge. Pearl Street. Sunday. No one around.

"Shit, he left us in Brooklyn," Delilah said.

Gorge stretched, cracking his limbs. "It's all right, the F train's not far."

Delilah gave him her hand. "Let's go."

"Not yet."

Gorge ducked back into the limousine and retrieved the bottle of whiskey. A thin layer sloshed on the bottom. He held the neck to his lips and breathed into it. The whiskey lit up and then caught fire. Light, heat, and smoke filled the bottle. Gorge tossed it into the limo. Delilah slid her hand into the back pocket of Gorge's pants, and they crossed the street and watched. The magical fire shattered the bottle and spread throughout the car. Soon flames engulfed the inside of the limo. Smoke plumed out. Glass cracked.

Gorge smiled. "A message for Bruno."

He and Delilah walked away and disappeared into the subway.

Gorge expected never to see Cleo Rice again—but three nights later she turned up teary eyed at Donnie D's, where Gorge was sitting in with SDSP. He stood at the bar with Delilah between sets, sipping a whiskey and a beer. His eyes hardened when Cleo squeezed her way through the crowd and approached them.

"Bruno isn't with me," Cleo said. "He's too pissed off and freaked out about what you did to his car to come near you."

"You're not? Stupid. Go away before this turns unpleasant," Delilah said. She turned her back on Cleo. "What the hell do you want anyway?"

Cleo twisted her hands together, her skin raw and cracked, several fingernails broken. Gorge recalled how beautiful even her fingers had seemed the night he met her, beauty now marred by bloodshot eyes and a face puffy from crying. Hair pulled back from her furrowed brow in a frayed ponytail, she wore no makeup or jewelry, no designer clothes, only jeans and a T-shirt with a simple leather jacket and child-like canvas sneakers.

"Did you mean it the other night when you said you'd help me?" Cleo asked.

Delilah didn't answer.

"If I had some help maybe I could… I don't even know what I want or where to go. But I don't want to be with Bruno Rice anymore."

Gorge suspected Delilah had the same idea he did.

Another lie.

Another trap.

Cleo, forever Bruno's pawn.

Yet he couldn't deny her naked vulnerability or the quaver in her voice.

"I don't sense any magic on her or in her right now," he told Delilah. "Best I can tell she's here under her own will."

"I didn't even tell Bruno I was leaving," Cleo said. "I couldn't think straight at the club that night. I wanted to go with you, but I was scared and confused."

Delilah locked gazes with Gorge, a question clear in her eyes.

Gorge nodded. "Not surprising. The magic Bruno used is toxic. It screws with every part of your mind. Eats away your personality. You can literally forget who you are after a while."

Delilah's shoulders slumped. She hung her head and rubbed her eyes. She had helped other women like Cleo in the past. Women equally abused or lost. Gorge knew the weary look in her eye, the fear of extending another helping hand only to see nothing change.

She shifted around to face Cleo. "You really want help? You're ready to give up everything Bruno gave you?"

Cleo nodded. "I'm sorry for everything we did to you. I'll still help you with Peter Peters, I promise. Peter's my friend. I still want to do that for you. I owe you that. Much more than that."

"Forget that. It doesn't matter," Delilah said. "What does is whether or not you want to live your life trying to be what people like Peter Peters and Bruno Rice want you to be. Or do you want to live how you want to and to hell with anyone who tells you different?"

"Answer that question," Gorge said, "and most of the other questions in your life go away."

"I—yes, I do. I mean, yes, that's what I want," Cleo said. "I'm done with all the bad shit. I want to be me again. I can't live another day this way. I mean it."

Delilah met Cleo's eyes. A possibility hung poised between them, a turning point for Cleo, a gamble for Delilah. Then Delilah's face darkened, and the potential vanished.

"No." She swiveled back to the bar. "I don't trust you. Go away."

Shock blanched Cleo's face. She sobbed as if Delilah had gut-punched her.

She turned to Gorge.

He shrugged. "Sorry. Later, Cleo."

Cleo backed away, staggered into the crowd, and then squirmed through it to the ladies' room at the rear of the club.

"Trust your instincts. Don't question yourself," Gorge said. "Don't look back."

Delilah rubbed tears from her eyes. "Yeah, right."

Finishing his whiskey, Gorge ordered another round. Delilah leaned against him, resting her head on Gorge's shoulder, staring at their reflection in the mirror behind the bar. He wondered what she thought, what she saw when she looked at herself, at him, at them together, their pale faces like ghosts in the gloom and flicker of the club. They looked so much like everyone around them yet were so different. Delilah drained her whiskey then buried her face in Gorge's hair. He put his arm around her and stroked her back. He meant to order another round, but then a man with small blue spikes of hair fake-punched him in the arm.

"Time to rock, Max. Ready for round two?"

"Yeah," Gorge said. "With you in a minute, Rack."

Delilah pulled back onto her barstool, tears gone, but not even a ghost of her usual smile.

"We'll leave after this set," Gorge told her. "Go to the diner you like on Lafayette then go home. You'll paint. We'll sleep in, get drunk in bed when we wake up, and ignore the world for a day or two."

"Yeah," Delilah said. "Perfect."

Gorge kissed her before he walked to the band and picked up his guitar. He threw its strap across his shoulder then plugged his cord into its jack. One of the bouncers wrapped his meaty fingers around the neck, muting the strings.

"Nice and easy, Max. Understand?" he said. "Like the first set. Don't piss nobody off. None of that shit like that night with Shake Appeal. All hell breaks loose here again I'll make sure it breaks out all over your sorry ass."

"Anything you say, Darren." Gorge blew the bouncer a kiss. "Didn't realize you were so interested in my ass."

Darren made a sour face. "Ah, shit, man, screw you. Do it like I told you."

Gorge stared at Darren's hand until he got the hint and let go of the guitar.

A woman screamed outside the ladies' room. Her voice lanced the music playing over the PA system and the grumble of the crowd. She screamed again. Darren ran. Gorge followed, a sinking feeling weighing him down, making him afraid to look at Delilah, who'd caught up and ran right beside him, holding his hand, her nails digging into his palm.

The ladies' room door hung propped open. A handful of women stood around the entrance, consoling a crying woman. Darren shoved past them into the lavatory. Gorge and Delilah stood in the doorway. Inside one of the stalls, its door jammed open, Cleo lay crumpled on the floor, head slumped sideways and resting on the edge of the toilet, legs splayed out in front of her, left sleeve bunched up past her elbow. A needle dangled from her arm below a rubber strap coiled around her biceps. A dribble of blood ran from where the tip had punctured her vein.

The fingers of her right hand still brushed the hypodermic's plunger.

Delilah rushed in and knelt beside her. Tears welled in her eyes as she tried to find a pulse in Cleo's wrist and then her neck. She held her cheek above Cleo's still lips.

"Shit," Darren said. "That's all we need, the cops back here again."

Gorge inched into the stall. His senses buzzed as Cleo's death energy gathered, preparing to leave her body. Kneeling on the dirty floor beside her, Delilah looked up at him, wet tracks streaming down her cheeks.

Gorge gripped her shoulder and knelt beside her, crammed into the tight space, amidst the odor of piss and stale vomit. The women in the hallway watched.

Darren picked up the payphone, calling 911.

"She isn't gone yet," Delilah whispered.

Gorge tilted Cleo's head back and laid his hand on her forehead.

"I didn't think..." Delilah said. "I mean, when I turned her away, I thought she'd go back to Bruno. I didn't know she was this desperate. I don't want her to die. I'll help her. Okay? I will. I'll get her to people who can fix her head so she can be herself again."

Gorge assessed the fear and compassion in Delilah's eyes. The mortal tradition of trying to save people from themselves mystified him. The Sidhe had no equivalent. In the Kingdoms, you took responsibility for yourself, sink or swim, and no one rewarded weakness with understanding or mercy. Healing people, rescuing them from danger or violence—those things the Sidhe accepted. But if you wanted to waste yourself away in a dissipated life, make yourself beholden to a cruel master, or shoot yourself full of poison, no one stopped you or tried to save you. It so rarely worked in the mortal world that Gorge wondered why anyone bothered.

"Sometimes it's better for things to end," Gorge said.

"No!" Delilah punched his chest. "Not this time. Do you hear me?"

Gorge sighed. "Loud and clear."

"Then do it."

"If I can."

Gorge felt Cleo's pulse weakening; her time approached. He set his other hand over her heart and then placed his lips on hers, shifting his body to conceal his actions from the crowd in the hall. He laced magic into Cleo's life force, into her blood, muscle, and skin. He tasted the heroin in her veins, shared for a moment its narcotic effects, and then gently pressed into her with his energy, pushing the poison back, healing the damage it had done, flushing new life into Cleo's body. He sampled an impression of her fractured, swirling mind and wished he could heal her psyche as well, but more magic would only worsen it. Green light flared where he touched her. Delilah hunched over them both, helping to conceal it. Gorge eased Cleo back from the precipice of death, using all the magic he'd gathered that night. When her pulse beat steady and strong, he let go of her and slumped against the side of the stall, half-exhausted.

Cleo blinked. Her body twitched. She sat up and stared at him.

"What happened—? Where am I—?"

"Toilet," Gorge told her. "You'll be all right."

Delilah wrapped her arms around Cleo. "Stupid, stupid," she said. "You don't have to do that, please don't do that, I'll help you, I will, all right? I'm sorry I turned you away. I didn't know how bad it was. I didn't."

Cleo hugged Delilah back, tears streaming from her eyes. They broke off their embrace, and Delilah helped her onto her feet and walked her out of the ladies' room.

Darren hung up the payphone and eyed Cleo as Delilah guided her into the club. "She okay?"

"No," Gorge said.

"Yeah, but she'll live? 'Cause her face was almost gray. She looked dead."

"Looks can be deceiving."

"What'd you do to her, man?" Darren said.

Gorge scowled. "Woke her with a kiss. Didn't you know I was Prince Charming?"

"Asshole," Darren said.

Gorge pushed past Darren and returned to the band, ignoring the curious looks of everyone he passed. The story of how

Gorge had saved a woman's life had already raced through most of the club, inspiring fresh awe in his fans. A hush fell over Donnie D's, broken by the hum of the ready amps. Gorge pulled his guitar into place. He spotted Delilah and Cleo at the bar, Cleo drinking from a glass of water. Then he met the stares of the crowd before he played a single roaring chord that towered over them.

SDSP kicked in on top of it, four musicians smoothing rough, fast noise into music. Gorge let them rev things up, waited for the audience to fall into the rhythm of the song then danced his fingers over the strings. His sound hit them like a shot of adrenalin. The crowd cheered; magic flew. Every note Gorge played returned to him, replenishing the energy he'd shared with Cleo. He dove into the song, lifting up the music, closing his eyes and hearing it in his mind how it would've sounded in the Kingdoms but could never sound here. The thoughts were bittersweet, a fleeting taste of his old home. He wanted to chase the Way of the Bone, but until he recharged, he didn't have the power to do so without the darkness infecting everyone who heard his music.

He mellowed his notes and opened his eyes.

The crowd danced, the lights flashed. Gorge glanced at the bar.

Brimmer, Jack, and Marty stared back at him. Jack frowned. Marty toyed with a drink. Brimmer smiled. They sat where Delilah and Cleo had been.

Gorge scanned the club but didn't see the women. He reached out for Delilah with magic but felt nothing. He pushed his senses further. His music turned darker as he did. The magic flared a notch. He felt Delilah nowhere in the club.

The song ended. Gorge slipped off his guitar, left it on its stand, and rushed to the bar, ignoring the surprised expressions of SDSP.

Looking only at Jack, he said, "What are you doing here? Where's Delilah?"

"She left with Cleo," Jack said. "We, uh, passed them on our way in."

"You're lying," Gorge said.

"He's not," Brimmer said. "They left. For real. We saw them go. Gals' night out."

"I didn't ask you," Gorge said. "Jack, tell me where they went."

"They, uh, left, man," Jack said.

"One more time before I make you regret your answer: *Where?*"

Jack and Brimmer traded glances. Marty sipped his drink.

"They're okay, Max. They're fine," Marty said.

"Yeah, we're just screwing around with you. You can take a joke, right?" Brimmer said. "They left in a limo."

"Whose?"

Brimmer shrugged. "I thought you were the limo expert."

"If you morons make me drag it out of you, I'll drag your tongues from your mouths along with it," Gorge said. "Or maybe I'll break your fingers and tear off your thumbs? Tell me now. Whose limo? Where did they go?"

"All the way." Brimmer laughed. "They went all the way."

Gorge's hand lashed out like the tip of a whip, striking the side of Brimmer's neck. He fell off his barstool, cracked his head on the bar, and landed on the floor. Before Jack could react, Gorge had his other hand wrapped around his neck. He squeezed. In the swirling shadows and din of the club, no one noticed; Darren had lost interest in Gorge the second he put down his guitar. Marty dropped his drink; the glass cracked on the floor.

"Bruno made us follow, Cleo. I swear. I didn't want to, but he forced us. I don't know how—*he just did*," Jack said. "He said do it—and we couldn't not do it."

"You're not telling me what I want to know," Gorge said.

"Lay off him." Brimmer grabbed the bar and pulled himself up. His voice turned rough and shaky. "You think no one can touch you? *Wrong*, shithead!"

Gorge let go of Jack and reached for Brimmer.

Brimmer flinched and fell sitting onto his barstool, his hands up in surrender.

"Easy, man, easy," Marty said.

"Back off, Max," Brimmer said. "I'll tell you. That's why we're here, anyway, to give you a message. The limo is one of Rice's. Cleo and Delilah got in, and it drove away. Cleo said they were going to the hospital so she could get herself checked out, but you know what—*hospital's in the other direction.* The rest you can figure out for yourself. Rice says you have something he wants. Now he's got something you want. It's all cool, though, because he'll make a trade. Go to his place at midnight tomorrow. Give him what he's after, he'll cut Delilah loose."

"Does he think this is a game and that I'm a fool?" Gorge said.

Brimmer shrugged. "You don't do it, Delilah dies. You go there before midnight tomorrow or she leaves Rice's house without his say so, she dies. Bruno made me wear this so you'll know what I'm telling you is real." Brimmer lifted his hand to show Gorge a silver ring set with slivers of iridescent crystal. "You know it?"

Gorge stared at the ring.

"What does the ring mean?" Jack asked.

"It means Brimmer can't lie," Gorge said. "It's the Ring of Truth. If you lied while wearing it or spoke an untruth—even unknowingly—it would set your hand on fire."

"Bullshit," Brimmer said.

"Try it," Gorge said. "Please."

Brimmer eyed the ring but said nothing.

"How the hell did Bruno Rice get his hands on that?" Gorge said.

"What? Can't figure it out?" Brimmer said. "Guess you're not as smart as you think you are. Or you're crazy. Did you really torch Bruno's limo? That's nuts. No wonder you buy his bullshit about a magic ring."

"Max, man, I'm sorry," Jack said. "I didn't want any of this to happen, but I couldn't stop him. I couldn't stop myself."

"You still think Bruno Rice will hand you the world on a silver platter?" Gorge said. "Do you, Brimmer? You hate my guts, fine, but what the hell did Delilah ever do to deserve being abducted and threatened with murder? Are you starting to understand what kind of man Bruno really is? How he uses people? I saved Cleo's life tonight, and this is how he repays it." Gorge inched closer to Brimmer, leaned into his face, let his glamour fade, and his fury blast through; Brimmer paled, and a fire of doubt ignited in his eyes. "I'll never forget your part in this."

Gorge stepped back and smashed three bottles from the bar.

He stormed back to SDSP, grabbed his guitar, and bringing his hand around in a blinding whirl, belted out an earth-shaking chord full of raw anguish. It shattered the song in progress, but then Gorge snatched up the melody and rebuilt it, driving the music to a higher place. Magic sparked out of him, igniting the band, raising them up. The song washed over the crowd with tidal force. People screamed, cheered, gave themselves to the music, let it fill their bodies and souls, let it all become like a single living thing—the song, the people, the moment they shared in space and time—all united by the desire to unleash primal emotions through the music.

Like a bold shaman, Gorge led them, soaking in more magic than he put out.

Reality blurred. The walls stretched.

Darkness seeped in through the cracks.

Gorge welcomed it. He didn't care what happened, who lived or died, or what got ruined.

He played to draw the things that lived there down from their distant perches to show them this bright spot of life and turn their fury against it. They stirred to the music, and their motion radiated across the darkness in concentric ripples across the fabric of the universe. Magic came on the waves. Black, frozen, deadly magic. Gorge sucked it into himself and banked it deep in his soul.

His hands flashed along his guitar.

He no longer felt the instrument; the music streamed fully formed from his body.

The sound grew and expanded. It pushed harder on the walls.

Everything shifted askew, and darkness spilled into Donnie D's.

...the Way of the Bone...

...the way to hell, the way home...

The things that lived in the darkness were still so far away.

...I will find the dark way...

Gorge had pricked up their senses, but he didn't have their attention.

He pushed harder. Let more magic flow. Filled the space with music that didn't belong in the mortal world. Sounds that screamed against reality and assaulted its fabric. What returned from the audience intoxicated him. Raw magical power blooming from fear and amazement and the unique sensation that runs through a body when music strikes it on a primal level and sets every nerve shivering. Gorge worried it might rip apart his body—still, he played.

Someone shouted at him. Shoved him. Punched him.

He ignored it.

He was immovable.

Unstoppable.

Only his music mattered.

SDSP dropped their instruments; Gorge continued.

Someone kicked over his amp, igniting volcanic feedback, and then yanked his cord out of it; somehow the music continued.

Among flashes of darkness and bursts of power burning through his senses, Gorge realized Donnie D's had erupted into chaos, not a melee like the night he played with Shake Appeal, but instead a frenzied, dancing madness as if the magic controlled the bodies in the crowd, pulling them apart and slamming them together, flailing them in time to the music like debris tossed on rough waves breaking in a storm. Only the band and Darren seemed immune, and Darren hit Gorge again, trying to shut him down. SDSP had already stopped playing and stood frozen in place, staring at Gorge, shielded by the magic with which he'd charged them. Gorge saw panic and tears in the faces of the audience and in some of them a wild elation at the raw power of the experience. A ring of space formed around Gorge, distance no one dared to close even as the tightness of the club formed an intimacy they were too shocked to flee. Only Darren came near him, striking Gorge again, yet failing to move him a single step. He grabbed for Gorge's arm. Gorge sent a jolt of magic into him, flinging him into the wall across the club. Then he played a last few furious notes before he screamed, spun around, and hurled his guitar against the bar. It cracked to pieces.

Threads of magic sizzled in the air.

Donnie D's fell silent.

The air around Gorge simmered.

The darkness retreated.

The crowd stilled. No one tried to stop Gorge as he left. They avoided him as if he were electrified.

At the door, Gorge hesitated. Magic swirled around him, charged higher than he'd ever been since his exile, but it still hadn't been enough to open the Way of the Bone. He lifted one hand over his head then left. Outside Donnie D's, he glamoured himself in to the night and began to think of all the awful things he was going to do to Bruno Rice.

CHŌRUS

GORGE PASSED THE REST OF THE NIGHT IN HIS APARTMENT, burdened by its loneliness. He couldn't sleep and had no appetite. He drank whiskey, but it tasted bitter. Patience never came easy to him.

Soon after dawn, he sat on the floor of Delilah's studio.

He stared at her paintings and drawings, his fingers idling over the strings of an acoustic guitar, picking out melodies, which he wove around the street sounds leaking in. The grind and rush of passing cars and busses. The murmur of conversation from the sidewalk.

By noon, the sunlight streaming through the high windows heated him and needled his eyes. He shifted to a shaded spot and continued playing.

The sun brought life to the colors on Delilah's canvasses. By dusty shafts of daylight, he saw more than a touch of the Kingdoms in her art, a sign the magic he'd given her over the years had changed her as much as living in the mortal world had changed him. Gorge was no longer purely fae, Delilah no longer entirely mortal, neither truly belonged to one world or the other, and no others lived quite like them. Their

only home, their only country existed in each other, and it had been so for decades, perhaps even from the moment they met.

Subconsciously, Gorge's fingers picked out the notes of a song he'd written soon after his exile, a ballad, "Soniella," about the woman who'd betrayed him and precipitated his fall from grace. He let go of the strings. The music stopped.

He had promised Delilah never to play the song in her presence, and it felt wrong to play it in her studio, surrounded by her art.

He wondered why he'd never written a song for Delilah.

The question chilled him.

He supposed, in a way, his entire life and all the music he played, he played for Delilah.

It seemed inadequate.

He wanted something hers alone.

A song she could claim.

One he could play and lift her out of all the awful things they'd gone through.

He cleared his mind of everything but music and Delilah's paintings all around him and began a new melody. It didn't come; it wasn't enough. He set down his guitar and walked to the covered canvas in the corner. He grabbed the edges of the cloth, hesitated, and then yanked it away, exposing the work in progress.

In the unfinished piece, he looked upon himself.

The desert burned around him in a whorl of scathing sands and searing blue skies, sunlight streaming through it like currents on a river.

Gleaming iron chains dangled from his body.

He knelt at the heart of a vortex of heat and light, head hanging, shoulders low, but with a noble, unbreakable bearing in his posture, an aspect that said that although he had been laid low, he hadn't been broken. Above him in the right corner of the canvas, a small figure that resembled him rose on brilliant fiery wings toward crystal sparks of musical notes. In the painting's focal point, though, hung a sterile, empty place at the center of the composition, a dead zone above his figure untouched by the light and energy in the rest of the image: the space his wings should've filled. The intimacy and understanding in the image humbled him.

He picked up his guitar and sat before the canvas, strumming, picking at scales until the song took shape. It came slowly, note by note, chord by chord, the melody smoothing itself true, but he struggled—and that seemed appropriate. No song written easily could possibly be worthy of Delilah. For this he had to delve into his heart and soul; he had to lay himself bare and capture what he found there in his music. Delilah deserved nothing less.

He played, circling back, starting over time and again as he charted his way to the proper tempo and lyrics that captured some essence of the bond he felt with Delilah. Hours passed. He grew frustrated, became exhausted, and whenever the effort wore him down, a glance at the unfinished painting reignited him. Hatred and anger held him back. He wanted to go now to Bruno Rice's house, burn it to the ground, drag Bruno kicking and screaming into the woods, and teach him what it really meant to cross one of the Sidhe, even an outcast—but those emotions had no place in a song for Delilah.

He set the guitar down and closed his eyes.

He imagined...

Delilah in her studio, full of confidence, hands brushing paint onto canvas, hair shifting in the light, the smell of oil paints and turpentine. She never liked him watching her work, would chase him away if she caught him. The floor creaked as if she stood there, shifting her weight from one leg to the other for a better reach.

He opened his eyes.

Delilah wasn't there, but the fire inside him cooled.

Only his feelings for her remained, pure and unclouded.

He picked up the guitar again, let time drop away, and played until the studio grew dark and the sun sank behind the neighboring buildings—until his song was right.

No, not his—Delilah's.

He played it one more time, every note perfect. He infused it with magic and sent it into the room, imprinted it on the walls and windows, on the canvasses and art supplies, on Delilah's smock, and on the air. When he finished, he covered the unfinished painting of him then left the studio. He cast more magic into the door lock, sealing the studio like a time capsule, preserving part of what he and Delilah shared in case one or both of them never returned. For one year, the door would open only for Gorge or Delilah; the spell would discourage anyone who tried, make them simply forget and give up. For a hundred years after that, anyone who spent time in the room would hear Delilah's song in the back of their mind and see the images of her paintings in her dreams.

Done, Gorge put away his guitar and rested.

GORGE TOOK A CAB TO BRUNO'S.

As the car carried him along the winding roads, he noticed a difference in the magic surrounding Bruno's home. It possessed a new, more potent aspect Gorge couldn't pin down.

The cab rounded the end of the driveway, and Bruno's mansion seemed very different in the absence of glitter and party noise. Shadows hung deep over the house and grounds. Lights burned only in a few first-floor windows to either side of the entrance. The house otherwise remained dark.

And silent.

Gorge paid the cabbie, got out, and stood in the driveway, filtering the night and all its varied energies, tasting the magic. The presence of the Sidhe, not surprisingly, registered as diminished; the fae liked to turn out for parties but not for the dead quiet. They weren't gone altogether, though, only subdued. He needed to watch how much magic he used, how much of himself he exposed—or let Bruno expose. Better not to draw attention if he could avoid it.

Other threads of magic twined around him.

Bruno's rotten magic, the magic he'd felt the first night he came here, turned his stomach again. The other, though, came clearer and stronger—much stronger.

An ace up Bruno's sleeve, Gorge thought.

He climbed the steps. The door opened.

Cleo stood in the entrance, wearing the same clothes from last night, her gaze downcast. She gestured Gorge into the foyer then closed the door, leaning on it to hold herself up. She looked drained, wounded, and terminally sad. Gorge wanted to hate her, to feel aflame with rage for her betrayal, but he couldn't imagine anything he could do to her worse than what she'd allowed Bruno to do.

"I'm sorry...." Cleo said in a hoarse voice; she'd been crying. "I didn't want to do that last night. I *meant* what I said. I didn't tell Bruno I was going, but somehow he still knew, and after you saved me, when I was sitting with Delilah, he was in my head ordering me to make Delilah get in the car. I told her I needed the hospital. She trusted me, and I... Max, Bruno's too strong. I couldn't resist what he put in me. Everything's blank after we got in the limo, like he knocked us out. I don't remember the ride, coming home, anything—and I didn't see Delilah again."

Gorge touched Cleo's cheek and pushed a lock of her gold hair behind her ear; then he gripped her chin and lifted her head. Still, she avoided his eyes.

"Make it right, now. Where's Delilah?" he said.

Cleo shook her head. "Bruno will hurt her if I tell you. He'll hurt me too."

Gorge made a frustrated sound partway between a grumble and a growl. "Then, let's play Bruno's game."

"He wants to see you in the parlor."

"Lead the way."

Gorge followed Cleo through the house, now clean, orderly, and ordinary, as if the party had never happened and all the sins Gorge witnessed that night were swept away with the discarded decorations and leftover food. Rooms that had hosted drunken celebrations now stood empty or cozily arranged, almost stuffy, lacking any sense of Bruno's excesses. The mansion played its part as Bruno needed, merely another prop in his illusion, a stage where he exhibited his wealth and took advantage of the people too eager to indulge themselves at his expense. A sweet trap, another con, like his nightclub. Cleo brought Gorge into a bright room and offered him a seat on one of the sofas. Gorge stood. She poured him a whiskey, which he took then poured onto the floor.

He said, "Where's Bruno?"

"He's coming."

"I feel his magic," Gorge told her. "I'm going to take it away from him—I'm going to take everything away from him. I hope you know that, Cleo. I'll make him pay for what he's done, and you, well, you're going to be left out in the cold. You won't have Bruno to pull your strings anymore or his money to buy you nice things. You're going to fall hard, and I don't think you'll ever get back up again."

Cleo stared at Gorge. In her watery eyes, he saw anger, shame, sadness, acceptance, and despair. She contained a squall of emotion pinned to a hard-edge of scorn directed at him and his desire to bring her world crashing down. Gorge saw that she knew she deserved every bad thing headed her way, yet he saw hope in her, too—that maybe Bruno would save her and her life would go on full of riches, every desire met. Gorge didn't need magic to see her mind teetered on the brink of collapse. Bruno had toyed with it too often and too deeply. Innocent in some ways, Cleo's soul sheltered a greedy core as deep as Bruno's. She hungered as much as every other mortal for those things that passed for treasure in this world.

She cried. Gorge smiled at her tears.

Cleo shivered and looked confused.

"You're cruel and arrogant," she said.

"Arrogant, yes. Cruel, no. I'm only honest. Truth is cruel." Gorge set down the whiskey glass and eyed Cleo. "You used to be beautiful. That's what I thought the first time I saw you—how beautiful you were, how truly rare in the mortal world, almost as beautiful as one of the fae. Has Bruno ever let you see them?"

Cleo nodded.

"Then you know what you squandered."

Cleo shuddered, suppressed a sob, and then slapped him.

The blow stung. Gorge chuckled.

"Don't laugh at me," Cleo said.

Gorge laughed harder.

"I mean it. Stop! Don't laugh." Cleo punched his arm.

Gorge's laughter trailed off. "The only reason I tolerated Bruno's presence was because I hoped you might be worthy of Delilah's friendship, but you're not fit even to stand in her shadow. The only reason you are alive is because she asked it. She would've taken you in, cared for you—been your friend for the rest of your life to save you. Can you say you would have done the same for her? You could've been so much more than you are, Cleo, and yet you're so much less than you ever wanted to be."

Tears streamed from Cleo's eyes even faster now. She spun away, opened the door, intending to storm from the room, then stopped and backed up as Bruno entered, with Brimmer, Jack, and Marty behind him. The stink of magic flooded the room with them.

"Don't be cruel, Max. You had your fun screwing me over and wrecking my car," Bruno said. "Don't be a sore loser now."

Gorge raised an eyebrow.

"That's right. You've lost, I've won," Bruno said. "Forget whatever you planned to do to me tonight. The only way I'll let Delilah leave here is if you do what I say—and then she'll leave *without you.*" Bruno gestured around the parlor. "I hope you'll be comfortable in your new home."

"I only have one home," Gorge said. "This isn't it."

"You mean the Kingdoms? I know about them."

"You know nothing," Gorge said.

"I know you're never going back there," Bruno said. "That you never can."

"When the time's right, I'll go back."

"No, Max, you won't because now you're mine. You'll stay here, and like everyone and everything else I set my sights on, you'll serve my desires." With a crooked smile, Bruno nudged Brimmer and said, *"Brimmer, get me a drink."*

Gorge felt a soft discharge of magic.

Brimmer walked to the bar and poured a glass of vodka.

Gorge identified part of what contributed to the magic that had come into the room. Brimmer still wore the Ring of Truth, but also, around his neck, Bruno wore a silver and platinum collar inset with a blue gem that glowed dimly, another artifact from the Kingdoms. Gorge knew it, had last seen it centuries ago during a time of war among the Sidhe, and although the collar contained great power, it alone couldn't account for all the energy swirling around the house.

Gorge pointed to the collar. "How did you get that?"

"You like it?" Bruno ran his fingertip along its contour. "Picked it up during my London days when I gadged about with a group of occultists obsessed with magical artifacts. It's come in handy over the years. Opened a lot of doors for me to a trove of secret knowledge I used to learn all about the Enchanted Lands and what they could do for me. What I could take from them. You know what it is?"

"The Voice of Reason," Gorge said.

"That's right," Bruno said.

"The last time I saw it," Gorge told him, "I cut off the head of the fae wearing it and took that from his severed neck. It isn't meant to be stained by mortal souls. Neither is the Ring. Give me both of them now so I don't have to hurt you when I take them."

"No, I won't be doing that." Bruno took the drink Brimmer handed him and downed it. "You can't touch me as long as I wear this, not if you know how it works."

"It casts a mild geas that persuades people to do what you want," Gorge said. "I'm not so easily persuaded."

Bruno shrugged. "There are other ways to make people do what I want. But I admit I'm very good with the Voice. It works especially well on ambitious or aspiring people like Cleo—or Jack, Brimmer, and Marty. They'll do anything I ask. But it works best on people who don't know it's working on them at all. Say, for instance, your pretentious little art whore, who right now sits on a bed beside a glass of wine laced with far too much barbiturate, which she'll drink if I don't come back inside the hour and use the Voice to tell her to not to."

Rage erupted inside Gorge, but he locked it up, ignored Bruno's jibe at Delilah, and kept his temper. He couldn't act until he knew Delilah's location. At Bruno's mention of her name, he tightened his senses and traced the lines of magic rising from

Bruno and spinning around the house, hoping to track them to Delilah.

He couldn't.

They only doubled back on themselves or dead-ended in clouds of ambient magic.

He couldn't say what kept her hidden, nor could he be certain Bruno told the truth, but with all the magic loose in the house, he couldn't deny the possibility—and from the strength of the magic, he suspected Bruno hadn't yet exhausted his arsenal of artifacts from the Kingdoms.

Not only a wizard but a rotten plunderer as well.

"What's that?" Bruno said. "Nothing to say at all? No smartass comeback? The magnificent Max Chaos—speechless? I guess this 'weak excuse for a wizard' hasn't done too badly, has he? That is what you called me, isn't it?"

"It is," Gorge said. "And I never lie."

Bruno scowled. "Let me tell you how this will work. First, you'll never see Delilah again. Get your mind around that now. But give me what I want, and I'll let her go, and she'll never see me or Cleo again. Don't and I'll let her die." Bruno paused to gauge Gorge's reaction, but Gorge betrayed none. He stood still, eyes fixed on Bruno's, waiting, listening. "Second, you'll play for me and let me record you. You'll play here, tonight, in a studio space I've prepared, and you'll play as long and as much as I say. After that, you'll remain here, well, *forever*, playing at my command. I know what you do with your music, how you pull energy from the people you play for, and gather magic—and I want all you have and all you'll ever produce. I want to find out if music really can change the world when millions are listening to yours—except your music will be mine, and you'll be my personal reservoir of magic. I'll get everything I ever wanted, maybe live forever. You'll know your girlfriend is alive somewhere without you. Not standard contract terms, I admit, but fair enough under the circumstances. After all, you did torch my favorite limousine. Now, it's time for you to play. *Come over here by me.*"

Bruno's command, amplified by the Voice of Reason, pushed into Gorge's mind, sending a current through his body. The collar's magic made listening seem like the smartest thing to do.

It promised him happiness and satisfaction if he obeyed. Gorge shrugged it off.

"Do what I say, dammit." Bruno's twisted smile danced. *"Apologize to Cleo for what you said to her."*

Gorge resisted the almost overwhelming impulse to comply. The force of the magic intensified in response; the Voice hollered in Gorge's mind, leading his thoughts in circles of rationalization, which brought him back again and again to the urge to tell Cleo he was sorry for how he'd treated her—*it's the most reasonable thing, the right thing, the thing that would be best for all involved.* Gorge almost did it if only to silence the Voice. The magic screamed at him inside his mind. He screamed back, shouted down its hold over him. He stood his ground till the power broke apart, and the Voice faded to silence.

"Go on, *say you're sorry,*" Bruno said.

Gorge looked from Cleo to Bruno and said, "No."

"What?" Bruno's smile vanished, and his face turned tomato red. *"Do it now."*

Gorge shook his head. "Cleo doesn't deserve an apology from anyone except you."

Touching the collar, Bruno focused on Gorge. *"Do it. You want to do it. You'll feel much better if you only apologize to Cleo. It's the right thing to do after all, the reasonable thing."*

"Stop it," Gorge said. "You're making a fool of yourself. You can't control me. I'll play for you to protect Delilah—that's my choice. And it is *a choice,* Bruno, because I could walk out of here anytime I want. I could punch my hand into your chest right now and squeeze your heart until it stops. I'll give you what you want, but learn your lesson here: You have no control over me but what I give you. You're mortal. Even with the Voice of Reason, you can't simply boss around one of the fae if he damn well doesn't want to be bossed. I'm no fucking leprechaun whose pot of gold you've stolen. Are we clear?"

Bruno's eyes narrowed with anger—but a touch of uncertainty twinkled there, as well, and that satisfied Gorge. "Have it however you want it as long as you get in the studio tonight."

"Another thing." Gorge walked up to Jack, Brimmer, and Marty. The three took wary steps back from him; they looked as if they were in a fog. "Send them away and don't screw around with them anymore, but make sure they never succeed, never get a recording contract. I want them to live with their failure."

"Not part of the deal," Bruno said.

"Make it part," Gorge said.

"They're going to be your band," Bruno said.

Gorge shook his head. "I don't need a band. Where you want me to take you, I can only go alone. You've heard me play. You know they'll only hold me back."

Bruno considered it then shrugged. "Brimmer, Jack, Marty, *piss off, I don't want you here anymore. In fact, I want nothing to do with any of you ever again.*"

Gorge felt the Voice of Reason reach across the air as its magic touched them then the power shifted away, and the men emerged from a haze.

"Are we done for tonight?" Jack asked Bruno.

"All done," Bruno said. "Free to go. In fact, *I insist you go.*"

"Why does he get to stay?" Brimmer pointed at Gorge.

Moving too fast for Brimmer to react, Gorge touched the guitarist's neck with a spark of magic. Brimmer twitched. All his hair stood on end. Then he collapsed on the floor.

"Because I'm the fucking star, you envious prick." He hunched down to say it to Brimmer's face, snatching the Ring of Truth from Brimmer's finger as he did, then slipping it in his pocket when he stood. "Take him home, Jack. If any of you has half a working brain left remember who was right about Bruno Rice."

While Jack and Marty struggled to lift Brimmer, Gorge stepped closer to Bruno, who retreated instinctively. He seemed to have forgotten the Ring and missed Gorge taking it.

"What?" Bruno said.

"Are we making some fucking music here tonight or not?" Gorge said.

"Yes."

"Then let's do it."

"Cleo will show you to the studio while I see to Delilah," Bruno said.

Walking through the house, Gorge knew Delilah was close. He felt his magic in her but too thin and diffuse for him to trace it. He tried to track Bruno's magic, but interference from all the threads of power twining around the place made it too difficult to parse—and then he lost him.

Cleo took him to the private rec room where she kept her collection of art.

The unknown magic crackled there; it set Gorge's skin crawling as he stepped into the room.

It rushed over him, chilling him like a cold draft. The room contained the magic. Gorge wondered if Bruno had come here to recharge himself before arriving at the parlor, thinking himself so clever for concealing the source of his power.

Cleo rounded the pool table and twisted a piece of the carved molding on the wall.

A secret door popped open. A staircase yawned beyond it. Cleo went first. The steps descended at least two stories beneath the mansion to a cellar that Gorge surmised sat beneath the basement. The dim space at the bottom of the stairs percolated with a sickening fog of magic unchecked by the veils that damped it down elsewhere in the house. It stank of blood, of dead souls and cruelty, of anesthetized dreams and euthanized love. The force pummeled Gorge. His guts lurched, and he shuddered, staggered, reached a hand out to brace himself against the wall—then yanked it back as the toxic energy passed from the wood into his fingers. Upstairs, he had picked up only shreds of this power and assumed it much weaker, but Bruno had hidden it well.

Bruno with his sound-proofed private rooms, his tinted windows, and his joy in spying on his nightclub clients. Bruno the liar...

...the sneaky bastard.

Using his low-rent magic to steal artifacts from the Kingdoms. Magic-proofing his floors and walls.

Leave it to a wizard to build a containment spell into his house.

Cleo flicked on the lights to reveal an expansive room cluttered with furniture, guitars and other musical instruments, and old books and records. Odds and ends of antiques and knick-knacks filled rows of shelves. A pair of glass-walled rooms occupied an alcove on the far side of the space: a performance studio—with a drum set, guitars, microphones, and music stands—beside a recording room with a mixing board and sound equipment. Gorge eyed a device on a table in the center of the recording room. An antique gramophone. An enormous brass horn mounted on a hand-cranked machine that played wax cylinder recordings. Something differed about it from the ones he had seen in museums, though. It looked alien beside the high-tech gear flickering with electric lights. The strongest magic Gorge had yet sensed here surrounded it, explaining much of the power he felt—but not all of it. One more thread remained unaccounted for, the one that gave him chills and nauseated him.

He moved around the room, sniffing out the source.

All around him pockets of faint magic rose from power imbued in the objects in the room. All of them. The mirrors on the walls, the books and the records, even pens on a weathered writing desk and the desk itself. A pair of eyeglasses. A telescope. A knife in a leather sheathe. A wooden globe. A wooden duck pull toy. All of it bristled with magic, but a weak, passive kind that worked without being noticed, only making the items better or more favored. None of it had come from the Kingdoms or the work of the Sidhe, and Gorge guessed Bruno had collected the items from other wizards in hopes of gathering power.

Cleo said, "You're getting warmer."

"What do you mean?" Gorge said.

"You're close to what you're looking for," she said.

Gorge eyed Cleo. A twitchy smile bowed her lips. She looked at a wardrobe against the wall. Built of dark-stained oak and carved with flourishes of laurels and stars, the wardrobe smelled of old clothes and aged wood—and, like nearly everything else in the room, of magic.

This magic possessed a different quality, though.

It didn't radiate from the wardrobe itself but from something inside it.

Gorge grabbed the handles and yanked open the doors.

In the heartbeat it took to grasp what he saw, his heart nearly turned black with a despair kept at bay only by a simultaneous surge of outrage.

The wardrobe had been emptied of shelves and hangers and fashioned into a cage with bars of cold iron mounted in the wood on all sides of it, including top and bottom; on the prison floor sat a bowl of scummy water and a stained metal plate holding moldy scraps of bread. Beside them in a still, soft mound rested the drying, ephemeral corpse of one of the fae. She had been young, five or six centuries old at most, and even in death, her beauty remained stunning. The tone of energy drifting from her remains told Gorge she'd been a musical fae, a songstress with a voice to make angels weep and put all the songbirds of the mortal world to shame. Her withered, colorless wings lay folded beneath her as if in her final moments she had laid down on them, looking for a last tiny scrap of comfort. Her blue dress of silk and lace draped her like a shroud. The lines of hopelessness etched into her sunken face told Gorge all he needed to know about her time spent in the cage.

He wept.

It took him another moment to realize that he knew her.

Toynia.

She had once sung in his chorus.

Her face so haggard and shriveled now, he barely recognized her.

Gorge shuddered, lowered his head, and let his tears flow.

He touched the bars and felt the deadly chill that could draw the magic right out of him or negate it and leave him powerless. Toynia's talent had been expansive, her magic as well, yet those simple bars trapped her.

The magic Gorge felt in Bruno had come from her.

Toynia's magic.

Dying, decaying.

Stale and fading.

A magic born of rotting beauty and dead glory.

Soon it would be altogether spent.

Bruno wanted him for this. He had used Toynia while she lived, and now he kept her body like an old battery, raiding her corpse for fixes of magic. The act represented a desecration no mortal could ever comprehend, a transgression heinous enough to invite the Kingdoms to unite for retribution if anyone there learned of it. More than ever since his exile, Gorge wished he could return home if only to deliver Toynia's body back to her people and show the Flock what Bruno had done. If the kings and queens and all the creatures of the Kingdoms saw how the mortal world treated the fae, perhaps they might even rescind his exile.

He could go home again...

...but why would he ever want to?

Cleo stepped to Gorge's side and touched his shoulder. "Max."

Gorge shrugged her hand away. "Shut up. There's nothing you can say now that won't make me want to kill you and Bruno even more than I already do."

"She's the one who told Bruno you were in this world."

"What?"

"Bruno found a faerie ring and used the Voice of Reason to lure her here. He imprisoned her here for more than a year and took everything he could from her. She never gave him your name, no matter what he did to her, but she couldn't keep everything a secret."

"Are you saying she died to protect me?"

"No. Bruno would've drained her to death no matter what," Cleo told him. "But she was loyal. She said no better musician than you had ever lived."

"She was gentle and beautiful, and Bruno destroyed her. He caged her to do it, but you...." Gorge faced Cleo, tears streaming down his face. He dropped his glamour to show her the depths of his grief and fury. "You curl up in bed with the monster and trade your soul for the things that glitter."

Cleo's face twisted, and she looked away. "He *is* a monster."

Gorge turned his back on her.

Cleo sighed. "Maybe... I'm one too."

Her feet scuffed, her body shifted, and too late Gorge realized her deception when a cold iron ring stung his throat and snapped in place as Cleo locked its clasp. Instinctively, Gorge tried to pull it loose, but it only seared his fingers and his neck; the more contact he made, the more he felt it sucking away his magic. If not for his shock and grief, Cleo never would've gotten the thing on him. He looked around the room for a tool he could use to pry it off but found nothing strong enough to do it.

"Don't fight it." Cleo skittered away, frightened. "Bruno said it will only waste your magic."

Gorge lowered his hands and let the collar rest on his jacket and shirt. It balanced if he didn't move too much, and if the iron didn't touch his flesh, it gave him little pain—but it trapped his magic inside him.

"He'll keep you here like he did Toynia," Cleo said. "You won't fit in the wardrobe. Do you want to see it?"

Cleo crossed to a tall shelf of records near the performance space and pulled several albums off it. She reached into the empty space and clicked something that released the shelf to swing away from the wall. Another hidden door, a stone space behind it. Gorge edged closer. Iron bars enclosed it like the wardrobe cage but large enough for Gorge to fit inside—and no larger. Being in the cell would be like living in a coffin.

"Like it?" Cleo said.

Gorge didn't answer. Instead, he grabbed one of the guitars scattered around the room—an electric blue-black Stratocaster— sat down, and picked through scales at random. Everything had gone wrong; he'd lost the upper hand by assuming himself immune to whatever Bruno could throw at him. No question he could overpower Bruno when it came to magic, but raw power offered no help while the iron ring around his neck hobbled him.

He needed to think; he needed music.

His fingers scraped over the strings; scales flowed into chords then into bits and pieces of songs he strung together.

Cleo listened to the tinny unamplified sounds, confused, and then wandered to the recording room where she set to work preparing the equipment for the night's session. Out of the corner of his eye, Gorge monitored her, hoping she might betray some clue as to where Bruno had hidden Delilah. He tried to cast his senses around the house, but the iron ring and the magical shielding stopped him. He had underestimated Bruno. Not that the man was any better a wizard than Gorge had given him credit for, but because he was far more cruel, cunning, and driven than Gorge had understood.

He picked at the guitar strings, playing rambling, bluesy riffs, thinking of Toynia, of Delilah, of all the things he'd lost. After a while, Bruno descended the stairs, sweating and panting. A pink welt bulged above his eye, and he pressed a blood-spotted handkerchief to his cheek.

"Warming up? Good," he said, his voice thick and sullen.

"What happened to you?" Gorge asked.

Bruno stomped his foot and whirled on Gorge. "Your little bitch did this. I went to let her go, and this is how she thanked me."

Gorge eyed Bruno's wounds. He didn't doubt Delilah had caused them.

"So, Delilah's gone? Free?"

Bruno waved Gorge off and headed for the recording studio.

"Answer me," Gorge said.

"No, she's *not gone*, not yet." A grotesque sneer twisted Bruno's lips. He raised the handkerchief to reveal four parallel, bloody gouges along his cheek. "I had to use the Voice to stop her going mental. She's difficult to control with your magic in her. I left her upstairs, asleep. She's free to leave whenever she wakes up. *Best* I could do."

Staring at the man's contorted face, Gorge felt a twinge of fear at the idea of Bruno Rice letting loose with his magic, of the man thinking he could possibly control it.

His fingers halted on the strings.

He hadn't feared anything since he was a child.

He wouldn't start again now.

Gorge stood up, swung the guitar over his head, and struck the body against the floor on angle that snapped it free from the neck.

Bruno and Cleo froze in the recording room and stared at him.

Gorge threw the broken guitar neck, bounced it off the glass. "You're wasting time."

Bruno nodded and poked his head through the door. "Right, fine. Find another guitar, try not to break it, and let's start."

"First, tell me what that is." Gorge pointed at the gramophone.

"Like that? I went through hell to get it. Tell you the story sometime. It's called His Master's Ear. It doesn't only play music, it records it. And it records magic. I can draw out your power, store it on the cylinders then play it back and take the magic when I need it. Listen."

Bruno took a wooden case from a shelf and removed from it a wax cylinder lined with grooves, notches, and ridges. He inserted it in the machine in place of the blank one there. He turned the crank to play it back; the gears wound up and faint sound emerged from the horn. The machine glowed. Bruno let go, and the crank turned itself. A voice flowed from the horn, the melancholy song Gorge had heard at the party drifting up through the floor of Bruno's rec room.

Toynia's voice.

Toynia's magic.

As rich and wonderful as he remembered it.

Light expanded from the machine. Cleo stared at it, mesmerized until Bruno pushed her aside, placed his hand near the horn, and drew the power into his fingertips. It lit up his arm as it soaked into him. The grooves and notches in the cylinder vanished as the music played, the recording erasing itself as it surrendered its magic to Bruno. His face grew younger, more vital, his body firmer, stronger. The magic revived him, but in his sloppiness, he lost much of the power, spilling it into the air.

Toynia's power.

Wasted.

Like her life had been.

Gorge grabbed the turning cylinder, cutting off the song. He threw it on the ground and kicked it to pieces. The aura around the machine blinked out.

The corona outlining Bruno's arm flashed and vanished.

Bruno staggered, doubled over, coughing, wheezing to catch his breath.

He dry-retched and his face reddened. Cleo rushed to his side.

Gorge left the room, snatched up another Strat, and picked out a happy tune.

Bruno recovered and came out of the recording room. "Prick. Do you know how long it takes to make those cylinders, how hard it is to gather the ingredients?"

"No, and I don't care. You don't deserve to hear Toynia sing," Gorge told him.

"Maybe that matters where you come from," Bruno said. "In this world, there's no deserve or don't deserve, no fair or unfair.

All that counts is taking what you want, and staying on top because if you're not on top then you're down in the shit."

"Spare me your tired philosophy." Gorge got up and entered the performance room. "I'll play now. Record me or don't."

Cleo came in after him. "Bruno says I have to take this off you or the magic won't flow." She reached up and undid the iron collar. "It goes back on before you leave this room."

Gorge saw the performance and recording room stood inside an iron grid invisible from the exterior. Magic would flow freely between the two rooms but not beyond them. When Cleo stepped out, she locked the door, completing the cage.

The space was near silent, except for sounds Gorge made, and it seemed very tight and lonely. The echo of a memory came to him of chains and heat and sand scraping his lips.

The knobs of scar tissue on his back ached.

The warm touch of blood trickled over his skin.

Gorge began to play.

Bruno hustled back to the recording room and put a fresh wax blank in His Master's Ear. He flipped switches on the machines, set tape in the recorder then pushed a pair of headphones onto his ears, and settled in behind the sound board.

Gorge stopped playing.

Bruno yanked his headphones off and activated an intercom between the two rooms. His voice crackled over the speaker. "What? Why'd you stop?"

"Where's Delilah?" Gorge said.

Bruno frowned. "I told you, she's in her room, asleep."

"I don't trust you. I need to know she's safe."

"I don't know what you expect me to do," Bruno said.

"I'll know if she's all right if I sense her, but you've got so much crap magic and iron around me, I'm practically blind."

"That's how it has to be."

"I have no reason to play for you if she's not safe."

"She's safe. *Play.*"

"I don't even need to leave this room," Gorge said. "Open the door. Remove the spells concealing her. I can feel her from here. I'll know if she's okay, then I'll play."

"No," Bruno said. "*Play now.*"

Gorge ducked free of the guitar strap and set the instrument in a stand.

Bruno stared at him, his frustration rising and reddening his face. He undid the collar of his shirt and stroked the Voice of Reason.

"Go on, play. It's the only choice you have. Delilah's safe, and it's best for her that she'll be without you. A mortal woman should be with a mortal man, not with your kind. Now you don't have to worry about anything but making music and gathering magic. Pick up the guitar. Play."

The words knit a haze around Gorge's mind. He knew the Voice of Reason created it, and he knew not to trust or agree with Bruno, but the intensity of the urge shocked him. Weakened by the iron, his mind let the magic of the Voice worm into it. Gorge swayed. He grabbed the Strat, slung the strap across his shoulders, and played a fast, ethereal riff.

Bruno settled into his seat, smiling, and donned his headphones again.

His smile...

...slithering like a serpent.

Nothing good comes of making Bruno Rice smile.

Gorge stopped playing. He shrugged out of the guitar strap, gripped the instrument by the body, and slammed its solid wood against the glass window between him and Bruno. The glass quivered. Gorge hit it again, and again, aiming for Bruno, who sat on the other side with his arms crossed in front of his face. Gorge dropped his grip to the neck and swung the guitar like an axe, a blow that formed a hairline crack in the glass as the guitar body snapped away in a mess of broken strings and splintered wood. Bruno screamed, jumped out of his seat, and slammed his headphones on the console.

"You're going to *play!*" Bruno said. "Cleo, bring him another guitar."

Cleo unlocked the door and carried a Telecaster with a sunburst finish into the room and handed it to Gorge. He folded his arms across his chest and refused it.

"Play." There was a plaintive, urgent tone in Bruno's voice.

"I've been alive longer than your people have had written history," Gorge said. "If you want a waiting game we both know how it will go."

Bruno slumped in his seat.

"Fine. Whatever. This is how *you* want it, not *me*. *I* was going to be merciful. *I* was trying to take the high road," he said. "Cleo, fetch the monitor."

Leaving the Telecaster in a stand and locking the door after her, Cleo walked to a corner of the cellar and returned pushing a television on a wheeled cart. Wires trailed it, tethers to an unseen hookup in the dark. She parked the cart by the performance room, screen facing Gorge. Beneath the television sat a video recorder. Cleo pushed a few buttons and adjusted a dial. Numbers in a digital display rolled backward.

"I wanted to spare you this to make your time here more bearable," Bruno said. "Switch it on, Cleo."

Cleo clicked a dial. The screen brightened and an image resolved.

"If you believed Delilah had gone on with her life, that your sacrifice had saved her, then staying here would've been easier for you," Bruno said. "So have it your way. Live in torture."

An image took focus, a room in Bruno's mansion.

Delilah sat on a bed. Chains and leather straps hung down from mounts in the ceiling. Gorge remembered the room from the night of the party; he could be there in seconds if he could get out of the recording studio. On a table by the bed waited a full glass of wine. Delilah reached for it—hesitated—then lifted it by its stem, holding it beneath her nose to sniff the aroma. She ran a hand through her hair and swirled the wine in the glass.

"You told me she was sleeping," Gorge said.

"I *tried* to let her go—*I did*—but she attacked me, so I told her to stay there, and drink the wine," Bruno said. "I can't let her leave. You understand that, right? She'll hurt me or expose me. And now that I've got you, I don't need her anyway."

"Stop her," Gorge said.

"No. Play," Bruno said.

"Stop her or not only will I never play for you, but I'll kill you," Gorge said.

"You can't even leave the studio unless Cleo unlocks the door," Bruno said. "You won't play? We'll see how tough you are after a few weeks without food and water."

"*Tell her to stop!*"

Gorge erupted and hurtled himself through the air. His fists thundered against the glass between him and Bruno. The window wobbled. Gorge pounded it, extending the crack he'd made to a jagged line. He grabbed the stool from behind the drum kit and hurled it against the glass. Through his anger and the din of his rampage, a voice drilled into his mind.

Bruno over the intercom.

The Voice of Reason pushing against his will.

Gorge hesitated, listened; he couldn't help it.

"I can't stop her," Bruno said. "It's too late."

The words sank in.

Gorge dropped a music stand to the floor.

"Why? Go! Now! Stop her."

Bruno slammed his hand on the console. "You crazy bastard! You're ruining everything. I can't stop her from drinking it because *she already has*. You're watching a bloody recording."

Gorge looked at the television again.

Delilah reached for the glass, lifted it by its stem, sniffed it... and then...

No... don't...

...drank.

She drained the glass, set it down. In seconds, she folded into sleep on the bed.

Her eyes closed. Her chest rose and fell.

Her hand slid off the bed and dropped the wine glass onto the floor.

Cleo worked a remote, and the screen flickered as time rewound.

Delilah reappeared, sitting on the edge of the bed, reaching for the glass, lifting it, sniffing it...

"I anticipated there might be a day I needed this to give you a little push," Bruno said. "Never thought I'd use it this soon."

Anger and grief scorched Gorge's mind.

He punched the glass, spreading the fine crack another half inch. Bruno recoiled.

Gorge grabbed the Telecaster, jammed the cord in, and placed his fingers on the strings.

A torrent of sound arced from the amplifiers. Magic came with it.

Gorge held nothing back.

He filled the studio with light.

He played hard and fast, his fingers stretching, his hands blurs of motion lighting up the strings as he tapped into the energy he'd gathered from the gigs he'd played. The poison power he'd absorbed from the darkness. The pure white light of an audience's admiration. He focused everything stored inside him toward Bruno and launched it out of himself in a storm of sound. If music and magic could pass between the two rooms that left Bruno nowhere to hide.

Yet, the magic refused to go where Gorge told it.

Gorge marked its path through the glass, but where it should've reduced Bruno to cinders, it warped and curved away to flow instead into the horn of His Master's Ear.

Bruno grinned as he watched the light show pass him.

He dropped the handkerchief from his face. His torn skin bled thin, black lines that trickled between his lips and made him appear as if his mouth was full of blood.

The wax cylinder spun; the stylus carved diameter after diameter of tiny, delicate marks into it, recording Gorge's magic.

Gorge attacked the guitar, drawing on every note and scale he'd adapted from the Kingdoms; he pushed out raw power, willing it to defy the recording device and blast Bruno. He summoned more energy than he'd ever expelled at one time since his exile. It tore at his body. Pain flared in his limbs. Blood dribbled from his scars, down his back, and pooled at his feet. The glass walls vibrated; the floors pulsed. Outside the studio, furniture shook. Bruno's collection of artifacts fell from their shelves or toppled over. Some cracked apart. Cleo backed away, bumped into the wardrobe, and then pressed herself into the corner it formed with the wall. The TV monitor glared magnesium bright before the screen exploded with a shower of sparks and puff of smoke.

Yet Bruno stood in the clear, watching the magic pour into His Master's Ear, another wax blank in hand, ready to swap it when the first one filled up.

Gorge amped up the music.

If he couldn't leave with Delilah then he had no reason to leave at all.

Pain electrified. Everything around him bowed and rippled, its solidity undermined by the music. He felt the darkness at the edge of his awareness and tried to call it down to obliterate Bruno and his house—but he couldn't bridge the distance. Too much of his power funneled into His Master's Ear.

Delilah's face filled his mind.

Her skin, translucent in the desert sun.

Black hair like liquid shadow.

Her touch so gentle yet strong as she lifted me and freed me from my chains.

Earthy scent of her breath.

Salt-sweet smell of her sweat.

Gorge carved her song out of the wall of sound he'd created and sang.

Dead man, discarded
True love departed
The darkness bleeds
Whisper fear's needs
Immortal, now mortal and pride must kneel
Shadow of her soul, light of her desire
in her eyes, I heal.

Playing with bloody, shredded fingers, performing with all the grace, power, and awe of the music he'd known in the Kingdoms, Gorge sang. His voice carried over the guitar's roars and shrieks, asserted itself through the screech of high notes and the juggernaut of heavy chords. His singing writhed in the air like a ribbon of solid sound. It touched Bruno and Cleo, even lost, dead Toynia, and filled the cellar with a web of light. Magic rose from Bruno's artifacts and antiques and flowed toward Gorge, sizzling and short-circuiting against the iron boundaries.

Lost way found again
scorched earth reborn
touch of her skin
soothes anger's sin
in her artist's eye, my broken wings heal
blood spills, scars never forgotten, never sealed, a dream
becomes real.

A net of pain tightened around Gorge's chest, stomach, legs; his head pounded.

He ignored his agony and played.

The sound grew; the light became blinding. Bruno's eyes widened in terror.

Gorge's wings appeared.

He cast off his glamour, and Bruno saw his true face. More than human, more than Bruno could ever hope to be, his face the face of a god. Behind him spread wings formed of energy that rippled and shimmered with iridescent light, magic flames filling the space where his natural wings had been torn away.

And the only thing it takes to make it all go away
is the sound of her voice asking me to stay.

The magic light flared.

Power chewed through Gorge, punishing his body from the inside out.

Bruno cowered in the recording room, still untouched.

The cylinder in His Master's Ear was nearly full. The energy around the machine sizzled.

Bruno crept across the floor to change cylinders, but then Gorge set his song afire with a blistering lead, and His Master's Ear exploded.

A flower of brightness enveloped it. Parts of it shot in every direction.

All the magic stored in it released at once, flaring only as far as the iron grid, obliterating the rooms with light, sweeping over Bruno and Gorge. The horn struck the cracked window between the studios; the thick glass shattered, scattering a thousand shards to the floor.

Cleo screamed.

The magic hit Gorge like an acid shower in a hundred-mile wind.

It staggered him.

One by one, the strings on the Telecaster snapped, each with a noxious, twanging screech, forcing Gorge to end his song. The reverberations settled. He dropped the guitar in a stand.

His hands ran slick with blood from his ripped fingers; the back of his shirt was soaked through with blood from his scars. He climbed through the broken window and stood over Bruno, looked into his vacant face, and saw no point in killing him now. Though his body still lived, the magic had demolished his mind. Blood dribbled from his ears and his eyes, from his nose and mouth, from under his fingernails. He sat splayed on the floor, unaware of anything.

The magic had also cracked the Voice of Reason. Tucked close to Gorge in his pocket, the Ring of Truth remained undamaged.

Gorge pulled the broken collar off Bruno. Dead, power exhausted.

He dropped it clanging to the floor.

The door to the recording room stood unlocked, a breach in the iron prison.

Cleo cowered by the wardrobe, staring at Gorge and trembling.

She'd fared better than Bruno, but not much.

No magic remained in the room, not even the last scraps of Toynia's power.

Gorge limped across the cellar, made his way upstairs.

He opened a bedroom door and whispered Delilah's name.

The wine glass lay on the floor, drops of red staining the carpet. Delilah reclined on the bed, so still Gorge thought she was gone—but then her chest rose once and fell.

A few seconds later, it did so again.

His hope flared.

Gorge felt her pulse, so weak it seemed intangible. The magic he had infused in her over the years had slowed the effects of the alcohol and drugs, and with magic he could save her—as he'd saved Cleo—but he was depleted and the all the magic in the house was gone; only the hum of the Sidhe in the woods outside remained. All that magic expended in Bruno's hidden rooms, and the Sidhe probably had no idea thanks to Bruno's secrecy and spells. He could ask them for help, but why would they help an exile—and if they did, they would demand a hideous price.

Gorge embraced Delilah and kissed her, felt her warmth fading.

"Don't go," he told her. "I wrote you a song. I want you to hear it."

The song...

Gorge scooped Delilah off the bed and carried her downstairs.

He found Bruno Rice's fastest car, a red Porsche, located the keys, and then with Delilah in the passenger seat, he sped into the night.

The speedometer crested 100 mph.

Too slow.

Gorge wove the Porsche through late-night traffic, his faerie reflexes allowing him to pick out a path as if the other vehicles stood still. Twice, police cruisers appeared in his rearview mirror, lights flashing. Gorge just pushed the car above 120 mph and vanished among the vehicles ahead like a phantom.

The ride became streaks of light and lines of dark pavement.

The East River a gleaming, black ripple reflecting city lights as he rocketed across the 59th Street Bridge.

Plunging into the narrow shadows of the city streets....

Gorge sat in a thin puddle of his cooling blood as the sun rose.

Its light filtered through the tall windows as bronzing dust motes danced in the air.

He played Delilah's song on an acoustic guitar, finished, then played it again.

He had lost count of how many times he'd played it now.

Delilah lay wrapped in a blanket on the floor beneath her unfinished painting of him.

Her chest rose, fell, rose.

Every so often her eyelids fluttered or her fingers twitched.

Gorge felt her strengthening, little by little, her body clearing the drugs as he reclaimed the magic he'd stored in the studio and healed her with it. It was working, but *so slow*—and fatigue crippled him. Drained. Wounded. Woozy. His head swam in a fog. He wanted sleep, but if he stopped the song, the magic would drift away, leaving Delilah on her own before she was strong enough.

He finished the song, played it again.

His steel strings were slick and crusted with blood.

His voice emerged in a scarred whisper.

The sun ascended and warmed the room.

Light stung Gorge's eyes, and his mouth turned dry.

Voices and engine growls rose from the street.

Gorge's head dipped.

The world darkened...

...and then he snapped himself awake.

He played a flat note.

Another.

Then the wrong chord.

He hadn't made such mistakes in centuries.

He rejected his exhaustion, focused on the song, on Delilah's paintings, on the magic in the air—but he was only a husk, almost as weak as the day he arrived in the mortal world.

His head dipped again...

Darkness.

A soft touch...

...caressing him...

...lifting him.

Moist warmth on his lips.

A sweet, familiar taste.

Gentle fingers in his hair.

He opened his eyes.

Delilah stared back at him. Deep indigo rings circled her glassy eyes. Her pale skin made her look delicate and wounded, almost ghostly—but *she lived.* She eased the guitar from Gorge's hands and set it aside. She opened the blanket cocooning her, drew Gorge into it, and pressed close to him, holding him tight as she wrapped them together.

"It's okay," she whispered, her voice so soft, Gorge wondered if it was real. "We can sleep now."

And they did.

For two days straight.

CŌDA

Bruno's "shocking mental breakdown" made headlines for two weeks, his crack-up attributed to age and illicit drugs. There was no mention of Cleo, nor any of Bruno's secret cellar. Brimmer Riggs had found him wandering his empty mansion and then taken him to a hospital, the fate of Disharmony Records left uncertain.

Someday, though, someone would discover the cellar and find Toynia's remains. Gorge couldn't allow any further desecration of her body. He and Delilah returned to the mansion to retrieve the poor fae's body.

It took little effort to break into the house. Only facing the stone cell Bruno had intended for him and the wreckage left behind by his outpouring of magic proved difficult for Gorge. In the end, though, he simply turned his back on it and left.

"This is a bad idea," Delilah said.

"Almost everything I do is a bad idea," Gorge said. "My choices almost killed you."

Delilah held the back of Gorge's head and kissed him.

"Fuck that," she said. "Bruno Rice and Cleo almost killed me. *You* gave up everything for me."

"Not quite everything." Gorge's gaze drifted away to the woods behind Bruno's mansion. "Besides nothing I had or will ever have means anything without you."

Delilah touched his shoulder. "Which is why this is a bad idea."

A gust of wind swept among the trees and stirred the blanket-wrapped bundle resting on the ground between them. A corner flapped, and a small, thin hand slipped out, its flesh like arctic ice, fingers dry and shriveled. Gorge tucked the hand back in and wrapped Toynia's corpse tight.

"What if they sense your magic in me? Or feel you here in the woods?"

Gorge lifted the bundle and presented it to Delilah. "They won't. I've got no magic left in me for them to sense. It'll take months to rebuild it. If there's ever a time it's safe for me to be so close to them, it's now. As long as you wear the Ring of Truth and keep to what I told you to say, the fae will believe what you tell them. Don't take off the ring no matter what. Don't lie and don't answer their questions. If they think you did this to Toynia, they'll torture you to death, and I won't be able to stop them."

Delilah took the bundle. "People where you come from are not very nice."

"People where I come from aren't people."

"Right."

Delilah snugged the bundle against her chest and started down a gentle hill into the woods.

"Delilah," Gorge called after her. "You don't have to do this. If you're... afraid, I mean. I'd understand if you said no."

"If I did then you'd only do it yourself, and where would that get us? I already said yes." Delilah balanced on the slope and glared at Gorge. "I'm not afraid. Whatever comes, you'll be with me, and I'll be with you. One way or another. That's all I care about."

Gorge said, "Show them the Ring right away after you open the door. If they don't see it first, they may not give you a chance to explain. If they offer you anything to eat or drink—"

"Refuse it," Delilah said. "I know. And no bargaining, and don't fall asleep. Say my piece. Get out of there. I've got it, now will you please just let me do it?"

Gorge nodded. Delilah continued down the hill.

Gorge sat on a large stone and leaned back to wait.

He stared at the clear sky through a mesh of indifferent leaves and branches.

A new song drifted across his thoughts, a fresh melody; he let it fill his mind and grow.

The day passed, night fell. Gorge slept against the tree.

Morning came. He dug food out of the pack and ate.

He played his guitar, played his new song. He waited.

Night came again, and he slept.

In the morning, he woke to Delilah crunching leaves and twigs as she climbed the hill.

He sat up and watched her.

The bundle was gone. She cried with her arms crossed tight over her chest.

Gorge ran to her.

"What happened?"

Delilah pressed her face to his neck but said nothing.

"It's all right, you're safe now," he said. "Did they hurt you?"

"They were grateful. They were glad to know Bruno had suffered, and no one ever asked me about you or anything else." Delilah glanced at the setting sun. "How long was I gone?"

"Two days."

"*No.*" Delilah recoiled and shuddered. She pulled the Ring of Truth from her hand and shoved into Gorge's. "It was only fifteen minutes. They listened, took Toynia. That's all. They offered me a reward, food—I turned it down and left."

"Doesn't matter," Gorge said. "You went through the door. Going even a little ways into the Kingdoms changes how time passes."

Gorge walked Delilah to the top of the hill and picked up his pack.

"They were so thankful," Delilah said. "If you'd been the one to bring her back, they might've forgiven you. They might've taken you back."

"I don't want to go back."

"Fuck, Gorge, how can you not want to?" Delilah wiped tears from her eyes. "It's perfect there. Peaceful. Beautiful. And the magic, oh, god, it's like being on fire with love and power all the time. Their whole world is full of light and energy, and it's all so much more intense and real. Why would you give up a chance to get that back? I can't be the reason that keeps you from it. Don't put that on me. I don't want to live with that."

"It's not on you," Gorge said. "It's on the ones who cast me out. It's on me. Don't be fooled by a glimpse of the Kingdoms. There's a deep, foul darkness behind all that light. The Kingdoms have as much suffering there as in this world." Gorge met Delilah's eyes. "I couldn't take you with me if I went back. It would be going into exile all over again."

Delilah stared into Gorge's eyes, yearning, searching; Gorge met her gaze, unwavering.

He raised a hand to show Delilah the Ring of Truth on his finger.

She took his hand in hers. They walked out of the woods, away from Bruno Rice's mansion. Into the shroud of silence that surrounded it, Gorge hummed the melody of a new song.

Unruly Fictions and Aggressive Guitars

(2019 Remix)

SOME STORIES COME OF AGE LIKE REBELLIOUS CHILDREN.

They refuse to cooperate. They talk back and put you in tough spots.

They leave their stuff scattered all around your desk, your mind, your heart.

They confuse you.

You love them anyway. You do your best with them and hope your bad habits and baggage don't influence them too much. You try to stop them from abusing adverbs. You make sure they're wearing all their commas, semi-colons, and periods in the right places when they go out of the house. But they take on a life of their own.

About all we authors can do with such unruly fictions is go with the flow, keep things on an even keel, and hope it all ends well.

The good ones surprise and delight us as much (we hope) as they do our readers.

The bad ones we lock away in bottom drawers and maybe pull out later to raid for ideas.

"Three Chords of Chaos" revealed itself as one of these tumultuous tales when Gorge first laid eyes on

the dumpster-diving scrape sprite. I hadn't planned it, but that poor guy was doomed the moment I finished describing him. Gorge whispered in my ear what he intended to do to him—and I couldn't persuade him otherwise.

I tried. I rewrote the scene, rearranged it, let other characters try to talk some sense into Gorge, gave that little garbage eater some pluck—all to no avail.

The more I pushed, the more Gorge pushed back.

He made it clear who he was, what he wanted, and left it to me deal with it.

So I did. He is, after all, the star of the show.

Which is one reason why "Three Chords of Chaos" isn't precisely the novella I set out to write. So there, my secret's out; of course no one would be the wiser if I didn't 'fess up. In fact, if you were to ask my editor, she would tell you the finished story is pretty close to the one I outlined for her back when Gorge was only another rough-edged faerie in a couple of short stories in the award-winning *Bad-Ass Faeries* anthologies. Back before he thought he knew it all. I could still get a word or two into that hard head of his then. How fast egos expand—even those of characters who exist only on paper. Gorge's became a gravity well, warping my story to suit him; though the fundamentals of my original plot didn't change all that much, the final tale is very different in detail and emphasis than what I'd envisioned.

The usual adjustments that come with writing occurred. Character names changed. Personalities shifted. Supporting characters came and went. Plot points tightened. Scenes shrank or expanded. Themes grew and sharpened. What changed most, though, was the story's balance. At the outset, I saw "Three Chords of Chaos" as much more of a period piece entrenched in the American indie and underground rock music scene of the late 70s and early 80s. I wanted to write as much about that era and its music as about the characters. I harbored notions of who Gorge was and why that time offered the perfect environment for him; exploring that provided an early, driving force behind the novella.

It seemed like a natural fit for my fallen faerie. Gorge shares a lot in common with the musicians and fans who defined influential rock music in those years.

Instinctive defiance of the established order.

Principled disdain for pure commerce.

Open-eyed cynicism directed at all kinds of authority.

A self-dependent, self-reliant DIY attitude.

An unflagging dedication to making good, challenging music.

Most of all, though, a near symbiotic relationship with their fans.

Many of the bands that shaped that era never became household names. Chances are you've never heard of some them, never listened to their music. They got scant radio play in their prime, and few ever released records on major labels. If you were listening to these bands back in the day, it's because you were plugged into something special. You went to concerts held in people's houses or dive venues or community centers. Or you read one of the fanzines of the day and mail-ordered singles and EPs based on reputation alone or a trusted reviewer's praise. Maybe you caught mention of some bands in the hipper music magazines and newspapers, but you never caught them on MTV, Top 40 radio, TV commercials, or movie soundtracks. The few of these bands I knew of at the time I encountered only because a friend of mine had a mixtape of their music made for him by one of his friends who'd raided an older sibling's records to make it. That tape was radioactive. My friend kept it hidden. It had songs on it with really bad words *in the titles*.

That tape was more valuable than gold.

It was the only real—albeit brief—exposure I had to indie underground music.

I grew up in the suburbs. My peers loved classic rock and hair metal or pop dance and power ballads. I started out on a different path; the first two albums I bought myself were *Synchronicity* and *The Best of Blondie*. A pretty good start for my nascent musical tastes. But then the wave of popular music and MTV bands swept me up, and though not all of that was bad, much of it was pretty shallow and none of it ever seemed entirely *real*.

It's my curse to have never been on the cutting edge when it comes to discovering new music. I tend to connect the dots about a year or so (often much longer) after bands break up. I did it with the Pixies. I did it with Soundgarden, Dead Kennedys, and Television. I've done it with half a dozen other of my favorite groups or songwriters. I walk into the party about the time everyone else is nodding off, the lights are on, and the only beer left is the cheap local brew. Sometimes I get lucky and catch on early, but my luck can also be cruel.

One indie band I clued into early was Hüsker Dü.

They received a lot of press in the early 80s for an indie band, some in publications that actually came my way once in awhile, such as *Spin* and *Rolling Stone*, and occasionally *The Village Voice*. Hüsker Dü blipped my radar so I started prowling for their albums. The first one I found was *Candy Apple Grey*, ironically their first major label release. I snatched it up, put it on, and waited to be amazed only to be deflated when the album made little impression on me. It's good but it didn't justify the hype. I had a lot riding on that album. I wanted a lifeline to reel myself in to the world of genuine, soul-searing, underground rock music that remained only a rumor to me. The people I knew whose tastes stood entrenched within the confines of radio songs often assumed "indie" or "underground" equaled "bad," and that's why the bands weren't more successful. My instincts told me different. I sought something to knock the scales from our eyes.

Candy Apple Grey didn't do it.

It didn't explain why the lifeblood coursing through the underground was much richer and more vibrant than that of the mainstream. It's taken me nearly thirty years to understand how cheated I was and what might've been if only that first Hüsker Dü album had been *Flip Your Wig* or *Zen Arcade* or *Metal Circus*. Those albums—when I finally gave them a chance—blew that old hype away.

What stings most is that I didn't listen to them until I began my research for "Three Chords of Chaos." In that time, though, my enlightenment has led me to a lot of music I'd overlooked and back to some I never fully appreciated when I first heard it. I spent a significant portion of my research time for this story with headphones on, immersed in the music that informs Gorge's back story. Black Flag. Dead Kennedys. The Germs. Hüsker Dü. Minor Threat. Minutemen. Mission of Burma. The Ramones. Richard Hell and the Voidoids. The Stooges. Sonic Youth. Television. Hell, even Mötörhead (technically not part of the American indie music scene, but who can deny Lemmy?). It's a double-edged sword: I missed out on a lot of phenomenal music over the years because *Candy Apple Grey* didn't light up the right synapses, but on the other hand I've got it all to listen to now, when good new rock music is damn hard to find. Better yet, it remains as fiery and inspiring as it must have been when it was first written, played, and recorded.

There's true life in this music.

There's heart. There's blood and sweat. There's pain, fear, and passion. There's anger and hope, desperation and arrogance. There's lowlife and genius.

It's like the Minutemen sang: "I work sweat, but I dream light years."

Like there is for Gorge, there's magic in it too.

The more I learned about the music and the musicians, about the bands and the upstart indie record companies, about the econo tours in vans held together with spit and prayer and the informal network of musicians and fans who traded information (like hobos in decades past marking friendly houses with secret symbols), the clearer it became that the scope of the underground music scene, the variety of its music, and the sheer power of its existence sprawled far beyond what I could hope to capture in a single novella. I set "Three Chords of Chaos" in New York City, but some of the brightest-burning indie hotspots lay in Los Angeles, San Francisco, Minneapolis, and Washington D.C. Even worse? The prospect of encapsulating in a piece of short fiction the range of a musical movement that spans from Minor Threat's hardcore, no-holds-barred guitar rage and vocal assault to Minutemen's quirky, funky punk to Mission of

Burma's jangly crashing melodies to Sonic Youth's trippy art punk to Hüsker Dü's blend of razor-edged guitar riffs and sixties-inflected songs—and a dozen or more other musical styles and philosophies.

It was a dark day when I realized there was simply no way that a novella-length piece was enough to tell a story that would do justice to all that.

Fortunately, Gorge gave me the answer.

Standing at the dumpster, tragic scrape sprite in hand, Gorge made it clear that *this* particular novella was about him. Maybe he'd be happy to share the stage and jam with the greats of the American underground, but "Three Chords of Chaos" was not going to be so much historical fiction as a journey with the greatest musician ever to be kicked out of the Realms of the Sidhe. The story is his—well, his and Delilah's. You may have noticed he's got a soft spot for her.

So I let Gorge take over.

He turned out not to be a total prick, either.

He gave me a good story and let me sneak in a fair few nods to the history and realities of the indie scene, to the good and the bad, to the spirit that shaped it, and the music that defined it. Maybe Gorge would've fit in among the bands and clubs of that time. Maybe not. He's got an epic attitude problem. But then his world isn't quite that world. It's a skewed version where magic is real, and a wounded, fallen, relentlessly pissed-off faerie can become an overnight rock god in the mortal world. In Gorge's reality, music equals power. Except for the magic, that's not too different from our world. The fact that music recorded when I was barely a teenager remains as potent and infectious today as it ever was—that the stories of the people who made that music and the trails they blazed have done so much to inspire countless other musicians as well as this story—speaks to that power. It hasn't faded but only grown, along with the importance and appreciation of those pioneering bands. It reaches beyond the music, too.

In today's independent and small press scene, I see much the same defiant, DIY, integrity that marked those indie musicians. It's quieter and less prone to spark fistfights, but the attitude is there. Sure, it's easier now to get the word out, to network, to find your fans, to record or publish your work, and put it in people's hands. (Imagine what pivotal indie record companies, such as Alternative Tentacles, Dischord, and SST, could've accomplished with the Internet instead of mail-order sales and handshake deals with regional distributors.)

One thing hasn't changed or gotten easier, though.

It still takes guts and a bottomless well of dedication to flip the bird to the mainstream and put your work or the work of others out into the world the way you want it to be—the way you *know* it should be—and bare your soul to your readers, your fans.

Gorge might say it's the only worthwhile choice.

He's never been known for choosing the easy path.

Like those indie musicians, he believes body and soul in his music, as authors must believe in their stories—and as sometimes they must trust them to lead where they need to go.

Whether or not you're into the music that inspired "Three Chords of Chaos," I hope you enjoyed the story. If you've never sampled the bands of that era, I encourage you to give them a listen. Despite the changes, I still mean "Three Chords of Chaos" to be an homage to that music, that era, its spirit, and the independent and punk musicians who lived it. Peppered throughout the story are a handful of Easter eggs, nods to some bits and pieces of the past. Also I've included a short list of recommended listening. It's incomplete by far, only a starting point, and it's not strictly true chronologically to the era or the movement, but all of it influenced my writing, all of it played—at one point or another and often at high volume—while I wrote this story. Check it out. It's pretty easy to find these days. I listened to a lot of it on Rhapsody (later Napster—and now dig much of it on Amazon Music Unlimited), which offers a wealth of albums from that time and the music that followed it. If you don't like one band, try another. Try ones not on my list. They're all unique; you're bound to find something.

No doubt, those who lived through this scene—those who experienced this music as it was created, or who sweat through the live shows, or helped make it all possible by giving a piece of their own personal magic, or those for whom music is a profession—will find mistaken assumptions or incorrect details

I didn't get quite right. I apologize for any inaccuracies. I hope those readers will find "Three Chords of Chaos" respectful of the spirit of the era and the power of music. There are many references and documentaries about this music. Two books were particularly helpful in my research: *Our Band Could Be Your Life: Scenes from the American Indie Underground 1981-1991* by Michael Azerrad (Black Bay Books, 2002) and *American Hardcore: A Tribal History*, Second Edition by Steven Blush (Feral House, 2010). Also helpful were the films *Punk's Not Dead* (dir. Susan Dyner, 2007), which provided perspective on the threads that run from punk's roots through to its present, and *Sid & Nancy* (dir. Alex Cox, 1986), which offered invaluable insight into the prototypical punk attitude, which now I think of it so does another Alex Cox film: *Repo Man* (1984).

Gorge isn't big fan of movies, but I'm certain he'd approve of that one.

James Chambers
April, 2013

Extended Version

IT'S NOW THE FIRST DAY OF 2019 AS I REVISIT THIS FOREWORD. Almost six years since the first publication of "Three Chords of Chaos." In that time, "The Way of the Bone," the original Gorge story, was reprinted in *The Best of Bad-Ass Faeries* (eSpec Books, 2017). The previous edition of "Three Chords" made it to the Bram Stoker Award® Preliminary Ballot for the year of its publication in the category of Long Fiction. Not a nominee, but still a nice bit of recognition. The world is a much different place now, and I'm a different writer in many ways, and music still seems as important as air most days.

For this "Remastered Edition," I closely revisited and revised the text with essential and always helpful input from my wonderful editors, Danielle Ackley-McPhail and Greg Schauer. They keep me honest. They challenge me to write better. And they always seem to understand what I'm going for even when I stumble. No author could ask for better editors.

I originally intended only to revise, polish, and clean-up the text for this new edition. New material wasn't part of the equation. Along the way I realized how much I missed Gorge, Delilah, and their world and how much I missed writing about music. A couple of loose ends from "Three Chords" always bothered me a bit so I decided to plunge back in and tie them up, which occurs in the brand new story (or "bonus track," if you will), "Feed the Fair Folk Sweet," a direct follow-up to "Three Chords of Chaos." This new edition also includes a new song, "Song for Delilah," which I hadn't planned to write. Greg convinced me to do so, and I'm happy he did, because I like how it turned out, what it says about Gorge and Delilah, and what it adds to the story. The cool, new liner notes for the songs were also Greg's suggestion, and I admit it wasn't until I tried writing them that I saw how much fun they would be.

For readers entering this world for the first time, you're jumping in with the full-on, remastered, hi-def, outtakes and all edition—the complete Gorge as of this writing. For those who read the previous edition, I hope this one will be like listening to an old favorite album in a fresh new way, finding all the things you enjoyed last time around and more.

Another interesting thing happened to me in the time between editions: My daughter entered her teen years and started high school. What does that have to do with "Three Chords of Chaos"? Well, one of the things she most wanted in 2018 was a record player. In the era of digital streaming with nearly everything ever recorded literally at our fingertips, she wanted to check out vinyl—and she wanted to do it with David Bowie records. Formerly a fan of current pop performers, she's grown, and her tastes have changed. I think she might be looking for the same thing in music I was at her age—something real, something honest, something inspiring. It heartens me to see our next generations seeking something that can't be found on screens, that can't be summoned up by a voice-activated interloper, and that lasts longer than an Internet outrage. It heartens me to see them value music full of sadness and joy, wonder and exploration, music that dares to take a chance and bucks the common sounds.

Music meant to be remembered and revisited.

If nothing else, revisiting "Three Chords of Chaos" has reminded me how much it's about that—but not only with regards to music. Isn't that what we hope for every time we open a new book or sit down to watch a new movie? Isn't that what creators should strive to create—something honest and lasting? Whether or not "Three Chords of Chaos" lives up to that ideal is, of course, up to readers to decide. I hope you'll find it worthy. I hope you'll enjoy it. And, at the very least, I hope you'll see (to paraphrase Minutemen) how this book works sweat but dreams light years.

Thank you for reading. Thank you for your support.

James Chambers
January 1, 2019

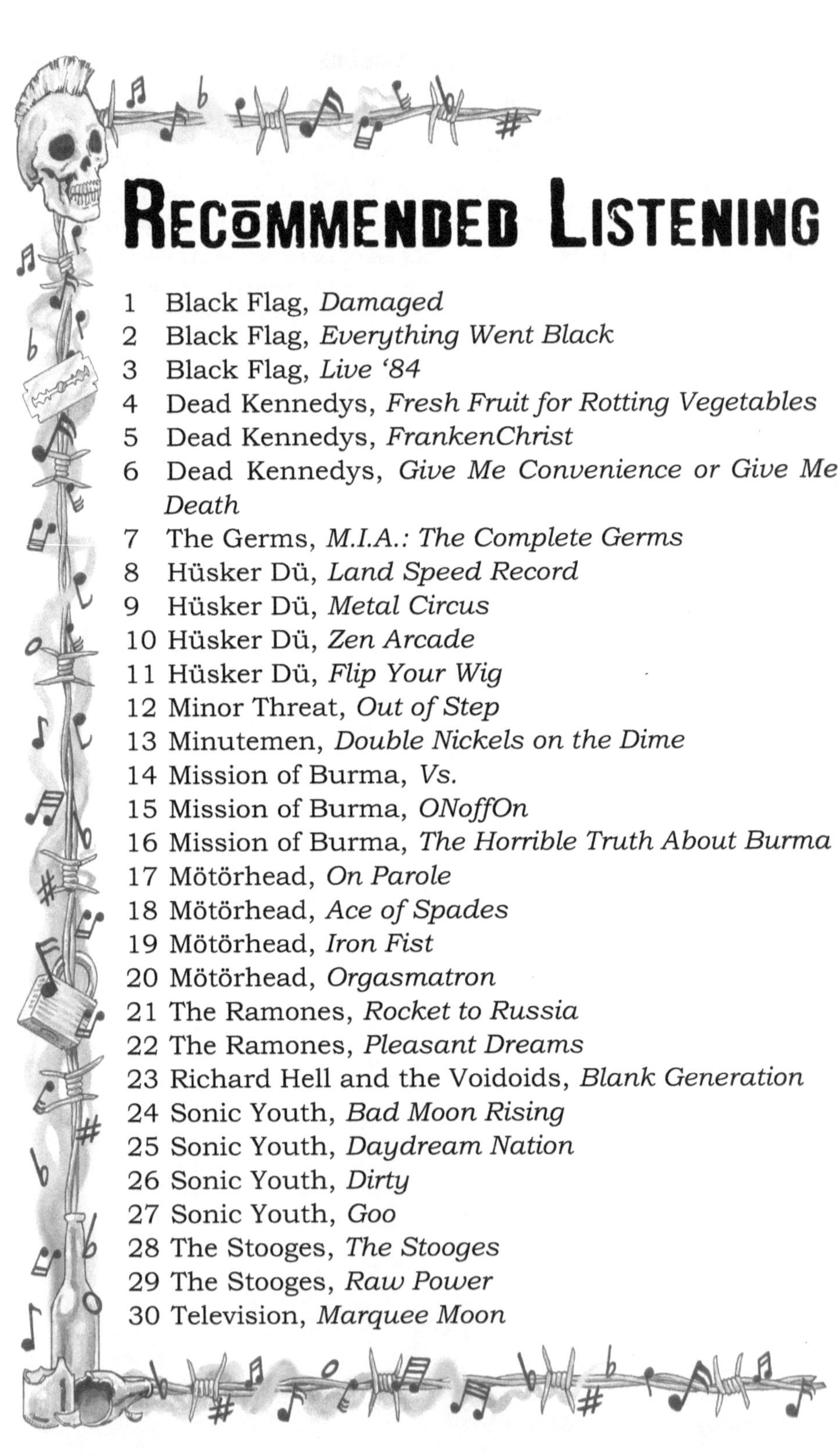

RECOMMENDED LISTENING

1 Black Flag, *Damaged*
2 Black Flag, *Everything Went Black*
3 Black Flag, *Live '84*
4 Dead Kennedys, *Fresh Fruit for Rotting Vegetables*
5 Dead Kennedys, *FrankenChrist*
6 Dead Kennedys, *Give Me Convenience or Give Me Death*
7 The Germs, *M.I.A.: The Complete Germs*
8 Hüsker Dü, *Land Speed Record*
9 Hüsker Dü, *Metal Circus*
10 Hüsker Dü, *Zen Arcade*
11 Hüsker Dü, *Flip Your Wig*
12 Minor Threat, *Out of Step*
13 Minutemen, *Double Nickels on the Dime*
14 Mission of Burma, *Vs.*
15 Mission of Burma, *ONoffON*
16 Mission of Burma, *The Horrible Truth About Burma*
17 Motörhead, *On Parole*
18 Motörhead, *Ace of Spades*
19 Motörhead, *Iron Fist*
20 Motörhead, *Orgasmatron*
21 The Ramones, *Rocket to Russia*
22 The Ramones, *Pleasant Dreams*
23 Richard Hell and the Voidoids, *Blank Generation*
24 Sonic Youth, *Bad Moon Rising*
25 Sonic Youth, *Daydream Nation*
26 Sonic Youth, *Dirty*
27 Sonic Youth, *Goo*
28 The Stooges, *The Stooges*
29 The Stooges, *Raw Power*
30 Television, *Marquee Moon*

Bonus Tracks

*New content exclusive to this edition

 Faerie Ring Blues

Rollin' Joe Linnet worked six steel strings like no mortal man should've known how to do—but only Gorge recognized it. He glared from the shadowy back corner of the bar, his anger burning hotter with every crying note the virtuoso bluesman played. Rollin' Joe enchanted the crowd crammed into Sam's Place in Los Angeles, all of them eager to get as close as possible to new talent before it rose out of reach. None of them doubted Rollin' Joe's rise; no one questioned his mastery.

Only Gorge knew better.

He watched how Rollin' Joe's hand wrapped the neck of his weathered Martin, how his fingers stroked the sweat-tarnished frets, and he knew the man's playing sprang from much more than mortal skill alone. Gorge sensed magic in the music. And in the man. Magic that damn well didn't belong to him. Although exile to the mortal world had robbed him of much of his own magic, Gorge still recognized the chords and scales of the Enchanted Lands even when they sounded like a broken-down hell played by a mortal on a mortal instrument in mortal air. He knew them as well as his own life story. To human ears, the music sounded magnificent, but it stabbed at Gorge's like daggers digging into his soul. He drained the bottle of beer in his hand, slammed it on the bar without taking his eyes off Rollin' Joe, and said, "How the hell does a second-rate blues guitarist out of some back-water, Mississippi river town learn scales it took me years to master?"

Delilah, beside him, put down her charcoal pencil and closed her sketchbook. She eyed the fury smolder-ing in Gorge's eyes and caressed the back of his hand. Only her presence helped Gorge keep his temper in check when such black moods came over him and stoked his hatred. He hated the Faerie Kingdoms, where he'd been the greatest musician in the Enchanted Lands; he hated its ruling council, the Flock of Eternity, who'd betrayed and exiled him. He hated the mortal world, his unwanted new home—and he hated most mortals, too. He loved only music and Delilah, who'd saved his life and helped him discover he could play the music of the Kingdoms here, despite the limits of mortal reality. Only that love kept Gorge from freeing the worst darkness inside him. He needed to be worthy of all that she'd done for him. He put his hand on hers and dampened the rage Rollin' Joe's music set boiling inside him.

Peace didn't come easy.

The joy on the faces of the crowd as they danced beneath a cloud of cigarette smoke and tapped their feet to the rhythm of Rollin' Joe's blues made him want to kick the guitar man aside, take the stage, and show them all the sound of music played with true magic. Instead, he clutched Delilah's hand tighter and waited for Rollin' Joe to finish his set. Not even Delilah could stop him then. The moment Rollin' Joe took his last bow, Gorge headed backstage. No one questioned him. In L.A. no one messed with a star, especially a short-tempered one whose latest recording looked sure to rank as one of 1958's biggest hits.

Gorge found the bluesman's dressing room and pounded three times on the door.

A woman opened it; her face lit up when she saw Gorge. Across the cramped room Rollin' Joe leaned back in his chair and drank from a bottle of beer. His eyes widened as they lit on Gorge, and Gorge read it clearly: Rollin' Joe saw Gavin Gray, L.A.'s star session musician, as Gorge had fashioned his mortal identity, knocking at his door and thought how far and fast his own star was rising.

"Nice set," Gorge said.

"Thanks, man. Glad you caught it." Joe leaned forward, thumping the front legs of his chair against the floor. He pointed to an ice chest. "Want a beer?"

Gorge kicked open the chest, grabbed two beers, and popped off the caps. He handed one to Delilah, and then introduced her to Joe and his girl, whose name was Jana.

"Gavin Gray, the living end," Joe said. "You've jammed with Gatemouth and Les Paul. Hell, you even sat in with Sinatra. The last record you played on, man, I listened to that record for a week straight," Joe said. "Fine guitar playing."

"I know," Gorge said.

"Here to check out the competition?" Joe tried a smile but it faltered.

"Something like that."

"Well, brother, I'm happy to meet you, but you got such a serious expression on your face, like I kicked your dog or you found me sleeping in your mama's bed, you're giving me the heebie-jeebies."

Gorge always concealed his faerie features behind a glamour in public, but the vestiges of his true face still leaked through, lending him an exotic, sinister look he never hesitated to use to his advantage. He gave Joe his best hard stare.

"Where'd you learn to play like that?"

Joe blinked and then peered down into his beer bottle. "My granddaddy taught me, mostly. But I sang the blues at a lot of low-down honkytonks and took my licks to learn it too. Taught myself a few tricks over the years." Joe lifted his head and winked. "You like 'em?"

"Bullshit. You didn't learn that music in any juke joint."

"Hey. Screw you, man. What? World ain't big enough for another good guitar player? What would you know about the blues anyway living out here in La-La Land having it made in the shade? Or maybe you don't like that I'm a black man. Is that it? People said L.A. would be different, told me I'd be leaving all that hate behind in Mississippi, but L.A. ain't different. People here got as much hate as anywhere. You got hate burning inside you, man?"

"Yes," Gorge said. "But not for you. At least, not yet."

He plucked Joe's Martin from its stand and started to strum and pick. He settled into the chords and scales from Joe's set, played some of the same riffs and songs, but he took them further and played them better than Joe could ever hope to, because the music of the Enchanted Lands ran through his blood and its magic belonged to him. The defiant light in Joe's eyes blew out. It satisfied Gorge to see it go, especially when a touch of awe replaced it. That softened Gorge's anger but only a little.

"I learned this music when I was a child. I can play things that make it sound like the children's music it is. I know where it comes from and what it means. You don't."

"Hey, man, I don't need this shit. I don't want a problem with you."

Jana stepped behind Joe and put her hand on his shoulder. Joe reached up and slid his hand over hers, an almost unconscious gesture. He sat up straighter with Jana behind him. Gorge glanced at Delilah, who lowered her beer bottle from her lips and smiled.

"Answer my questions, and we have no problems," Gorge said, still strumming the guitar. "You met someone from the Kingdoms who helped you play the way you do."

"What Kingdoms? Shit, I told you, I practiced. I played. I suffered."

Gorge laughed. "That's not what folks are saying."

"What do I care about a lot of useless talk?"

"They say you're like Robert Johnson. Went away an average guitar player, came back a couple years later playing blues like no one had ever heard before. They say you learned to play in a graveyard, sitting at the hoof of the Devil, or from Robert himself down in Hell."

"That talk about Johnson is superstition. Good publicity, s'all. If Robert hadn't died young, everyone would've forgotten it by now. It's folklore, myth. No truth in it."

"There's more truth in myths than you might think. Did you make a deal with the Devil, Rollin' Joe? Robert died young. Will you? Did you sell your soul to be the best? You vanished from sight for a couple of years. Where did you go?"

Gorge's playing intensified. Music filled the room, and a faint, red light flowed around Gorge, around Joe's guitar, and along its strings. Gorge drew on the music of the Kingdoms, mastering all that Rollin' Joe had played and then layering on more complex combinations and melodies. The light danced over the sound hole. Gorge picked harder and faster. His fingers sped up and down the guitar neck in a blur, forming chords then fingering riffs between them, stretching the instrument to its limits, bending his notes and popping harmonics with stunning precision and rich emotion. He spun a hard, chunky rhythm like a freight train rolling through the night then spun into a tight, melodic riff. The red light filled his eyes, where it deepened to crimson. Rollin' Joe nodded and tapped his foot as he recognized the song: Robert Johnson's "Cross Road Blues," about a man desperate for a ride home before dark. Gorge played it haunting and rich. Joe held steady meeting Gorge's stare, but when Jana's trembling fingers tightened on his shoulder, he glanced up at her, at the tears welled in her eyes.

Gorge played on.

Joe held up a hand, signaling him to stop.

The red glow faded as Gorge wound down.

"You scaring my girl, Gray," Joe said. "No need for that. I'll tell you."

"I'm listening."

Joe popped the ice chest open, grabbed two more beers, and popped the tops. He handed one to Gorge and drank half the other at a gulp.

"I did like they said, all right. Went down to the crossroads, and I met a man who wasn't really a man, and me and him, we made a deal, only he didn't want to be paid in cash money. I spent some time with him. I listened and learned. Seemed like only a few weeks, but when I left him, two whole years had gone by. *Two whole years.* How that can be, I'll never understand. The last day I saw him he blew some dust onto my hands. He took my guitar and tuned it. When he gave it back to me it felt charged up. Electric. That charge ran into my hands when I touched the strings. After that I could play like you heard tonight. Good enough to be the best."

"What was his name?"

Joe shrugged. "He answered to Nick."

"Where did you meet him?"

"Outside my hometown in Mississippi, but you could find him anywhere two roads come together as long as they're the right roads for you. The crossroads ain't no one place. It's a thing of the soul, a way of feeling, of playing the music. You got the right feeling inside you, Nick will come. He can find you anywhere."

Gorge played a few more exquisite notes, and then placed Joe's Martin in its stand. He stood and polished off his beer.

"Thank you, Rollin' Joe." Gorge walked toward the door, putting his arm around Delilah's waist to lead her out of the dressing room.

"Hey, how long he give you?" Joe said.

"How long for what?" said Gorge.

"Before he comes to collect your soul. I figure you know him by a different name, but the way you play, you must've made a deal with Nick too. He gave me seven years, but I'm figuring to renegotiate when the time comes."

"Oh, yeah?" Gorge said. "Well, good luck with that."

Gorge parked the car at a dusty desert crossroads, got out, and waited. He and Delilah had driven most of the night to a place on the edge of Death Valley, not far from where Delilah had found him wounded and chained to a rock after his exile from the Kingdoms. That had been three years ago, 1955. The place still held meaning for him and that imparted it with power; he'd despaired here, found salvation here in a mortal woman's arms, and here he'd discovered his foolish betrayers had left him enough magic to start over, gathering energy to himself to rebuild his power. He had thought that made him unique in the mortal world: a lone faerie stripped of his wings and his status and cast out of paradise. Maybe not. Someone from the Kingdoms had bargained faerie magic to Rollin' Joe, and anyone dealing music from the Enchanted Lands to mortals had to have a good reason to risk the wrath of the Flock—as well as Gorge's. Exile or not, he'd been the greatest musician in the Lands, and he still considered the music his.

Reclining on the hood of their car, Delilah shaded her eyes with a newspaper as the sun climbed the horizon. The morning brightness painted her pale skin with bronze light and shadow, a sight that filled Gorge with wonder. On the surface, Delilah would never be as gorgeous as the most stunning faerie maidens, but her soul and her heart and his love for her made her the most beautiful woman Gorge had ever met. She caught him watching her and smiled. Gorge looked away and paced. The latent heat in the air prefaced a day of savage temperatures.

"Where is he?" he said.

"You sure it works how Linnet said?"

"He wasn't lying. I'd have seen it in his aura."

"I guess we have to wait and see what happens."

"It could be days."

"We can't stay out here that long without more food and water, but I'm with you for as long as it takes."

Leaning over the car, Gorge kissed Delilah. She curled her hand around the back of his neck and stroked it.

"Thank you for that," Gorge said. Then he rounded the back of the car and took his acoustic guitar from the trunk. "I don't plan on waiting that long."

He removed the guitar from its case then sat on the ground and settled back against the car's front grill. With a glass slide over one finger, he started with "Cross Road Blues" but wove into it the music of the Kingdoms. He followed it with another Robert Johnson song, "Hellhounds on My Trail," then "Me and the Devil," and after that he improvised, entwining earthy, heartsick blues rhythms with ethereal melodies from the Enchanted

Lands. He played for hours, lingering on the edge of a trance. Whenever clouds dimmed the sun, a faint glow manifested around him and his guitar. Delilah found a shady place where she could listen to the music, and then she took out her sketchbook and passed the time drawing.

Sometime after noon, Gorge took a break.

The high sun cooked everything beneath it. Gorge wished they'd brought more water. The dryness reminded him of the days he'd spent here in chains, certain he would die, before Delilah rescued him. The wounds where blackjack sprites had eaten away his wings still had never fully healed; sometimes they wept blood.

Gorge blew on his callused fingers and resumed playing, recalling the pain.

The afternoon faded and surrendered to twilight.

A three-quarters moon mounted the night sky, and a chill crashed the air. Delilah climbed into the car and wrapped herself in a blanket.

Still Gorge played.

Short of midnight another guitar answered Gorge's call.

The music snapped Gorge alert. He fingered a plaintive reply.

The two guitarists traded riffs awhile, and then, picking his trail by moonlight, Gorge walked into the desert in the direction of the sound. Delilah followed him.

Soon they reached the intersection of two dirt paths barely more than hardened ruts in the earth. At its center stood a grizzled, old black man in a black suit, playing a red Dobro, its steel body gleaming in the starlight, its built-in resonator lifting the man's music into the night. He wore a black fedora and dark sunglasses, and a scraggly wedge of gray and white hair extended from his chin. He nodded to Gorge and let his music talk for him. After a while, the dark man turned and walked deeper into the desert, stepping faster when he saw Gorge and Delilah steady behind him. He continued playing, and Gorge kept up, sometimes strumming rhythm for the dark man's lead, sometimes picking lead to the dark man's chords. They passed around a low, rocky hill and came into a circle of stones, a formation familiar to Gorge: a faerie ring.

The dark man silenced his guitar.

Gorge did likewise.

Their music rolled away into the sounds of night creatures and the sigh of the lazy wind. Gorge sensed beings, perhaps even faeries, from the Enchanted Lands nearby in the darkness.

"You know Rollin' Joe Linnet?" Gorge said.

"Sure do."

"Your name Nick?"

"You can call me that. Or Old Scratch, or Papa Legba, or Anansi, or Loki, or plain old Jack. Whatever you like. I answer to all of them. Didn't think I'd ever meet you, no sir. Sure hoped I wouldn't. Optimistic of me, that's no lie."

"You know who I am?"

"You're Gavin Gray. You didn't come here to sell me your soul in exchange for being the best, better than anyone else who ever lived. I know that. So tell me what you want."

Gorge inched closer to the dark man and studied his face. The shadows deepened his wrinkles to crevasses, but the color of his brown skin possessed a strange, translucent tone. The man's face grated against something in the back of Gorge's memory.

"I know you," Gorge said.

"Yeah, you do."

"I don't recognize your face. Who are you?"

"A touch of glamour lets people believe I'm whoever they want to see. You talked to Rollin' Joe so you wanted to see old Nick and that's what you got. But that's not who I am."

The dark man removed his hat and glasses, and then he gestured with two fingers, waving his hand as if wiping his face clean. His features ran liquid, rippled, and when they solidified again, the man had a faerie face. His ears narrowed to points, and his eyes shimmered like crystals. The sight of the face stoked Gorge's anger to a red-hot rage, but he held it tight inside himself.

"Rade," he said.

"Been a long time, Gorge. We've both seen better days."

"You know him?" Delilah asked.

"Rade and I grew up together, performed together. Then we went to war side by side against the Unseelie. Rade changed after that."

"Untrue. I only realized I'd never be as good a musician as you. So I followed my talents. I was an excellent soldier and an even better general."

"I never could beat you with a bow," Gorge said, "though I could hold my own against you with a sword."

"When we were younger maybe, but even then you never matched me in strategy and tactics," Rade said.

"As you never matched me in music."

Rade nodded.

"If not for me, you would've been the greatest."

"Maybe, maybe not." Rade tilted his head at the vast, indigo sky. "No one's ever the best, not really. They say there's always someone better."

"That's not what you told Rollin' Joe Linnet."

Rade stretched his arms and rolled his shoulders. Brilliant green wings sprouted from his back and spread out behind him. They swirled with the substance of a thick mist, translucent, yet powerful and cohesive, shaped like a dragonfly's wings. Gorge spied the awe in Delilah's expression, and it saddened him that she would never see *his* wings.

"It's different for mortals," Rade said. "Being the best for a short time has weight for them because their lives are so brief. When you live as long as we do, you need more because when your time on top passes, it leaves you emptied out, and there's still a long road ahead of you."

"Why the disguise, with the crossroads?"

"A show for the mortals, that's all. I'm bringing a legend to life. Go down to the crossroads, get down on your knees, and make a deal with the Devil. Fame and fortune is yours for the taking at only the cost of your immortal soul. I'm making bargains."

"Faerie bargains, worthless bargains. What do you get out of it? I know you don't care a scrap about taking their so-called souls."

"I get magic. I give a little of mine to the humans so they can play the music of the Kingdoms. They take it into their world. People hear it, love it, and they pass energy back so the magic grows in the musician. When it grows enough, I take my payment, claim all the power they've built up, and they never play the same again."

"Why would a general in the army of the Faerie Kingdoms need to gather magic among mortals?" Gorge said. "All the power of the Kingdoms is yours to command."

"It isn't enough."

"It's more than enough. It always is. You've fallen out of favor." Gorge's lips twitched in a half smile. "Have you been exiled too?"

Rade shook his head. "Only punished. Severed from the usual sources of magic for a time."

"What'd you do?"

"I executed two Unseelie spies during a time of truce. Those thieving dark faerie bastards deserved it, but the Flock made an example of me to keep the peace. When I'm in the Kingdoms, I'm confined to my home for the duration of my sentence, but no one cares what I do here. I need magic because my rivals are trying to banish me from the military. I can't let them take advantage of me."

"How many mortals have you used?" Gorge said.

"A dozen, maybe more. Some last longer than others."

"The music of The Kingdoms isn't yours to dole out."

"It's more mine, now, than yours," Rade said.

"It stopped being yours when you turned your back on it."

"And you lost it in exile."

"But I never abandoned it!" Gorge's voice rose. "The Flock took it from me. She took it from me. I can still play."

"Have you been trapped here so long that you've forgotten what the music really sounds like? We can fool the mortals playing its echoes, but don't try to fool yourself. What you play here isn't anything compared to what you could do back home."

"I'll get back there, in time."

"The Flock won't ever let you back," Rade said.

"Then I'll destroy them."

"You can try."

"I'll destroy you, here, tonight," Gorge said. "I'll take your magic."

"If you're willing to put every last bit of magic inside you at stake, then let's have a contest, like when we were young. No one ever wants to pay my price. When I come to collect, they all try to cut a new deal. Sometimes I offer them a duel with the Devil. If they prove the better player, I let them off the hook. They never do, but losing breaks their spirit. How about you? Winner takes the other's magic, all of it, and if you lose, I get your mortal woman too. Or have you forgotten how you took my woman when you took the music from me."

"I never took anything you weren't ready to give," Gorge said. "Better for you that Soniella chose me anyway. I saved you from her treacherous nature."

"The way you were breaking rules and playing forbidden music, you should've seen it coming. You didn't know her as well as you thought you did. That's okay. Love blinds." Rade rubbed his hands together. "So, do we have a deal?"

"No, Delilah stays out of it."

"Forget it then. You don't have enough magic to make it worth my while."

Delilah stepped beside Gorge and slid her arm around his waist. "Go ahead. Do it."

"I won't risk losing you."

"You're better than him. I heard it on our way here. Maybe there's more magic in him, but he doesn't know how to play in this world as well as you do. Remember what you did to Rollin' Joe with only a few licks?"

"Maybe," Gorge said.

"Definitely. Do it. Put this jerk in his place."

"If I lose, he'll take you to the Kingdoms. Once you've eaten their food and drank their wine, you'll never leave. You won't want to. We'll be separated forever."

"It won't happen." Delilah held Gorge tight and kissed him, her breath warm and sweet. Afterward she said, "You won't let it."

Gorge studied the intensity in Delilah's dark eyes. She loved him; she believed in him. To refuse the contest would betray her trust in him, as much as it would wound his pride. He weighed his chances against Rade, but regardless he couldn't walk away from the challenge. He couldn't let Delilah down.

"If I win," he said to Rade, "I take all the magic in you, and you give me the list of mortals you've bargained with, so I can collect in your place when their time comes."

"If I win, I take what little magic you have and your woman."

"That's the deal. Who'll judge?"

"The music will."

Rade swung his Dobro into position and strummed a chord. The sound caught Gorge off guard, coming into him with a physical presence that vibrated in his bones. He followed every note Rade played, soaked in the rhythm and the melody, and deciphered the combination of mortal and faerie music he contrived. A green glow appeared around Rade, and the stones of the faerie ring burned with the same light. The harder Rade played, the brighter it became, and then when he stopped, the illumination faded out with his last note.

Gorge played next, making sure to cover all the same ground as Rade, but taking it further, playing more complicated chords, more elegant melodies, infusing the music with raw emotion, with pain and passion, like a true bluesman. The light returned with the music, glowing red for Gorge, and it brightened the entire ring.

When Gorge finished Rade took what he had played and worked it into something new and dazzling, changing time and rhythm, playing parts of it to make it look easy for him, while Gorge, bound to the mortal world, had to struggle for it. Rade finished with a long, fast series of complicated riffs, working his fingers all the way down the neck of his guitar from wailing high notes to growling rumbles. He let the last chord resonate for several moments, before cutting it off hard.

Gorge responded, already straining. Rade's magic strengthened his hands and fingers; Gorge did all the work himself. As the stones lit up around him, Gorge realized he'd been careless to agree to the contest within the faerie ring. The circle gave Rade the advantage through his stronger connection to the Enchanted Lands.

For Gorge the stones offered no help at all.

He looked to Delilah. Her confidence in him remained strong and bright. She didn't see the burden building in him, couldn't hear the subtleties of the music, or understand the ground on which the contest occurred. She simply saw Gorge and refused to believe he could lose. Gorge wanted to preserve forever the love he saw in her eyes. More, though, he wanted to deserve it. He attacked his guitar with renewed fury, playing with anger and sadness Rade could never summon. He stepped closer to Rade as if pushing against him with the music, and then he finished.

Rade's face narrowed with uncertainty for a moment before he launched into his next round of playing. The moment, though, gave Gorge hope.

The night deepened, and they took turns testing each other's limits. The faerie ring lit green then red, green then red, and there seemed no limit to how far Gorge and Rade could go. Shadow-shapes emerged and flitted through the shimmering light, creatures from the Lands: sprites, gnomes, and goblins, drawn by the echoes of music resounding back through the faerie ring. They circled the ring and watched the duel.

Gorge's fingertips tore and bled. The pain only hardened his resolve. He finished a violent, wailing run of chords and riffs, leaving the stones burning red.

Rade chased him, tracing a searing melody until a few bars in—he missed a note.

He recovered before his green light winked out but then one of his strings snapped with a metallic twang. The light gathering in the rocks flared and then died.

"No," Rade whispered.

Throwing down his Dobro, he leapt across the ring, drawing a switchblade from inside his suit as he moved. He crashed into Gorge and sank the knife deep into Gorge's chest below his shoulder. Gorge toppled, struggling to hold onto his guitar with one hand, while Rade seized the instrument and pulled. Pain dizzied Gorge, but he held tight until Rade smashed an elbow into his face, stunning him. Then Rade leapt away with Gorge's guitar.

Rade laid his fingers on the string, but Gorge kicked his feet out from under him before he could play a note. He spilled onto Gorge, still clutching the guitar, desperate to pick up where he'd left off. Gorge grabbed the guitar body and then curled his legs under Rade and kicked him upward and away. Rade's grip broke, and the guitar fell aside.

Gorge sprang to his feet. Screaming, he yanked the knife from his chest. A stream of blood trailed the blade. He brandished the weapon at Rade to keep him from getting up, and then kicked him in the side, knocking him to the ground. He seized his guitar and starting with the very note Rade had missed, Gorge finished out the round, turning all the stones red. After he stopped playing, they stayed lit, painting everything inside the faerie ring crimson. The swarm of gathered creatures jumped and danced with excitement.

"Don't ever come back here," Gorge told Rade. "You're not welcome. The music in this world is mine. *All of it is mine.* Do you understand?"

Gorge grabbed the back of Rade's head. Streams of green light exploded from where he touched his former friend's scalp. Rade's magic flooded into Gorge. When he backed off, the magic had healed his chest wound.

He knelt and extended an open hand. "The names."

Rade pulled a small, tattered notebook from inside his suit jacket and handed it to Gorge. The pages held lists of names, places, and dates, some crossed out, some not. Gorge shoved it into his pants pocket, and then he collected Rade's guitar and gave it to Delilah. Bathed in crimson light in the center of the ring with his own guitar in his hands, Gorge looked more like the Devil than Rade ever had. He eyed all the little beings from the Lands bopping and buzzing around, too amazed to leave, but too frightened to come any closer.

"Remember what happened here tonight," Gorge told them. "Remember who won."

Seven years passed. Gorge took note when Rollin' Joe toured America and then Europe, playing a thousand smoky blues bars on his way. The man's records sold as well as blues records did, and critics raved over them, until Joe became known as a king of the blues. Then one night he came back to L.A. to play the first of three sold-out shows at Sam's Place, and Gorge was there, knocking on Joe's dressing room door after the very first set. Jana answered, and Gorge saw Joe right away, sipping a cold beer, looking like barely a day had passed since Gorge had last seen him. Almost nothing in the dressing room had changed. Gorge walked in with his guitar case in hand and Delilah beside him.

"Seven years are up," Gorge said.

"Hoped I'd never see you again." Joe sighed. "It's been a good seven years. You ever find Nick?"

"I found him. We had a contest. I sent him back where he belongs. Now your bargain is with me. I'm here for what's due."

Gorge sat down across from Joe and took his guitar from its case. He began to play, weaving a spell of music the way he had the night he'd first met Rollin' Joe.

"Play," he said.

"Don't much feel like it just now."

"Play and maybe I'll let you renegotiate."

Joe turned away from Gorge and looked at Jana. Gorge caught Jana's slight nod. Then Joe turned back and picked up his guitar.

"Well, maybe a little."

He tuned his instrument.

"You two are still together," said Gorge.

"So are you and your woman," Joe said. Then he laughed, and added, "Having a good woman makes for a good life, but it makes for bad blues. Some days I got damn little to be blue about with Jana around, but then being a black man in this country is plenty to darken my mood. Jana keeps me from going over the edge."

Joe joined in with what Gorge was playing, and they began to trade riffs, playing rhythm for each other's lead, bringing the blues to life in the dank little room. Light floated in the air. Gorge ignored it. He had done this a dozen times now, played the contest, played by the rules of the bargains Rade had struck, and every one had turned out the same. He had gained a lot of magic in seven years. Rollin' Joe Linnet was the last name on Rade's list. Once Gorge took his magic away, it would be done.

Gorge concentrated on the music. He liked what he heard. For a mortal, Joe played the music of the Kingdoms with respect and skill. He always had, but Gorge had been too blinded by his rage to notice. He glanced up at Jana, her face striking in the flickering glow of the light flowing out from the music. Where

Gorge had seen fear the last time she'd heard him play, he now saw pride in Joe. He admired that. He saw in Jana's face that she knew what it would cost Joe to lose the music he'd played for so long, but win or lose, she'd wanted him to take the chance offered and play one more time before it all ended. More than that, she wanted to *hear* him play one more time, and as Gorge realized that, he guessed Jana knew how hollow the years ahead loomed without the music, but she expected to be there with Joe anyway.

Gorge and Joe played much longer than Gorge had ever bothered before when he came to collect. Although he could've taken the magic from Joe at any moment and almost did several times, Gorge couldn't stop thinking how much Jana and Rollin' Joe Linnet reminded him of himself and Delilah, especially on that night in the desert when Gorge had challenged Rade. He felt a sudden connection to the mortal world and an unexpected bond with the bluesman. Joe must have picked up his guitar, thinking he'd lose to Gorge, or at least not sure if he could win, and yet he'd done it for the same reasons Gorge had challenged Rade.

Gorge didn't take Joe's magic that night.

Instead the two men played a while longer, both of them working their six steel strings the way no mortal men should've ever been able to, and for as long as the music lasted, Gorge's anger ebbed, but only a little. When the music was done, he put away his guitar, left without saying a word, and headed home with Delilah at his side.

Feed the Fair Folk Sweet

Gorge scented stale magic on the air. Nancy Asp radiated an invisible, noxious cloud of it.

Unnatural. Misplaced. Torturous. Not her own. No magic belonged naturally to the singer/songwriter who led Your Uncool Niece. Seeing the dark circles of loss haunting her eyes, Gorge didn't care to know where or how she'd obtained it. He only wanted her out of the small kitchen in his apartment and away from him and Delilah. He wanted nothing more to do with the troubles that came with stolen magic. Mortals playing with power to which they had no right had left him so sick that even the flashes of anger, defiance, and guilt sparked by Nancy's sallow, sunken face submerged into his malaise almost as quickly as they came.

He should've slammed the door shut when Delilah brought her home. Delilah had taken pity after Nancy approached her begged for her help in the art supply store, yet another stray for her to help. Despite all the times they'd burned or betrayed her, Delilah never hardened toward the hard-luck stories. She never abandoned hope, a trait so purely mortal and inexplicable to Gorge it only made him love her all the more.

He rattled his fingers on the Formica countertop and glared at Nancy, seated at the little, art deco kitchen table. Car sounds and voices filtered in from the street, the mid-afternoon din of New York City. Delilah offered Nancy a mug of steaming tea, which she took with both her quivering hands to steady it. Chipped black polish on nails chewed raw decorated her spidery fingers. A stack of tinny costume jewelry bracelets jangled around her left wrist. The flourishes of a woman compensating for poverty with flash and quantity. Gorge rolled his eyes as she sipped the tea and then set down the mug, her hands still wrapped around it.

"What do you want?" he said.

Nancy flinched at his tone. "I want an explanation. You owe me that at least, Max."

"I don't owe you anything."

"Come on, Max, that night we jammed at Dresden Underground we *rocked*. You brought us to the edge of something great, put the whole fucking world right at our fingertips and then... and then..."

"Then I took it all away? Is that it?"

"What was so awful about Bruno Rice you had to burn it all down?"

"What makes you think I had anything to do with Bruno Rice self-destructing? Recording company executives crack up all the time."

"Brimmer said you torched Bruno's limousine. That true?"

Gorge failed to stop the curl of a wicked grin that came to his lips. The irony of Nancy, awash in bad magic, challenging him with the truth amused him. No one who stank of power like she did came by it honestly.

"Oh my god, you did it, you really did! Why? You convince Bruno to sign my band for Disharmony Records and then burn his car? What the hell's wrong with you?"

"It's what was wrong with Bruno."

"Brimmer told me you two had a huge falling out and you went after Bruno like a wild dog. Why'd you make him promise to sign us if you were only going to pull that shit? You sank our deal before we ever set foot inside Disharmony's office, man. Not cool."

"You're better off without Bruno Rice. Better off without Brimmer Riggs too. Shake Appeal's going nowhere with him except the dustbin of rock history. If Marty and Jack have half a brain between them, they'll dump Brimmer for a real guitar player. He's only sniffing back around you now because he thinks Your Uncool Niece is going to hit it big. Your sad, little ex is nothing but a wannabe looking for coattails to ride."

Nancy rubbed her eyes. "I know who Brimmer is better than you, asshole."

Delilah set a comforting hand on Nancy's shoulder. "Ignore him. He's a prick when he's under the weather."

"He's not wrong, Dee." Nancy shook her head. "Brimmer is who he is. I know that. But he told me stuff about Max and Bruno, about weird shit that went down with Bruno before he crashed and how Max Chaos dropped off the face of the earth right after it."

"Here I am. Still, painfully, on earth."

"Yeah, here hiding out," Nancy said.

"Recuperating. Bruno's not the only one who suffered," Gorge said. "The difference is I'll recover."

"At least tell me what happened."

"I'd like to, Nancy, I really would—except it's none of your damn business."

Nancy let out a harsh laugh. "You know some people say you're the devil and you put Bruno through hell?"

"Do they? Bruno put a lot more people through hell all on his own, including himself."

"He hurt so many people, worse than you could imagine," Delilah said.

Nancy looked at her, confused.

"Hey, what do people say about you, Nancy?" Gorge said.

"What about me?"

"You're ripe with bad magic. You've been playing naughty games when you don't understand the rules."

Nancy sniffled and lowered her eyes.

"Brimmer shared a few of Bruno's secrets with you, is that it?" Gorge frowned. "Maybe he stole one of Bruno's enchanted trinkets to play with? He promised you wondrous things, a life like you could only dream?"

"I don't know what you're—"

"Stop. You asked me for help." Delilah's voice upended the growing tension as Nancy realized Delilah's sympathy extended only so far. "Yeah, losing a record deal sucks, but there are much worse things. Now are you going to tell us the truth? Otherwise, you can show yourself the door right now."

Nancy shrugged free of Delilah's touch and scraped her chair back petulantly. She slipped off her leather jacket, and then pushed up the right sleeve of her black blouse to expose her pale forearm. Three rows of scabs marred it from her wrist to the crook of her elbow. Seared lines—now dried and crusted dark red—scribed intricate symbols that brought a frown to Gorge's face.

"Okay, yes, I didn't believe Brimmer at first, but I figured what the hell did I have to lose giving it a try? I was down, really down. The record deal fell through before it even started, and I didn't think My Uncool Niece would get back on its feet," she said. "Brimmer spun a crazy story about how you used magic to help you play better than you really are."

"As if. On my worst day I'm better than you'll ever know. That's not how magic works, anyway."

"Yeah, I get that now."

"Let her talk, Gorge," Delilah said.

"Gorge? Why'd she call you Gorge?"

"It's my name. Max Chaos is my stage name, like I'm sure Nancy Asp is yours. But go on telling us how you made bad life choices and need us to bail you out. Please."

"Jerk," Nancy said. "Brimmer had a wax cylinder. The kind people used to record music a hundred years ago. A real antique. He got it from Bruno Rice. Said if we listened to it, we could take its magic, and it would let us play like we did the night you jammed with us. Must've hit a dozen Chelsea antique shops before we found a working cylinder phonograph. We played the music, and…"

"And what?"

"Something came to my apartment. A demon, or a ghost, or whatever. It's been messing with me ever since. It scarred my arm. It empties my drawers. Tears up my furniture. It slams things around all night. It won't let me sleep. Brimmer took off. I didn't know who else to ask for help. I figured if part of Brimmer's story was true, maybe all of it was, and you'd know how to help me undo this."

"Because I'm so well known for helping people," Gorge said.

"Can you read her arm?" Delilah said.

Gorge nodded.

"What does it say?" Nancy said.

"You're in a lot of danger, Nancy."

"I am? Shit. Can you help me?"

"A month ago, sure, yeah, but right now, after what happened with Bruno, I don't know if I'm strong enough. Why should I anyway? You shouldn't screw around with things you don't understand. The music and magic on that cylinder were stolen, probably from a beautiful, gifted singer who suffered only because of her talent. Bruno Rice imprisoned her, forced her to sing, and drained all the life and magic out of her while she did— until she withered and died. Is that what you want in your music? No demons or ghosts. Only raw human greed and mortal sadism. You tried to cheat the music. Now you're paying the price."

"At least tell me what it says on my arm."

"The lines are from a very old song: 'To those who feed the fair folk sweet, fore'er grows our affection/To those who steal, or lie, or cheat, ne'er ends our contempt.' Underneath it reads: 'Bring us the one in exile,' which isn't part of the song."

At the mention of "exile," Delilah's expression darkened. Gorge waved off her worry. Nancy stared at her scabby arm.

"What's it mean?" Nancy said.

"Figure it out for yourself."

"You really want to leave this in her hands? Is that safe?" Delilah said.

"She brought it on herself. What can I even do as weak as I am?"

"Dammit!" Nancy set her chair wobbling as she shot up and yanked her jacket from the seatback. "Doesn't anything matter to you?"

"The music matters," Gorge said. "Now you should run along. You opened a door you should've left closed. Not my problem. I can't help you."

Nancy brushed past Delilah on her way to the door. She hesitated as she opened it.

"The night we played at Dresden Underground you said my band played brave music that people would never forget. Did you mean that?" Nancy said.

"What difference does it make?"

An edge crept into Nancy's voice. "Did you *mean* it? Tell me. Because if you didn't, if you just blew smoke up our asses, then the music means nothing to you. And if the music does matter can you really turn your back on whatever you heard in us?"

Wisps of silvery air only visible to Gorge drifted around Nancy. Decaying scraps of magic. Her mortal body incapable of sustaining them, yet unable to expel them. Gorge sensed the talent that had drawn him to her and her band, the latent music in them that had inspired him to make Your Uncool Niece part of his music, the one pure thing in his existence in the mortal world besides his love for Delilah—and to share with them a taste of greatness they would never achieve on their own. He had given them that gift then taken it away, a deeper loss than a mere record contract, one that left a gaping, impossible-to-fill hollow in Nancy, one he couldn't blame her for striving to soothe.

He knew how such emptiness ached. From the moment he arrived in the mortal world, he had sought to feed a similar void within himself, through Delilah, through music. He had filled it and then let it empty many times, only to refill it through the same dedication and tenacity he still saw in Nancy.

Gorge sighed. "Yes, dammit, I meant it. I don't say things I don't mean. Then and now, the music is what matters."

Nancy's studio apartment reeked of the same misplaced magic that polluted her body. In the absence of his own magic, the low, foul power clinging to the place hit Gorge like a punch to the stomach. He hadn't performed in weeks, hadn't yet begun to regather the magic he'd spent to keep Delilah alive after Bruno Rice had poisoned her. His lungs ached with every breath he took here. He felt feverish and woozy, as powerless as the mortals among whom he lived.

Gorge shivered and shoved his hands in his pockets. He could stand it, though. He had suffered much worse in his time. He forced himself to the center of the space and observed it.

Sparsely furnished with an old futon, an easy chair, and an assortment of milk-crates for tables and shelves, the room declared its inhabitant's devotion to music. Concert posters covered much of the walls, most half-torn down, flaps dangling from yellowed Scotch tape and thumb tacks. Batting protruded from fresh tears in the easy chair's upholstery. Nancy's clothing lay in chaotic piles on the floor, strewn from their crates.

In the room's brightest spot, near a sunny window overlooking the fire escape, a guitar rested in a stand. Sheets of music lay spread out all around it on the floor, on Nancy's guitar case, on a stack of notebooks. Bits and pieces of Nancy's musical mind. A battered, old music stand held blank sheets, a pencil, and an open spiral notebook scribbled with lines of lyrics in progress. A faded, fuzzy state university pennant taped to the window gave the only clue to Nancy's milk-fed, Midwest origins, the only hint of a life before this one.

In the kitchen nook, utensils littered the floor, their overturned drawers dumped beside them, shards of broken dishes jumbled in the mess. The cupboards all hung open, doors askew on their hinges, boxes of food toppled inside, crushed and spilling out cornflakes, flour, or cracker crumbs.

On the stovetop stood an antique phonograph loaded with a familiar wax cylinder.

"That's the thing from Bruno's." Nancy pointed to the wax cylinder. "For a day after we played it everything was amazing.

Brimmer and I wrote, like, four or five new songs each right after we listened to it. We jammed and felt really close, closer even than when I thought I loved him. Air and sunlight came in the window like energy waves from another planet, sweet and clean, damping the city noise. We heard nothing but the music and our own breath. It sounds weird, but my apartment felt as if it stretched itself bigger, and whenever we stopped playing, we could hear faraway tunes. So damn inspiring. We didn't think about food or water, not even each other, nothing but music until we crashed asleep. When I woke up, Brimmer was crying, full-on sobbing. Something bit my leg. I thought it was a rat, but I saw it run under the counter, and it… well, it wasn't a rat. Brimmer saw it too. That's when he grabbed his stuff and bolted. I haven't heard from him since."

"I doubt you'll ever hear from him again," Gorge said. "What bit you?"

"I know how crazy it'll sound, but I'm telling you the truth even if I can't explain it."

Gorge nodded. "Go ahead. I don't doubt you."

"It was a tiny, ugly man dressed in a scrap of paper bag with a bottle cap hat. He ran off with my blood on his lips, and before he hid in the cupboard, the little fucker flipped me off." The easy chair creaked with Nancy's weight as she settled into it, her shoulders sagging. "That's when I felt the burns on my arm. It happened while I slept, I guess. I tried to stay here and get rid of… whatever had come, but it wouldn't stop tormenting me. I couldn't stand it. I left, walked for hours, no idea what to do, and then I started hitting the all the clubs and shops where I'd ever seen you, hoping you could help me. I finally saw Delilah at Pearl Paint."

Gorge entered the little kitchen and took the wax cylinder from the phonograph.

Smooth and pliant, its recording now erased, its magic expended. Bruno Rice had recorded Gorge's magic on a similar cylinder, destroyed when Gorge overloaded it. He didn't feel the remnants here of Toynia's magic as he expected, no echoes of the gentle fey singer Bruno had held captive and drained to death. Instead he felt hints of his own magic. One of the blank cylinders Bruno had kept at hand must have soaked up enough of his excess power for Brimmer to discover it when he rummaged through Bruno's estate.

He closed his eyes for a moment, and when he opened them again, he placed the cylinder beside the phonograph. Grabbing a skillet from Nancy's floor, he smashed the wax several times then dropped the skillet and sifted through the cylinder's debris. He pulled out a glittering kernel embedded in wax fragments and scraped it clean with his fingernails. It resembled an oversized peach pit, but dry, smooth, and hard like a corn kernel. Its surface glistened with the prismatic sheen of oil on water.

"This seed held the magic within the cylinder. It's spent now."

Gorge slipped the kernel into his pocket.

"Is that it? Will this all go away now?" Nancy said.

Gorge snorted. "Are you serious? We've only begun. You attracted something very unpleasant when you released the magic it held."

High-pitched laughter cackled through the apartment, echoing from behind the walls.

The door to the bathroom flew open with the force of a hurricane wind, slamming against the wall. Everyone jumped. Nancy cried out, leapt to her feet, and bumped into Delilah, clinging to her as if her nerves could take no more agitation. Half a bar of old soap shot out of the bathroom. It bounced off Nancy's chest. She yelped then raised a hand to block the mostly curled-up tube of toothpaste that followed.

Gorge rushed across the room and slammed the door shut.

More laughter. From within the bathroom and behind the walls, from under the furniture and within the kitchen cupboards.

The cupboard doors rattled then flapped open and closed like clumsy bird wings.

The refrigerator rocked in place. Water spewed out of the faucet in short bursts.

The air in the apartment thickened with an odor of slimy rot, decaying cardboard, and stale food. With a spark and a wisp of oily smoke, Nancy's college pennant ignited and then smoldered to ash, adding a singed, papery odor to the mix.

Nancy's sheet music and notes quivered, rising on a phantom whirlwind.

"No!" Nancy shouted. "Not that! No!"

She grabbed at the pages, clutching them against her chest to keep the wind from taking them. She snatched them from the air, scooped up stacks from the floor. Her feet slid on loose sheets, tripping her, scattering the pages anew as she fell. Peals of laughter mocked her where she lay.

Delilah helped her back to her feet.

At the center of the apartment stood Gorge, alert, his gaze darting from place to place. He discerned telltale shadows that preceded each upset of the room, traced the echoes of laughter as they traveled behind the walls. He plucked a two-tined, meat fork from the edge of the kitchen mess then turned, body tense—and as a cracker box rustled in an open cupboard, he shoved the fork in and down like a miniature spear.

A high-pitched shriek came from cupboard.

The activity in the apartment ceased. The laughter died.

Gorge swept the cracker box onto the floor, revealing an unwelcome, glaring face.

The fork tines embedded in the wood pinned a miniature man in place.

He struggled to free himself, barking out a string of foul curses as he failed to budge the fork. The creature wore a tunic fashioned from a Hershey bar wrapper and shoes made from worn-out thimbles. A Pepsi bottle-cap hat rested on his head, strapped on with half a rubber-band. He shook his fist then flipped Gorge the bird. Gorge grabbed the little man with one hand, the fork with the other, and released him to his grip.

"Here we are. This the little bastard that bit you?"

He showed his restless captive to Nancy. She shook her head.

"No?" Gorge turned the sprite so he could look him in the eye. "One of his friends, then. How many of you are there?"

The sprite wriggled and fought Gorge's grip. "Let me go!"

"No," Gorge said. "Answer my question. Are your friends around? Why are you here?"

"That's two questions. Can't you count? Dumb mortal!"

The sprite thrashed and tried to bite Gorge's finger. Gorge finger-flicked his head, knocking the bottle cap askew.

"Oowwww!" the sprite said.

"Stop that," Gorge said. "Tell me what I want to know."

"Or what?"

"Or I'll make you."

"Make me? Ha! A dumb mortal make me tell something I don't want to? Not likely. Do you know who I am? Do you know *what* I am?"

"You're a scrape sprite. You eat garbage. Your own kind can barely stand to be around each other, which means if you're not alone, you're after something special."

The sprite straightened his bottle cap and furrowed his brow. "Huh, okay, so you know what I am. Fat lot of good it'll do you!"

To hammer the point home, laughter erupted from all around the apartment, rising out of shadows and crannies, from the pile of debris on the kitchen floor. The sprite placed his thumbs to his cheeks then waggled his fingers beside his face and blew Gorge a raspberry.

"You can never stop us!" the creature shouted. "We are legion! We will spill your milk and dump your drawers! Hahaha!"

A cheer came from the unseen mischief-makers.

"We will tear your seat cushions and stuff old shrimp in your pillows!"

Another cheer, louder, mixed with hoots and hollers.

"We will dishevel your papers and stuff hair down your drains!"

Louder cheering. Nancy whimpered.

Gorge tightened his grip on the sprite so that his next words wheezed out, high-pitched and shallow.

"We will... crack your eggs and spill them... on your head!"

The cheers began, but Gorge cut them off by stamping his foot and hollering "Enough!"

He used his stage voice, capable of electrifying a crowd without the slightest touch of magic. The laughter and jeers died out. "What you'll do is tell me what I want to know, and if you won't do so willingly then I'll make you."

"Yeah, right, like to see you try," the sprite squeaked out.

Spying a clear plastic container in the kitchen mess, Gorge grabbed it with his free hand then clutched it against his abdomen and prized off the lid. He shoved the sprite in then clamped the lid down tight. He wrapped a loose guitar strap from the floor of Nancy's music area around the container and tied it off. The scrape sprite thrashed against his prison and pled for release in a muffled voice. Gorge used a pair of scissors to punch two small air holes in the lid, each strike narrowly missing the sprite.

"Shut up. You're going nowhere," he said. He handed the container to Nancy. "Hold this. Keep it close. The cowards shouldn't bother you while you have one prisoner. Since there are so many of the little bastards, we're going to need a few things to deal with them. Have you got any cash, Nance?"

Nancy lifted her gaze from trying to see the sprite through the air holes. "Uh, not really, I haven't worked or had a gig for a while. I've got a little money stashed away, but that's, like, for emergencies only."

"Would you not call this an emergency?" Gorge said.

An hour later Gorge and Delilah returned to Nancy's apartment to find her curled up with her arms around her knees at one end of her futon, the captured sprite at the other. She eyed the container like a cat stalking a snake in a terrarium. Delilah carried in two plastic bags full of items from the Korean grocery on the next corner. Gorge dragged along two bulging, eye-wateringly stinky bags of trash.

"What's all that for?" Nancy said.

Delilah set to unpacking an array of cleaning supplies on the kitchen counter, along with a hammer and a box of nails.

"What do you know about faeries?" Gorge said.

"What, like, fairy godmothers?"

"No, the fey, the good folk, the kind little bastards that dwell in the woods."

"Man, this is the Lower East Side, no woods, no faeries."

"Now, yes, but once the whole city was a green island of grass and trees. The past doesn't disappear when the present comes along. Things that lived here then live here now. Differently and in secret, but they live. You called them into your home, but you haven't shown them proper respect and gratitude or given them what they demanded so they're giving you the works."

"What—what do they want?"

"For you to show them the exile."

"I don't know who that is."

"So you've got a real dilemma. But we're going to fix it."

"How?"

"First we clean this damn place."

"With bags of trash? They reek of garlic and fried pork. Are those from Lucky Wok Kitchen?"

"They are."

"What for?"

"All in due time, Nance."

Gorge tucked the trash bags outside the front door and then joined Delilah in the kitchen. He opened a box of trash liners and started filling them with litter from the kitchen floor while Delilah collected batches of utensils and dumped them into a layer of warm, soapy water in the sink.

Gorge paused to glare at Nancy. "We're not your personal housekeepers."

"Oh, uh, right, yeah."

Nancy hopped up from the futon and set about tidying up her scattered music materials. Once she put them back in order she took over washing utensils while Delilah collected broken kitchenware.

While they cleaned, the sprite in the plastic box beat his miniscule fists against the sides and cried for the mortals to stop their damn scrubbing up. Gorge sensed other sprites watching them, rushing around the apartment unseen, upset. Now and then he heard one gasp or protest: "Not the trash! He's taking out the trash!"; or "She's cleaning the spoons! How horrible!"; or "Our lovely, lovely mess! No!"

Soon the three of them put the apartment to rights again, drawers returned, cupboards organized and tidily closed, and bagged trash disposed of down the incinerator chute in the hallway. Gorge created a special cleaning fluid of lemon juice, mint leaves, ginger, and lavender flowers mixed with a touch of bleach and dish soap diluted into ice-cold water. A crisp, clean aroma suffused the apartment. Anguished groans came from the sprites. With a cup each of the custom cleaning fluid, fresh sponges, and paper towels, Gorge, Delilah, and Nancy wiped down the apartment, leaving no crevice unwashed. At last, Nancy emerged from the sparkling clean bathroom, smearing sweat from her brow. The apartment gleamed, light and inviting, cleaner than it had been in decades.

Gorge carried the remainder of his cleansing brew to the futon.

The captured sprite gagged. "Take it away! Take it away!"

"Tell me your name," Gorge said.

"No, no! Get it away from me!"

Gorge gathered a drop of the fluid on his fingertip and then dripped it into one of the air holes. The sprite shrieked then choked and coughed.

"There's more where that came from," Gorge said. "Enough for you to bathe in."

"Bathe? Horrible! N-no! Please! Anything but that!"

"Tell me your name."

A murmur raced around the apartment: "Don't!" Don't tell." "Keep him in the dark." "Take one for the team." "Spit in his eye!" "Keep our secrets."

Gorge dripped another drop through the air hole. The sprite doubled over and dry heaved, his eyes tearing up.

"All right, all right, no more! My name is Runch. I'm Runch!"

Gorge nodded and wiped his hands dry on his jeans.

"All right, Runch, why did you and your friends come to this place?"

Runch ignored a fresh round of squeaky, whispery protests. "We was called by magic. She played with magic we was looking for, *his magic*, the one we hate."

"Who do you hate?"

"The one in exile! He killed one of ours innocently picking through garbage! Stamped him flat underfoot! Now we'll kill him!" Runch punched and kicked the plastic. The hidden sprites echoed him in chorus, their tone hateful. "Except we can't find him! We can't feel his magic anywhere in this gloriously dirty city. We looked for days and days, and then, ah! Here in this mortal hovel we feels it. Except he's not here! We know he's trapped in the mortal world, but where? *Where?!*"

"Ah, well, that's a problem isn't it," Gorge said. "But aren't you a ballsy lot coming here from the Enchanted Lands on your own seeking revenge?"

"Not revenge!" Runch shouted, and a dozen voices seconded him: "Not revenge!" "No revenge." "No, no, it's justice we want." "Yes, justice." "And garbage!" "And justice!"

"That's right! Justice! And garbage! But mostly justice!"

Runch did an awkward dance, throwing his weight against the side of his prison in an effort to flip it over. It only rocked on the futon.

"He's not here, though. Shouldn't you look elsewhere?"

"We still smell him," said Runch. "Not far, not far, but his trail goes nowhere. How is it possible his magic is here but not him and leaves no trail?"

"It's a real riddle," said Gorge.

"We hates riddles." Runch spit on the bottom of the container.

"Hate riddles!" "Riddles are awful." "Waste of time." Waste of breath." "Riddles are the worst." "I think riddles are fun!" "Shut up!" "Yeah, shut up, you!" Who asked you?"

"If I give you the answer, will you leave?" Gorge said.

"No! Give us the exile!" said Runch.

"I can't do that. I can solve your riddle and offer you some premium trash." Gorge opened the front door and pulled in the bloated, plastic sacks from Lucky Wok Kitchen. "It's right here in those bags. A good three days' worth of discarded Chinese take-out."

"We know. We can smell it. Soooo good." Runch shook his head. "But we don't trust you."

"Why not?"

"No one treats us scrape sprites fair. But what would you know, mortal? No one uses your kind for fishing bait, or training treats for silver wolves, or shims to level their cabinets."

"Or drain stops!" "Or bookmarks!" "Or seasoning for Oak Frond Stew!" "Boot scrapes!" "Poison tasters!" "Cat toys!" "Chimney scrubbers!" "Paint brushes!" "Archery targets!" "Mug handles!"

"I understand," Gorge said. "But that only happens where you come from, right? No one does those things to you in the moral world. That's why you come for the garbage."

Runch scrunched his face. "The exile stomped one'a us under his shoe. Does that count?"

"Maybe he had a good reason. Listen, we've got the best garbage anywhere in this world. You should enjoy it. Why get hung up on one smushed scrape sprite when a world of tasty refuse awaits you?"

"He's got a point!" a hidden sprite called out.

"What about justice?" another cried.

"Garbage tastes better!" a third said.

"Garbage!" "Justice!" The voices crashed into a heated din of arguing.

"You'll explain the terrible riddle?" Runch said.

Gorge nodded. He dug the seed from the wax cylinder out of his pocket and waved it close to the air holes in Runch's container.

"Get a whiff. Recognize the magic?"

"The exile!" said Runch.

"Yes, a mortal wizard captured some of his magic in here." He pointed to Nancy. "She let it out. She didn't know what she was doing. She's a dumb mortal, like me. The exile is very far from here, maybe even dead. So there's no point to you staying here. We've cleaned thoroughly. You know what that means?"

"Yes, damn you," Runch said.

"Promise never to bother Miss Nancy Asp again and all that fine garbage is yours."

Runch seemed to think it over, then nodded. "Done."

"Done!" "Is it done?" "Did he say done?" "A deal?" "We struck a deal?" "For garbage!" "Tasty, tasty trash." "What about justice?" "First dibs!" "No fair!" "Must share, must share!"

Gorge undid the guitar strap and released Runch. The scrape sprite crawled free. Gorge hefted the garbage bags.

"Follow me," he said.

A dozen scrape sprites, male and female, all dressed in Runch's manner crept from the shadows and in-between spaces of the apartment. They lined up behind Runch, some wiry and bowlegged, others rotund and knob-kneed, a few as thin as pencils.

"Hey! Wait just a dagblaggit minute!" Runch said.

Several of the sprites chewed on their fingernails. Delilah and Nancy looked to Gorge for reassurance.

"Yeah?" Gorge said.

"How does a dumb mortal know so much about us scrape sprites? We don't advertise that scrubbing our marks from the domicile routine, you know. Top secret, that is."

"I'm not a typical mortal," Gorge said.

"Oh, how so?" Runch said.

"I read a lot of books"

"Books! Hah! Stupid mortal. All this wonderful trash everywhere in your world and you waste your time with words on paper? Haha!"

The crowd of sprites burst into laughter and then resumed marching out the door. Some nodded to Delilah and Nancy or tipped their bottle cap hats. Gorge led them into the hallway, to the hatch at the end, a chute straight to the building's incinerator. He untied the bags, releasing a disgusting reek of concentrated leftover rotting Chinese food. The sprites swooned.

Gorge opened the chute. He tipped one bag then the other into the opening, spilling their contents, and thrust them down. The sprites leapt after them, each one diving through the hatch, crying with glee as they chased the refuse-delicacy into the void. After the last one, Gorge closed the chute.

He hastened back to the apartment where he grabbed the hammer and a box of nails then rushed back and nailed the hatch shut. He descended floor by floor, nailing each one closed until no way out of the chute remained.

In the basement, he fired up the trash incinerator and left it burning as the odor of charred pork and burnt rice wafted out along with the screams of the sprites.

Later, upstairs, Nancy thanked him.

"They're really gone? I mean, dead?" she said.

Gorge shrugged. "Scrape sprites, well, they're not really alive. They have no souls, and they're as dumb as rocks. They're made of stray magic, the refuse of spent magic really, bits of magic trash that clump together and form a creature that thinks it's alive. Really, they're living off the echoes of the fey. And they're devilishly easy to fool."

"Why did we need to clean?" Delilah said.

"Once they infest a place, they mark it as their own. They wouldn't have ever left unless we gave them what they wanted or erased their marks. Easier to get rid of than cockroaches if you know what you're doing."

"So who's this exile they wanted?" said Nancy. "Any idea?"

"Not clue, Nance, not a clue," Gorge said.

 Way of the Bone

A DOZEN UNDRESSED PEOPLE LAY SCATTERED AROUND THE room like wilted flowers.

Gorge spotted his drummer, Dev, sprawled across one of the sofas, still garbed in his immutable costume of denim and motorcycle boots, snoring, his limbs entangled with three women sleeping nude. Empty beer and liquor bottles littered the floor amidst booze puddles drying in the hazy morning sunlight. Pills peppered the coffee table, and a torchiere lamp protruded from the cracked screen of the wall-mounted television.

Picking a clear path through the carnage, Gorge opened the first adjoining room and peeked inside. Roald, his guitarist, sat meditating by the open balcony, bed empty, room clean. Gorge retreated quietly and closed the door. In the next room his bass player, who looked like he hadn't yet slept, entertained four women in a bed disheveled with hurricane frenzy. Three of the women stared at Gorge's naked body with open lust. The fourth pressed her face against a pillow as she moaned with ecstasy.

"Sound check at four o'clock this afternoon. I'll have your balls if you're late," Gorge said. "I fucking mean it, Tank. Don't screw up this gig."

The bass player lifted his head from the soft arc of a perfect buttock and nodded.

Gorge cherished the abandon these people brought to their celebrations, chaos sweetened so much by their mortality and the real prospect of dying for a good time. He had known excess before his exile but diluted and bland in comparison, inconsequential and therefore cheapened. His mortal musicians and their groupies lived on the hard edge of a genuine abyss, and he found it addictive. The drugs and alcohol didn't affect him the same way they did the others, but he got off well enough on the atmosphere of risk and blind defiance. This was the way to live: one's ego and libido unchecked, forever flipping the bird at convention.

He returned to his own room and opened the curtains. His skin soaked in the midday heat. An old melody from the Faerie Kingdoms came to mind. He sat on the edge of the bed, picked up his guitar, and strummed while he sang. The song conjured his past when every day had been a thousand times more glorious than this one, and he had been worshipped and lived among kings. But the melody—heard perfectly in his head—could never be played as intended here. He set down the guitar in frustration and told himself, as he had daily for more than half a century: *Now I am free.*

Behind him Delilah uncoiled from the sheets and cupped herself against Gorge's back, wrapping her legs around his waist. Her skin, still damp with sweat from a morning spent in passion, plastered itself to Gorge. The gnarled knobs of flesh above his scapulae tingled as

she cleansed their weeping scars with a moist washcloth from the nightstand. She caressed them with her fingertips, her lips, and then dried them with a soft towel.

Delilah hugged him tight and whispered in his ear. Her words reached him on the palanquin of her honeyed breath.

"Tell me again about how it was in the Faerie Kingdoms," she said.

Gorge caressed the silky tops of her thighs.

"Which version do you want today?" he asked. "The paradise I sacrificed for my life here with you, or the gilded cage from which I broke free to save my soul?"

"How do *you* see it today?"

"Today, I see through new eyes. Today the Kingdoms are a delicate fruit rotten at its core, which I will destroy before it spreads its taint."

"How will you do it?"

"I will open the Way of the Bone."

Delilah glided her tongue over Gorge's neck and slid her hands along his chest and abdomen, toward his cock. He stopped her with a gentle touch.

"You'll keep me here all day if I let you," he said, flashing a wicked grin. "I've got interviews, a sound check, and preparations to make."

Pouting, Delilah rose, and moved to the bathroom. Gorge watched, captivated by her swaying, blue-black hair and the sublime way her curves and muscles shifted when she walked. She hadn't aged since he met her more than five decades ago; he'd brought enough magic with him for that at least when he'd been banished here.

While Delilah sang in the shower Gorge dressed in black leather pants, a faded orange Killing Joke T-shirt, and a black jacket. Before he left the suite, he dialed up the Motörhead playlist on Dev's iPhone, cranked the Bluetooth speaker to full volume, and then let the door swing shut as the feverish opening riff of "Ace of Spades" kicked in. Guitars roared. Bass and drums thundered. Then came the shouts of a dozen sleeping people blasted awake.

Checking himself in the elevator wall mirror, Gorge spent a touch of glamour to fix his appearance. He never let the public see him absent black lipstick, eyes circled with kohl, and wild, short spikes of black-and-silver hair rising from his hawkish face. His transformation to a human body had dampened his native faerie features, but the remnants provided for an exotic appearance he liked to emphasize. His plans demanded he play the monstrous rock god to perfection today. When Red Gorge played Madison Square Garden tonight, they wanted the devout attention of millions watching their live-televised performance. It was the first step in the last leg of the journey Gorge had begun before he'd been cast out of the Kingdoms.

On the twelfth floor a black man built like a pro wrestler met Gorge and guided him toward the concierge suite. "They're gathering," he said.

"I saw them, Snow," said Gorge. "They've been all around us the last few days."

"I counted a couple of dozen different types, but mostly blackjack sprites."

"Vicious, little attack dogs." Gorge grimaced. Bloodthirsty blackjack sprites had chewed his fiery, gossamer wings from his body before they'd left him in iron chains in the desert.

"There are some I still don't recognize," Snow said.

Gorge nodded. "You take to my training exceptionally well, but some things will always stay beyond your ability to perceive them. I sensed a trio of elementals, probably the Winds of Change. A handful of fey from the Choruses are here too. As if they could turn song against *me*."

"So, how do we play it?"

Gorge squelched the wise-ass comment that rose to his lips and put a reassuring hand on Snow's back. "We stay alert. Take down any of them that come within ten feet, and we do what we've always done—play the fucking show. Let them come. They think I'm weak. They expect if they punish me long enough, I'll repent, give up, or die. They have no idea how close I am to destroying them."

"Glad to hear it." Snow opened the concierge suite door. "Keep your guard up, boss, 'cause me, I got bills to pay."

Gorge laughed then shifted his attention to the young man waiting inside the suite. Silver piercings glinted on his face. Gorge sensed his nervousness and played on it, sizing him up with a stony glare, before he flopped onto an easy chair across from him.

"So, what the fuck do you want to know?" he said.

The man stammered, introducing himself as Kenny Choi, editor for *Guitar Gun* magazine. For half an hour he questioned Gorge about his early underground recordings, his influences, what he thought about streaming music services and the resurgence of popularity for vinyl, life on tour, and other topics. Gorge replied with whatever rude and indifferent answer occurred to him, grinding hard on his punk-inflected image.

"So, uh, *Way of the Bone*, your new album, out last month. The singles, especially the title song, have been burning up the charts, but it's kind of a concept album, right?" Kenny said. "What's the inspiration behind that?"

Gorge counted silently to ten and then said, "It's my fucking life story."

"Wow. So, like, it's a metaphor?"

"Yeah, exactly." Gorge slid into his stage voice, its effect on Kenny immediate. "It's about a musician who was the greatest musician who ever lived. Imagine having headphones plugged directly into the music of the spheres, and that's the kind of music this guy could make. He composed symphonies that brought tears to the eyes of the dead. His songs made virgins' loins tremble. They made royalty melt. And though he lived in a place where musical talent was a natural gift nearly everyone possessed, no one played better than him. So, this guy, he becomes friend to kings and queens, the confidante of emperors and empresses. They even initiate him into the Flock of Eternity, the 1,000 entrusted with all the secrets of the great Kingdoms."

Gorge kicked his feet up on the coffee table in front of him and sneered. "Except it all turns out to be a steaming load of dog shit."

He dragged out his pause to let his story breathe in Kenny's mind. When he sensed the reporter about to ask a question, he continued.

"It was all nothing more than a way for these uptight pussies to break him, to keep him in an invisible prison, and make sure he did what they wanted. When he'd finally had enough, he spurned their laws and castrating traditions, and pursued music they'd forbidden. So they mutilated him and cast him down to what they considered Hell. But he only got stronger there and rose again. He reclaimed his music, and with it came serious fucking magic. Now he's going to bring darkness down on all Creation."

"The Way of the Bone?"

"The dark way. The music that makes devils of men."

Kenny scribbled in his notebook. "Giving me fucking chills here, man. Tonight's so gonna rock."

"I know," Gorge said, satisfied with the light he'd fired in Kenny's eyes.

He wanted everyone who heard his story to believe in its meaning if not its facts, even if only subconsciously, so that when they retold it or wrote it down, they imparted some of their belief to others. Gorge's tale resonated powerfully with the band's fans, especially the young, so many of whom sensed that better worlds existed beyond this one, although they could never reach or properly perceive them. They grappled with anger they didn't understand, with rage born of soul-deep frustration and the primal knowledge that they were unjustly cut off from great glory. They were left only to dream, and Gorge was happy to inspire them. It had taken years to gather so many fans, and tonight as Red Gorge performed *Way of the Bone* in its entirety, millions would listen enrapt in Gorge's story, focused on *his* life and desires. He would gather the power needed to wedge open the Way of the Bone. His gain would seem small for the effort spent to obtain it, but the power would enable him to collect more from around the world, until he could finally, fully open the Way, and bring all the wild, dark, slavering things in the universe right to the doorstep of the Faerie fucking Kingdoms.

Kenny stood. "Thanks for the interview, man. It was awesome to meet you. I've been a fan for practically my whole life. Your music is the real fucking deal."

"No shit. Keep dreaming, Kenny."

"Count on it."

As Kenny pocketed his digital recorder and his notepad and turned toward the door, Gorge spied it: a faint, bronze shimmer along Kenny's spine, like a shirt-seam dusted with glitter. He recognized it at once and flew from his chair, shoved Kenny to the floor, and wrenched free the glimmering, semi-invisible thing that had grafted itself to the editor's back. Kenny howled. The door banged open. Snow barreled in as Gorge stood, wrestling a flickering winged lightning bolt. The creature whipped around, trying to fly free, dragging Gorge against the coffee table, but Gorge held tight, squeezing so hard, his knuckles turned white, until the thing gave up, shimmered, and became fully visible. The slender creature had a snake's body topped by the miniaturized torso, arms, and face of a man. Its wings were like white crow's wings, and at the end of its tail dangled a knobby, spiral stinger.

"Holy... shit..." Kenny said from the floor.

Snow wrapped a hand around the gun holstered under his jacket. "You okay, boss?"

Gorge nodded. "Look what I've caught."

"A dragon pixie."

"Correct. It's a type of servile homunculus."

"We're compromised."

"No, don't you see? They don't know what's coming. They sent this pathetic little thing to find out. They're as fucking clueless as ever. Isn't that right?"

The dragon pixie trembled and hissed at Gorge.

"Don't you know who I am? What I am?" Gorge said.

"They call you the Death-Singer, black-hearted from the day you were spawned."

"Yes." Gorge smiled, pleased. "And well they should."

"Holy... *shit,*" said Kenny. "It's all fucking real? The magic shit? That's so mind-blowing!"

"Snow?" Gorge said.

Snow yanked Kenny to his feet, maneuvered him into the corridor, and said, "See you at the show tonight, kid," before he slammed the door shut. Turning back to Gorge, he asked, "So, what do we do with it?"

"Do you understand, little pixie, what I'm about to ac-complish?" Gorge asked.

"You think you can open the Way of the Bone, but they'll stop you," said the pixie. "She'll stop you."

"She? Who?" said Gorge.

Realizing it had said too much, the pixie clamped its lips tight.

"Is it Soniella? I don't fear Soniella," said Gorge. "The Flock has no idea what's coming, else they wouldn't have sent you here to find out. They'd just have killed me outright. But the law is the law. They sentenced me to exile, not execution so they can't do that. I know them much better than you, little wyrm. There's nothing more revealing of someone's nature than being the object of their hatred and subjected to their torture. You're about to learn that firsthand. I'm only going to release you after I've blinded you, sliced out your tongue, and cut off your hands, so you can't share anything you know with my enemies. You'll be my message to them. I'll leave you your ears so that when the great destruction arrives on a crashing wave of sound, you may witness it before your makers return you to the clay from which they sculpted you."

The pixie squealed and thrashed, but Gorge pressed it against the table. It lashed out with its tail, landing its stinger deep in Gorge's arms several times. Gorge ignored the wounds, and when Snow handed him a knife, the first thing he sliced away was the pixie's tail, chopping off its sting with a single blow. The rest went fast. Soon Gorge released the decimated creature out the window, cleaned up the room, and called for his next interviewer.

They ended the sound check with "Soniella," the ballad Gorge had written for the woman who'd been his lover in the Faerie Kingdoms. She had also been his betrayer and tricked him into surrendering himself for exile. Only Delilah knew the story, so when she stormed backstage during the song, her fury seemed inexplicable to all but Gorge.

Her reaction upset him. They were each other's sanctuary, each the only one the other trusted with their life and soul. In his old existence Gorge had never known such devotion, but he found it essential in this world of cruelty and filth. She had found him in Death Valley, ruined and chained to rocky ground. Mistaking her camera for a weapon, he attacked her at first, too weak to do any damage, but then she freed him and gave him water, brought him to her city apartment and nursed him. From

Delilah he learned how to live in his new flesh of dust and ashes. If not for her, he'd have shriveled up and dried in the desert sun until he rotted away to dander to be blown across the sand.

He found her in his dressing room, drinking beer and scratching a charcoal stick across one of her countless sketchpads.

"I'm sorry," he said.

"It's fine. It's just... you promised me you'd never play that fucking song again."

"I need to prepare myself. I think she's here."

"How can she be?"

"I caught a spy this afternoon, and he said, '*She'll* stop you.' He couldn't mean anyone else. Agents of the Kingdoms will attack tonight, probably during the concert."

"Shit," said Delilah. "Why send her?"

"They think I won't be able to fight her. Maybe they think I still love her."

"Do you?"

Gorge met Delilah's dark stare and said, "I love only you," feeling the nearly palpable truth of the words as he spoke them.

"Will she try to kill you?"

"No, she's of the Flock, and so, supposedly, above such things. But she knows my music better than anyone else. She might be able to disrupt it. There are faeries from the Choruses, elementals that control the wind, blackjack sprites, others. Everything must be played perfectly for the Way to open. If they distort the sound or stop us from playing our full set, it could exhaust the magic I've gathered in this world and leave the Way closed."

"Will you die?"

"No," said Gorge "You might if they wipe me out, and I can't replenish my magic soon enough. Last time, I had an edge, having brought some with me from the Kingdoms. This time I'll have to spend everything I have to crack open the Way. After that, I'll be starting at empty. It could take a century for me to recover fully."

"Find her and kill her now."

"There's no time. I'll be the strongest I've ever been as a mortal during the concert. Better to face her then. Soniella will only show herself when the balance of my spell is most exposed. I'll be ready. I won't let her harm you. I won't let her destroy what we have." Gorge lifted Delilah's chin toward his face. "I promise you. You're my night-haired beauty. You saved me, and I'll save you. We're meant to be together for all time."

He kissed her, stirring to the heat of her lips. He folded himself against her on the couch, feeling her tremble and clutch at him. They slid out of their clothes and moved together, and afterward lay there until it was time for the show to go on.

Four songs into their set, Red Gorge had already driven the crowd into a frenzy.

The audience danced and slammed against each other, screamed lyrics from raw throats, and surrendered to the deep rhythms rising from the band. Their faces resembled ghost buoys bobbing on a dark sea. Dev, Roald, and Tank played like never before, the best Gorge had ever heard them: tight, fast, and with a will that would've left entire cities dead in their wake had they been an army on the march. They thrived on the excitement of the crowd and the fulfillment of their deepest wishes of greatness; it flowed into their music. Gorge worked his voice to its limits, ascending scales in rapid succession as he wove ethereal song over the hard terrain of the instruments. Together they created Red Gorge's signature sound: the grinding, irresistible progress of guitar, bass, and drums elevated by transcendent melodies and Gorge's unearthly voice. In the Kingdoms, where many more notes and musical scales existed, their music would've sounded crude, but in this world, it surpassed anything people had ever before heard.

As Roald bit into a guitar solo, Gorge raised his microphone stand and speared it against the stage. He drifted from the spotlight while guitar notes blistered the air. At the side of the stage, Delilah and Snow looked distracted by worry, and to Gorge they seemed immeasurably fragile, like paper and wax toys vibrating in the barrage of sound blasting from the arena's speakers. Part of him wanted to grasp Delilah's hand and comfort her. Another part wondered why he bothered with such a trivial creature such as a human woman who should've died ten years ago—and the moment that thought formed he knew his enemies stood nearby. He hadn't even noticed their attack begin, so subtle had it been, influencing his thoughts. Now he'd sensed the arrogant taint of the Kingdoms creeping into him.

It knocked him momentarily off balance and he almost lost his cue, but then he launched back into the song with a roar that shook the walls. The audience responded with thousands of voices that together barely measured up to the power of Gorge's amplified voice. The band tore into the song's climax with terrifying force, and didn't skip a beat launching into the next one. The others sensed Gorge's urgency and played with fantastic speed, as the lyrics emerged from Gorge like a cyclone slamming cars together along a rain-slashed highway. The arena rumbled. The force of the audience's energy connected with Gorge. A feedback loop opened as he absorbed it, skimmed away what he wanted, and kicked it back to them through the music. It was the moment he'd been working toward; the opening had begun.

The people nearest the stage thrashed to the beat, writhing like panicked animals. Security guards struggled to contain the melee from the rest of the crowd. Gorge watched the sea of people shoving, dancing, fighting, some even fucking in the dark. He swelled with pride for what he'd wrought. Like a living thing, the song grew around them in the shadows, stretched itself in the flashing stage-lights, reached its thunderous crescendo, and then segued straight into the next number, the title song from *Way of the Bone.*

Dev assaulted his drums and Tank's fingers ripped along the bass. Rhythm ruled for two measures then Roald's hands moved over his guitar strings, creating a riff that filled the arena like a jet of molten noise. The world wavered, as if the walls and roof, the advertising posters, and the overhead jumbo television screens were peeling back from reality so that the audience existed only within the music. Gorge rose at the edge of the stage and sang:

Born in a moment
Born in pain

Nothing's ever the
same again

Chained in the desert
Chains in my mind
Wings bit off by
my own kind

Once, lord of lyrics
Once, prince of peace
Now a demon let
off his leash

And I will find the way
the Dark way, the way home
the way to Hell
the Way of the Bone

His voice soared, hounding the melody along a gouging assemblage of sound that lifted and enhanced it. A hundred voices joined in, a thousand, then ten thousand, and more as the crowd sang—and then Gorge sensed even more energy streaming to him from voices around the world watching the broadcast. The seal on the Way of the Bone loosened. The arena faded away. Power flowed into Gorge, and he sensed the universe trembling at his hubris, for the Way of the Bone would bring only death and stir only the carrion eaters and the blind things that stood hungry in the night. It was the forbidden Way, submerged in the deepest pockets of reality, and Gorge was slipping his filthy fingernails in around the edges to pry it loose for his pleasure.

Empress loved me
King smiled down
Until I stepped upon
hallowed ground

Music surrendered
Love became dread

Cast away, scarred, and
left for dead

But I will find the way
the Dark way, the way home
the way to Hell
the Way of the Bone

First came the blackjack sprites, swarming across the darkness like oversized wasps. Gorge swept his gaze in their direction as he repeated the chorus and vaporized them on a burst of sound, hurling them back to the Kingdoms. Next came the Winds of Change, howling, driving down on the band, forcing Roald and Tank to the stage floor, rattling Dev's drums like dice. Red Gorge played on, kept the rhythm, and hit every note with practiced precision and the smoldering passion of fifteen years of hunting a dream. The Winds clutched at the sounds. Gorge watched the whirling elementals as they lashed out with airy tendrils, trying to grasp individual notes, to warp and change them, but the music carried on unaltered. His enemies hadn't had half a century to become acclimated to this world like he had, to understand how music worked here. As he started into the song's final verse, Gorge funneled some of his power upward to create a countervailing gale that sent the Winds of Change home.

Sing to me of shadows
Of stars gone dark
Of death and lies,
the hideous art

A light glowed across the arena. As Roald and Tank drove into a synchronized barrage of notes, a new sound rose over the music, although only Gorge heard it at first. It came in harmony, three voices singing a gentle tune ill-conceived for how sound worked in this world, yet effective nonetheless, especially when joined by a fourth singer with a much more powerful voice.

One Gorge knew intimately.

Soniella.

She flashed across the black expanse.

She'd brought three of her best from the Choruses. They sang, but not to disrupt Gorge's song as he'd anticipated. Like him, they were singing to open a way. The light glowing around them grew brilliant, almost blinding, at least to Gorge, who perceived it fully, and perhaps to Snow and Delilah, whom he'd trained to see as he did. The audience could only glimpse enough to think it was part of the light show.

Notes flowed outward from Soniella and her singers, rising from their lips like delicate snowflakes etched from candle flames. They amassed to form a ragged, swirling oval, and through its heart Gorge saw the place he'd once called home: his conservatory in the Kingdoms, untouched from the day he'd last left it. The half-finished composition he'd been writing still sat propped up beside his instruments. The faeries' magic slowed time, so that each single note Red Gorge pumped out lasted what seemed like minutes, while Gorge stared at the indescribable beauty beyond the opening, astonished by how it exceeded his memories, how much sweeter the air flowing out of it was than the air of this dingy gutter world, how much more sublime were the sounds.

Soniella descended to the stage. Gorgeous beyond Gorge's capacity to describe with a mortal mind, she stood bathed in light and clothed in transparent, iridescent cloth that revealed every measure of her perfection. Her hair moved like liquid gold, and from her back sprouted glorious double wings of blue and yellow. Once their beauty had been equaled only by Gorge's wings, and when they'd flown together entire villages had stopped to watch them pass. Gorge met her eyes, dizzying in their depths, and watched her lips move as she sang, struggling to form the sounds right in mortal air. Then her singers held a long, trilling note. Reality seemed to freeze.

"Come back to us, Gorge," Soniella said. "We wronged you. We see that. Return and be restored. My guilt has never faded, and I miss you, my love."

Gorge's eyes wandered over Soniella, over the view of the Kingdoms, and then he looked at Delilah, who, in comparison, appeared crudely formed, like a statue fashioned of cinder and silt. The sight of Soniella's glorious wings caused his wounded shoulders to ache with phantom pain.

"We can heal you and restore your wings. You'll fly again. You and I can be as we once were," said Soniella.

Gorge had never considered that the Flock might offer him reconciliation; that all he had forsaken might be restored, his lost glory renewed. The entire arena swirled awash in magical energy, barely contained by his and Soniella's efforts. Yet he felt cold to his core. Here lay a choice he'd never anticipated. His anger, nursed for decades, seemed like surf breaking over an eternally rocky shore. It would be madness to refuse. He stared into his conservatory, remembering his days there, and his eyes took in all the wonders he'd once possessed. Its allure ached within him—until he spotted a crystal square engraved with musical notations and carved to act like a prism, always surrounded by color. A gift from Soniella. Once he'd cherished it. The memories it held were the most potent Gorge possessed from the Kingdoms—and the most painful.

Gorge peered into Soniella's flickering eyes. Working magic in the mortal world strained her, but she'd accumulated a great deal of power since he'd last seen her.

Gorge let her approach and embrace him.

He whispered, "I have a gift for you, love," then kissed her and stroked her dusty, silken wings, holding her close enough to feel the tension leave her as she decided she'd won him over. He pressed his lips against hers. She let down her guard. Gorge inhaled, sucking a blast of magic from her body and into his. His power surged as hers withered. He made a claw of his hand and ripped away the top quarter of her left wing. Shoving her aside, he released a burst of energy, nearly all he'd accumulated that night, and Soniella's spell shattered. The brilliant opening vanished, taking with it the three singers. Gorge's view of the Kingdoms closed. The music thundered back to full life and speed.

Gorge sang:

My gift to you
My gift to them

Nothing's ever the
same again

And I will find the way
the Dark way, the way home
the way to Hell
the Way of the Bone

The song rumbled toward its end. Soniella—shocked and wounded—ghosted to nothingness and faded back to the Faerie Kingdoms. Roald led the band to a crashing finale, and when the music ended, Gorge alone sang out:

And I will find the way
The Way of the Bone

The crowd exploded with applause, and Gorge collapsed to the stage.

He struggled with what magic remained inside him to keep the Way open, but he lacked the power. Everything around him snapped back to substance as the Way slammed shut. He would gather no more magic tonight.

The band rushed to his side. He couldn't move, couldn't stand.

Delilah shoved past Tank, knelt down, and took Gorge's hand. Before she could speak, he grabbed the back of her neck and pulled him to her, kissing her, and as he did, he released all the magic left inside him, delivering it to her body, recharging the magic already there. He watched Delilah quiver with shock, and then Gorge's eyes shut, and saw only darkness.

Gorge ached when he awoke. Delilah's face at his side eased the pain. There was sunlight and quiet. Gorge lay in a hospital bed.

"Shhh, don't move," Delilah said. "You collapsed. The doctors don't think there's any permanent damage, though."

"She came to take me home and I said no," Gorge said.

"What do you mean?"

"Soniella offered to give me back my old life, my wings. I refused."

Tears welled in Delilah's eyes. She held Gorge's hand, pressed it to her cheek.

"You feel so cold. You sent all your magic into me. It filled me up when the Way closed. Why, when you were so close?"

Gorge shut his eyes and pictured Soniella as she'd appeared last night: glorious and vibrant and powerful, and yet deep in her eyes there had dwelled black terror curling like venom in a place where he only ever saw warmth and love from Delilah.

"If I'd exhausted my magic, you would've died. What would opening the Way mean without you beside me? What would anything mean without you? The magic is my gift to you. In the Kingdoms, they fear me. That's enough for now."

Gorge pulled Delilah into bed beside him. It was only in the halo of Delilah's warmth that this life felt right and his way felt good. She nestled her head against Gorge's chest and they lay there, each listening to the other's breath, to the indifferent rhythms of the city outside, to the breeze humming past the half-opened window.

Gorge chose then to remind himself, as he did everyday: *Now I am free.*

Lyric Sheets

*New content exclusive to this edition

BECAUSE WE SAY SO

D.S. Dent, Hash Reynolds, and Mickey O'Nanist
Reprinted by permission

Eyes jailed, lips sealed
Hands tied, tongue tied
Listen up like a goooood boy
Forget questions
Believe lessons
Accept because we saaaaaay so

CHORUS
No cryin'
No, no cryin'
Don't be such a crybaby
No cryin'

Wake up, dress up
Clean your face
Paint yourself like a goooood girl
Work hard, buy hard
And when you fuck
You'll fuck because we saaaaaay so

CHORUS
No cryin'
No, no cryin'
Don't be such a crybaby
No cryin'

Thou shalt not kill
We have a pill
To make sure you're a goooood boy
And when it's time
For you to die
You'll die because we saaaaaay so

And you better not cry about it!

Words: Dent
Music: Dent, Reynolds, & O'Nanist
© Bowery Sludge Records

Liner notes: The trademark song of the short-lived punk trio, Social Contract Dispute, "Because We Say So," achieved only street notoriety due to SCD's inability to complete a studio recording and subsequent break-up. Bootleg live recordings are known to exist.

FAERIE RING BLUES

Gavin Gray
Reprinted by Permission

Some stories begin at the beginning
Some stories begin at the end
This one begins with a broken heart

CHORUS
This I tell you true, my friend
Yes, this I tell you true my friend

One woman rips your heart out your chest
One steals your soul and makes you bend
This one holds dear life in her hands

CHORUS
This I tell you true, my friend
Yes, this I tell you true my friend

You live your days, picking at the scabs
Hoping weeping wounds will heal
Waiting for her love to be real

CHORUS
This I tell you true, my friend
Yes, this I tell you true my friend

Down in the circle
Where bargains are made
Where gifts are given
And prices are paid
The Devil's in the details
And the sad songs are played
The lonely stay lonely
And dead loves are laid

Some stories, they begin with a wish
Some stories end with a promise
The circle takes, the circle breaks

CHORUS
It's the faerie ring blues, my friend
Yes, the faerie ring blues, your end

You've got the faerie ring blues, my friend
Yes, the faerie ring blues, your end

Words: Gavin Gray
Music: Gavin Gray
© Blues of a Nation, Inc.

Liner notes: Released in 1958, "Faerie Ring Blues" marked a shift in the career of Gavin Gray that would see his music increasingly peppered with references to magic and myths. Intended to preface a full album of blues music that never materialized, "Faerie Ring Blues" remains a curiosity in the discography of one early rock's most enigmatic artists. Gray's detour into blues gave way to a long stint as a top session guitarist throughout the 1960s.

SŌNIELLA
Gavin Gray w/ Gorge
Reprinted by permission

Siren, goddess, fury, lover
Devoured me with the sharpest bite
Outshined the music that was my life
Filled my soul with milk and honey
Before you left me only tears
Gifted me with all your fears

Misled by your call
Lured by darkness' pall
Hated by them all
Wingless now I fall

CHORUS
Soniella, Soniella
Never sing your name again
The way I sang it then

Tempter, genius, devil, master
Emperor of the realm of sound
For you I laid my empire down
And drank deep of your nectar
Poison sweet and betrayal deep
Isolation all you left me

Cheated by your call
Raged by darkness' pall
Hated by them all
Wingless now I fall

CHORUS
Soniella, Soniella
Never sing your name again
The way I sang it then

You turned love to hate
And destiny to fate
You killed the beauty
To fulfill your duty
Yet still the darkness waits
Yes, the still darkness waits
And forever, my heart hates

Exile, mortal, survivor, lover
Fall then rise, my way regain
Healed, I learn to contain my pain
Hold clear the black heart you bared to me
Save a scrap of love, hoard the dark
Never, Soniella, forget your part

Destroyed by your call
Bled by darkness' pall
Hated by them all
Wingless now I fall

CHORUS
Soniella, Soniella
Never sing your name again
The way I sang it then

Never sing your name again
The way I sang it then

Words: Gorge
Music: Gavin Gray
© Ethereal Melodies
Liner Notes: This posthumous collaboration with Gavin Gray
appeared on Red Gorge's first album, *MusicMage.* Gorge report-
edly purchased the rights to all of Gavin Gray's unpublished
music in order to secure this one song, for which he wrote his
own lyrics. The track rose to number three on the hard rock
charts. Despite the song's popularity, it rarely makes the cut for
Red Gorge's live shows, having been performed in concert only
three known times.

Burning Chains Broken
Gorge w/ Red Gorge
Reprinted by permission

Dark sounds, darkness inside
Forbidden verse
A lover's lies
Life cast aside
In her greedy kiss, my soul is mastered
Rage stills, a lost world forgotten
Life shattered, the truth lies battered

CHORUS
And the only thing it takes to make all my pain go away
Is the sound of her voice asking me to stay

We may live forever
Or die today
Our hands entwined
Mortal life defined
In her grasping arms, lives a country unknown
Lungs fill, breath of the mortal world
A crude home, I'm no longer alone

CHORUS
And the only thing it takes to make all my pain go away
Is the sound of her voice asking me to stay

Music before her
Man's lost daughter
Chains break away
And skin burns fade
Heart falls to flesh
Flesh falls to soul
Soul calls magic
Souls find home

CHORUS
And the only thing it takes to make all my pain go away
Is the sound of her voice asking me to stay

Lost way found again
Scorched earth reborn
Touch of her skin
Soothes anger's sin
In her artist's eye, my broken wings heal
Blood spills, scars never forgotten
Never sealed, a dream becomes real
And the only thing it takes to make all my pain go away
Is the sound of her voice asking me to stay

CHORUS
And the only thing it takes to make all my pain go away
Is the sound of her voice asking me to stay

Words: Gorge
Music: Gorge w/ Red Gorge
© Ethereal Melodies, Inc.

Liner Notes: The first single released from Red Gorge's influential *Way of the Bone* LP, this electric ballad featured eight simultaneous guitar tracks and a mesmerizing melody. Although a difficult play for radio programmers, it effectively heralded one of the greatest hard rock albums of all time, and helped put Red Gorge on the path to superstardom.

THE BALLAD OF RED GORGE

Gorge w/ Red Gorge
Reprinted by permission

Born in a moment
Born in pain
Nothing's ever the
same again

Chained in the desert
Chains in my mind
Wings bit off by
my own kind

Once, lord of lyrics
Once, prince of peace
Now a demon let
off his leash

CHORUS
And I will find the way
the Dark way, the way home
the way to Hell
the Way of the Bone

Empress loved me
King smiled down
Until I stepped upon
hallowed ground

Music surrendered
Love became dread
Cast away, scarred, and
left for dead

CHORUS
But I will find the way

the Dark way, the way home
the way to Hell
the Way of the Bone

Sing to me of shadows
Of stars gone dark
Of death and lies,
the hideous art

My gift to you
My gift to them
Nothing's ever the
same again

CHORUS
And I will find the way
the Dark way, the way home
the way to Hell
the Way of the Bone

And I will find the way
The Dark way
The Way of the Bone

Words: Gorge
Music: Gorge w/ Red Gorge
© Ethereal Melodies, Inc.

Liner Notes: Stripped down, bare bones, Red Gorge at its best, "The Ballad of Red Gorge," the third single from *Way of the Bone*, spent six weeks at number one and became a centerpiece of Red Gorge's live shows, often inciting frenzied excitement. Japanese promoters prohibited the band from playing it on their 2002 tour, due to its reputation for inciting mayhem, ironically leading to riots by unhappy fans. Notably, Red Gorge has left the song off of all three of its live recordings.

Song for Delilah

Max Chaos (?)
Reprinted under Fair Use for purposes of criticism and research

Heart of a vortex
breathing heat and light
My head hangs as my
shoulders fall, laid low
wounded and made small

Burning sand beneath my knees
Burning wings a memory
Dark dead zone untouched
The emptiness is your kiss
The void your embrace

What you see that isn't there
beats inside your heart
so fine
Your heart beating with mine
Breaking chains of malice and rage

You close my eyes to show me
I shut my eyes to see

CHORUS
Your brush dispels the emptiness
Your hand destroys my loneliness
Your body ties me to this earth
Your love frees me from memories

In your hair, shadows and light
turpentine and oil scent
sky black against your pale flesh
Breath of honey, goddess might
in your soul cools my fire

You're gone yet feelings remain
Pure unclouded as the sun sinks
behind the skyline, and I
raise my hands to the shadows

This lock I bind will hold for a year
This spell I wind last a century
Return to me and be healed
Or leave behind your song of dreams

CHORUS
Your brush dispels the emptiness
Your hand destroys my loneliness
Your body ties me to this earth
Your love frees me from memories

This lock I bind shall hold
This spell I wind shall last
This song I play shall heal
Your dream of us shall never pass

Lyrics: Max Chaos (?)
Music: Max Chaos (?)
Liner Notes: "Song for Delilah" has never been recorded or published but is attributed to Max Chaos based on reports from dedicated concert-goers during Chaos's heyday on the New York punk scene, circa 1980-1984. Chaos has never confirmed the song's existence or his authorship. Common belief holds that he performed the song only twice in public, during his brief return to Lower East Side clubs following his falling out with Bruno Rice. If so, Chaos never shared the title of the song, reputedly written for his lover. The lyrics printed here are generally recognized by music researchers as associated with "Song for Delilah" if not a precise record. They were reconstructed by Nancy Asp of the short-lived punk group, Your Uncool Niece, who claims to have transcribed them from memory after a performance by Chaos at Dresden Underground.

About The Author

James Chambers is an award-winning author of horror, crime, fantasy, and science fiction. He wrote the Bram Stoker Award®-winning graphic novel, *Kolchak the Night Stalker: The Forgotten Lore of Edgar Allan Poe*. *Publisher's Weekly* described *The Engines of Sacrifice*, his collection of four Lovecraftian-inspired novellas published by Dark Regions Press as "...chillingly evocative..." in a starred review. His story, "A Song Left Behind in the Aztakea Hills," was nominated for a Bram Stoker Award.

He has authored the short story collection *Resurrection House* and several novellas, including *The Dead Bear Witness* and *Tears of Blood*, in the Corpse Fauna novella series. He also wrote the illustrated story collection, *The Midnight Hour: Saint Lawn Hill and Other Tales*, created in collaboration with artist Jason Whitley.

His short stories have been published in the anthologies *The Avenger: Roaring Heart of the Crucible*, *Bad-Ass Faeries*, *Bad-Ass Faeries 2: Just Plain Bad*, *Bad-Ass Faeries 3: In All Their Glory*, *Bad Cop No Donut*, *The Best of Bad-Ass Faeries*, *The Best of Defending the Future*, *Breach the Hull*, *By Other Means*, *Chiral Mad 2*, *Chiral*

Mad 4, Dance Like A Monkey, Dark Hallows II: Tales from the Witching Hour, Deep Cuts, The Domino Lady: Sex as a Weapon, Dragon's Lure, Fantastic Futures 13, Gaslight and Grimm, The Green Hornet Chronicles, Hard-boiled Cthulhu, Hear Them Roar, In An Iron Cage, Kolchak the Night Stalker: Passages of the Macabre, Man and Machine, Mermaids 13, No Longer Dreams, Qualia Nous, Shadows Over Main Street (1 and 2), *The Side of Good/The Side of Evil, The Society for the Preservation of CJ Henderson, So It Begins, The Spider: Extreme Prejudice, To Hell in a Fast Car, Truth or Dare, TV Gods, Walrus Tales, Weird Trails,* and *With Great Power*; the chapbook *Mooncat Jack*; and the magazines *Bare Bone, Cthulhu Sex,* and *Allen K's Inhuman.*

He has also written numerous comic books including *Leonard Nimoy's Primortals*, the critically acclaimed "The Revenant" in *Shadow House, The Midnight Hour* with Jason Whitley, and the award-winning original graphic novel, *Kolchak the Night Stalker: The Forgotten Lore of Edgar Allan Poe.*

He lives in New York.

Visit his website: www.jameschambersonline.com.

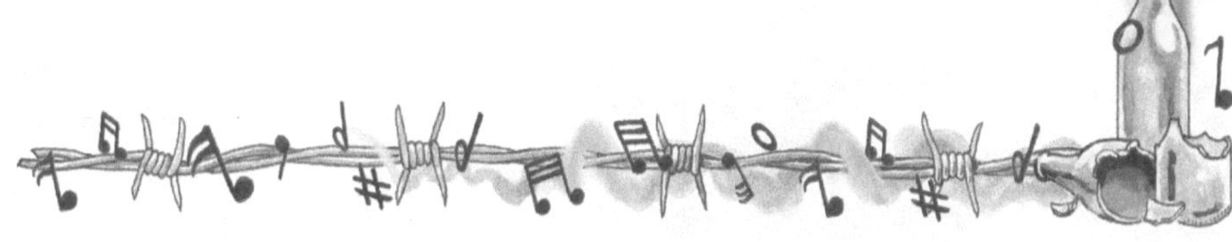